'A very, very good novel. Not a wasted word. Helen
Slavin has a highly original talent and is very
much a writer to watch'
Beryl Bainbridge

'Imaginatively told with a true sense of magic'
Daily Mail

'Annie Colville sees dead people. That surprise is
given away on page one of Helen Slavin's debut novel,
but there are plenty more to come – not least the deathly
hold of the unravelling story'
Scotsman

'Witty and heart-warming and a little eerie'
Independent on Sunday

'A funny, offbeat debut that won't let you go'
Woman and Home

'Warm and witty . . . unassuming and disarming'
The Times

'Quirky, irreverent and a little bit spooky, this book will
charm, move and scare you in equal measure'
My Weekly

'Wicked sense of humour . . . vivid imagination'
Australian *Guardian*

Helen Slavin is the author of *The Extra Large Medium* and *Cross My Heart*. She was born in Lancashire in 1966. After the University of Warwick, she had a variety of jobs as a temporary secretary before moving to Wiltshire. There, she got married and had a son and a daughter. She has written for radio and television, including scripts for the BBC series *The House of Eliott* and *Down to Earth*.

the
STOPPING
PLACE

helen
slavin

POCKET
BOOKS

LONDON • SYDNEY • NEW YORK • TORONTO

First published in Great Britain by Pocket Books, 2010
An imprint of Simon & Schuster UK Ltd
A CBS COMPANY

1 3 5 7 9 10 8 6 4 2

Simon & Schuster UK Ltd
1st Floor
222 Gray's Inn Road
London WC1X 8HB

www.simonandschuster.co.uk

Simon & Schuster Australia
Sydney

A CIP catalogue record for this book
is available from the British Library

ISBN: 978 1 84739...

PART 1

On the boulevard of broken teeth

Last night I dreamed that all my teeth were broken. Not just crumbling or broken like bottles, but oddly chipped and some with angular holes cut through. If you looked in, and I could because this was a dream and I was in two places, me looking up at me, it was like looking out from a cave. You could see sky, some sort of rocky outcrop with seapink growing on it. The wind was blowing in there, nothing too gale-like, not yet extending a light flag or anything. Just enough to blow the cobwebs from you, refresh you. But of course the cracks in my teeth were too small to crawl through, and then I woke up.

TOSHOKAN WA DOKO DESU KA?

Where is the library?

No, there's no extra charge. Usually we only hire out the language tapes for six weeks, but Swedish is impossible and so Mrs Atkinson is running an initiative scheme. If you can come back in not six but eight weeks and speak Swedish, she'll let you hire out your choice of CDs (spoken word or music) or any DVD free of charge for a year.

If you really wanted to don the full bearskin of Scandinavia and take on the challenge of Idiomatic Icelandic (accompanying CD and pocket-sized course book), you'd have to put a reserve on it. One of the book club ladies, Ellen Freethy, has it and appears reluctant to give it back. Each time she renews it she twists her mouth around the words, '*Takka fyrir, eg er ath laera Islensku,*' and then, in English, 'It does seem to be taking a while.'

It's been quite a long while actually; she's been at it since February last year. Clearly Icelandic is beyond impossible. *Svolitid.*

Swedish isn't impossible. You just have to work at it. I did it in four weeks. Rent out some films. Root out the

Hem Ljuva Hem homes and gardens magazines from the newsagents in the city, the one down the little side street by the theatre. It all helps.

Of course I haven't claimed the prize, because apart from anything I don't think Mrs Atkinson is letting library staff in on the scheme. Let's face it, Mrs Atkinson doesn't appear to let the library staff in on any scheme. The Grand Scheme of Things, and we are all in absentia. She lurks in the archive with those white gloves on, rubbing shoulders with the university bods we get in here, disapproving of Martha's affairs. Well, just one affair: Mackenzie Tierney of Tripp Tierney Associates, the architecture practice that has been given carte blanche to remodel the sagging bits of town. There have been other affairs that Mrs Atkinson didn't object to, although it is plain that it matters not one whit to Martha whether Mrs Atkinson approves or not.

I've had the teeth dream repeatedly these last few weeks. The twinned senses of unease and relief on waking are hard to reconcile, so I don't bother. During library hours there are a hundred and one ways to combat it. Out of hours is a different proposition. I am only signed up for the Thursday session of Intermediate Japanese but since the teeth dream began I have found myself at the foot of the stairs in the technical college on Wednesday and Friday evenings too.

The first Wednesday it was raining. I had missed my bus. There was the prospect of the long evening ahead. I missed the bus again on the Friday. Since then, I've just convinced myself it is intensive learning.

That was the same Wednesday evening that they advertised the Archivist course which I've also had on my mind. I should probably ask Mrs Atkinson for careers advice but I can't find the courage—clearly I should also sign up for Assertiveness

Training. Martha is the one being groomed for greatness, and even if I did take the course it isn't likely there'll be a vacancy come up here. Mrs Atkinson has her archive all sewn up. There's only one pair of white gloves.

The other staff members all have much busier lives full of children and divorces and, in Mrs Milligan's case, divorcing children. She weeps into her tea at least three days a week and I want to go over and hug her, the urge scorches me, but I don't know. It isn't my business and she would be the first to scorn me for it.

On Tuesday I was sitting by the window so that I could see out into the war memorial gardens beyond us; she sat on the sofa with the wooden arms. It's G-plan; Harvey says he could get a bomb for it on eBay. It is Mrs Milligan's island refuge, her bouclé-covered life raft. Harvey was chatting about his online fundraising, telling us all about the last-minute bidding rush for the complete set of Harold Robbins first editions, when Mrs Milligan started to weep. Tears dripped silently into her tea. She struggled with her face, it trembled, the edges started to go. Every nerve in it must have been quivering. I wasn't looking, I wouldn't do that. I could see her reflection in the window. No one did anything except talk louder, Martha suddenly very interested in Harvey's online auction.

Martha has responsibility for the book club and the author visits, and she dresses like a gypsy. That's not a criticism, by the way. She puts tones and shades together that make you feel you've been seeing the world in black and white all your life. In winter she's velvet and raw silk and wool. Have you ever seen raw silk? Just the sight of her coming through the door each day makes you want to jump up and wave your arms. I'd love to dress like that.

I don't know what's happening with Mrs Milligan's son other than her heart is breaking on his behalf. She's not bemoaning the grandchildren she hasn't been given. She's not going to burn the ex as a witch or vilify her for the betrayal. She's not apportioning blame, she's just destroyed because she can't stop it happening to him. She can't kiss it better or make it go away, and what she is thinking about, the thing her heart beats for, is him.

I suppose it must be odd to have children. Babies, who then morph into children and god-forbid teenagers. I suppose she thinks of his first day at school, the time she had to give him the Heimlich manoeuvre to get a Lego brick out of his throat, that first Goth girlfriend. When he careened off his bike in the park she could catch him before he skinned his knee. Now there isn't anything to be done.

But of course, there is. I have to reshelve.

Martha just leaves the trolleys sitting there. If stacking the returned volumes were left to Martha the shelves would be almost bare. The borrowers would have to rummage behind the counter.

Martha likes to sit at the desk and play libraries. She's recently acquired a pair of spectacles which I think are more of a fashion accessory than an aid to sight. They are sleek rectangles in tortoiseshell plastic the exact same shade as her eyes, and when she dons them there's a sudden hazel–green–chocolate intensity of eyes, lashes, brows and frowsy hair. The light from the cupola above catches in the chocolates and bronzes of her auburn hair. Even the odd grey strand looks lustrously silver. There are other days when she looks like the Gorgon Medusa. Hair snaking, eyes turning you to stone. The days after the Affairs—the Affairs who have been and done and seen how much blood can be squeezed from Martha's heart.

Martha's heart, gnashed at, chewed over, and she still persists in scooping it up off the floor, picking the bits off it and cramming it back in her ribcage. If scars make things tougher then surely Martha's heart must be as weatherbeaten and leathery as a medicine ball.

Martha likes to tappity-tap at the computer keyboard as if she's realigning NASA satellites. In fact, when the system crashed last week it took her an hour to work out Mrs Milligan had tripped over the cable and pulled out the plug. But despite that, Martha looks the part. When the borrowers come through the revolving doors into the lobby they are greeted by Queen Victoria, perched on a plinth in all her stony majesty. Then it's a few steps past the double doors to the media library, cross the stairs to the archives, through the chickenwired fire doors towards the desk—and there's Martha, looking like an intellectual. Colourful and bohemian.

And this afternoon the French teenagers are in. The council's Twin Town Spring Exchange Programme has begun. Somewhere in the library at Soissy-sur-Seine a renegade band of English teenagers are trampling the carpets and monopolising the terminals. There is also a young French man, a university student in his twenties on a different university exchange programme, who is a conversation assistant at the secondary school. He's from Bordeaux and he is Sequoia Forest Man, you just have to keep looking upwards until at last he looks down and his tousled sandy blond fringe falls forward like a landslide.

We are all supposed to be made the same I know, ten fingers, ten toes, two eyeballs. But we are different. He is called Joaquim and he is simply and utterly different. His hair, that sandy blond colour that you don't find on English heads. It has this texture that's unlike anything I've ever seen. The

9

colour is so golden, I suppose because it is sunny in Bordeaux. But there are tinges of red in there, the flare of orange when he runs his hand through it to push his overgrown fringe back. He does that a lot when he's writing emails home.

His hands too, they're like farmers' hands. Big and square, and the back of them is surfaced like a contour map of some Pyreneean commune. The mountain range of his knuckles, the valleys between. And then the gnarled plain of skin, forested with vaguely gingery hair, the rivers of his veins. His nails are very clean and clipped. The very crisp bright blue of his eyes. His lips have a purse to them, where the French comes out.

Ouh. Huit. Oui.

No. It's not what you think, it's just that he's in here a lot and what else is there to do? Am I supposed to ignore him? Look away and not smile?

The French students are, conversely, not foreign. Teenagers are the same ill-mannered arrogants all over the world. I imagine there are teenagers in far-flung and desperate places, places where we send the Christmas charity shoeboxes, and they'll be just as bolshy and arrogant and complaining. I can see them opening the lid and finding the toothbrushes and soap and gloves, and wishing it was an Xbox instead of a shoebox.

They barge you in the library's revolving doors. They spin you. They trap you. They all think they are so clever. What a shock they will all get when life kicks in. They think they hate school and that they know so much and I for one will not warn them. Let it be a surprise. A big, fat, nasty one.

Only the nasty surprise is saved for Mrs Milligan, trying to tidy away the reference volumes they've left on the desks. As fast as she is shelving the *Encyclopaedia Britannica* so the tall, thickset one with bleached-blond hair is taking them off the shelf. The local schoolgirls have christened him Face because they all think he's gorgeous. The girls are standing spectating, taking this childishness for entertainment. They giggle and gasp as if he is swinging from a trapeze. My legs are shaking as I stand at the desk because I can hear the situation beginning to fray at the edges. I'd like to shock them all into submission, bark out, '*Damare! Yame!*' which is Japanese for 'Shut up! Quit it!' but I can't. The words choke down into my throat like small stones.

The other boys are restless now, and the short dark one who competes with Face starts to peel books from the other shelves. The volume lifts, the words spit and spatter. Face shoves the short one into the table, which totters, and just before the riot begins, here is Mrs Atkinson to the rescue in her magician's gloves.

'If you don't mind, this is a library. The rule is quiet. If you wish to chat then I suggest you take yourselves down the street to the Boolean Engine Internet Café.'

Mrs Atkinson does not have children, but is getting divorced. She doesn't talk about her life outside the library; what we have found out about her husband and the circumstances, we've learned through idle gossip and hearsay. Of course, when you hear the idle gossip it isn't any wonder she doesn't talk. It seems sometimes as if the gossip is about another Mrs Atkinson, because at work nothing gets by her.

However we understand that Mr Atkinson is in information services, and is on a fast track to foreign parts when the divorce comes through. He is going to set up library systems and information services in portakabins across Belize with the help of Carmen, his International Information Systems Administrative Assistant. She's leggy with fake fire-red hair and until recently she was a lapdancer at a club called Movers and Shakers at the far end of town.

I wonder what Mrs Atkinson is like in real life, when she takes off the white gloves and goes home. I imagine her in the supermarket, alphabetising the tins. Anyway the magic gloves aren't working at this moment because the teenagers haven't vanished. It is nothing overtly sinister, just that unruly way they have of not coming to heel, of not doing as they're told. Mrs Atkinson looks as if she is directing traffic, waving her hands in sweeping, ineffectual gestures. I concentrate on the computer screen but it's no use, I can see her and them on the periphery of my vision. I can hear her and them. Face begins to mimic her. Almost catches Mrs Milligan on the cheek with his flamboyant gesture. That does it.

'*Cessez-donc! Allez-vous-en. Toute de suite. Allez-vous-en,*' snaps Mrs Atkinson.

The short dark combatant says with deep, low, scorn, '*Baisse-toi grandmere.*'

And she stoops. Eagle-like. '*J'EN AI SOUPÉ. C'EST TOUT. ALLEZ-VOUS-EN.*' She's speaking in a booming voice. She has this trick of somehow making it an octave lower when she's shouting. It's wonderful to hear, deep and sonorous. Operatic, almost.

Her voice expands outwards and there is suddenly silence. In the space where no one knows quite what to do, Mrs Atkinson points a white-gloved finger at the exit. The teenagers file past meekly. As the last one spins through the door and a tearful Mrs Milligan scuttles to the toilets, the whole library is looking at Mrs Atkinson.

This is why she's chair of the twin town committee.

After half an hour I am still at the desk, blind to the screen in front of me, imagining that Mrs Milligan might have drowned herself in the U-bend or escaped through the tiny window into the freedom of the Memorial Gardens. Then she slides into the seat at the computer. Her face looks washed and brushed up, her eyes pink instead of red. And I look away.

We're open until eight now, Monday through Thursday, and Martha is pushing the boundaries of that with her author events. Tonight a local horror-story writer called Devlin Kennedy is coming in for a cheese-and-wine book reading that doesn't even start until eight. This is the library as speak-easy. It is supposed to be closed up, dark; but no, you and a small group of others are allowed in for illicit cheddar and zinfandel. Although 'small group' is an understatement. There are always far more people in the library at night, and all the events Martha has organised have been full.

In the summer, of course, I can leave and it is still light. There is still time to get a baguette from the Miss Muffet Bakery and have an impromptu picnic by the war memorial.

In the winter the library takes on a bookish cosiness. The darkness outside is sparkled by the lights of the buses as they pull up and the brash fluorescent lighting we have in here makes everyone look paler, harsher. Except for Martha, who looks more porcelain and fragile. The carpet smells different too; it begins to hold the damp of the puddles that are trodden into it from outside, and people's coats and jackets have that winter-time coldness smell woven into their fibres. Martha has an Astrakhan coat, a tulip-shaped creature she bought at the vintage shop in the city. I want to steal that coat. I have to put my hands in my pockets over that coat.

It's been so cold of late I've wondered if the lake might freeze over. I was daydreaming about swimming under the crusted surface in the darkness when Joachim arrived to go online. He sat Gulliver-like at the computer, the chair too small for him, his long legs folded, knees almost under his chin. A couple of moments passed while I flicked through a copy of *Fauna Britannica* that had just come back in, before I reshelved it. The staffroom door was creaking open and closed as Harvey organised extra chairs.

The author events are held in the children's library, for the floorspace. It's at the front of the building, there is a big half-moon window and the whole room curls round. It reminds you of a chapter house in a cathedral. There is even a domed ceiling to match the one in the main library. I love that dome, the sky is always visible. The council hate it because the flashing always needs attention and in bad weather the rain drips straight through to Geography 910.

Martha was just coming through from the lobby with the cases from the wine shop, so when Joaquim had a problem there was only me to deal with it. It was nothing really, just some glitch on the server. Martha came over with a glass of wine. 'Here you are Ruby, something deliciously French,' she said, and then seemed to give me a knowing little look, a sly wink. She walked back towards the children's section and I saw in the on-screen reflection how she nodded something to Harvey and he looked over.

Then Joaquim's screen flickered into life; he was connected and I left him alone. I have an instinct for that. I know when it is time to go.

KENCHIKUKA

Architect

_____

'I said I needed this section on A3.' Mackenzie Tierney screwed up the page slithering out of the photocopier. He had rushed into the library looking for Martha to do some last-minute photocopying for some meeting and had found only me.

'You'll have to do, Rosie.'

Mackenzie Tierney is crisped and clipped and tall enough to block out the light when he stands before you. Salt and pepper hair shaved to number four. A set square of a man disguising physical confidence under expensively bagged clothing. A leather jacket, a linen shirt. Sometimes when he approaches the desk his eyes are so dark brown they are deeper than black. It is as if he isn't real, that somewhere inside the thin dark tunnels of his eyes lurks the real Mackenzie Tierney. That inner person is a very bad idea.

I caught the elevation as it rolled off the copier, handed it to him and looked directly into his face, or tried to. He was looking down, about to make a note on the original with one of the library's green Venus pencils. My hand shot out.

'Don't.' I hadn't intended my voice to sound so like a slap. Tierney looked up. If you were useful to him he would see you, otherwise his gaze glanced across your surface. You were a smudge on his lens.

'Calm down Rosie, it's pencil. It'll rub off.' The dark eyes bringing me into charmed focus. *Yes, I see you now, you will be beautiful if you will just behave for me.* He reached again, jabbing the pencil at the plans.

'No.'

This time he shook my hand off. Like a cobweb. 'I don't have time for this.'

I grabbed his hand as tight as I dared, shaved my voice down to a steely whisper. 'Mark that and I'll throw you out.'

'Oh for pity's sake, get serious Rosie.'

I snatched his pencil from him and threw it. Harder than I planned. It broke against the wall.

'Ruby,' I said.

He gave a supercilious look and then began to riffle and crumple his way through another set of plans.

'What are you going to do to Kite House?' I asked above the clacking of the photocopier.

'You've seen the place? It's a wreck.'

That was true enough. Kite House stood above the town and once upon a time it had commanded the view. Then, as they built the plastics factory and the dual carriageway, the windows at Kite House had been boarded up as if to close its eyes against the march of industry below. I thought it looked like a house asleep. I liked to walk out there and look at it in the rain, loving the sound of the water dripping and pattering in the broken gutters as I sheltered inside the old laundry.

'That's not an answer,' I heard myself snarl.

Tierney looked up sharply. 'There isn't an answer.

Nothing's set in stone yet.'

'Oh. Is that code for, "I'm razing it to the ground to build contemporary urban living space"?' I hoped I'd managed to keep my voice low.

'Listen Rosie, this project's at a delicate stage. I hope I can trust you with…' Something metallic glinted in his eyes. 'Can I trust you?'

How do you operate eyes like that? My God, the optical nerve of it!

'Doubt it.' At first I wasn't certain I had replied aloud. But Tierney wasn't listening, had accepted that I was bending to his will. Moved on. Busy now, reckless in his hurry with the documents, letting them slither and slide from the table as he sorted through. I squatted onto my haunches to salvage them from the floor; he stepped backwards, his heel almost nipping my fingers.

'Sorry, didn't see you down there.' An apology delivered down the ridge line of his fly. 'No damage done I hope Rosie.' His eyes lashed across me, smart and smirking. I stood, placed the rear elevation on the table.

'Rita,' I said, more tersely than I'd intended.

'What?'

'Ruth.'

He didn't like this game.

'Roxanne.'

I enjoyed what I'd managed to do to those eyes.

'Roberta.'

A flicker of uncertainty crossed Tierney's face, then he looked away, began screwing up more bits of paper, ripping it all off the feed. Tossing it over my head towards the bin. I could feel the concussion of air his hand made beside my cheek. Felt his eyes upon me.

'Let's do this again shall we?'

Instead of stepping beside me, he reached round me, corralling me in his arms as he lifted the photocopier lid and adjusted the document slightly. His fingers drummed on the control panel, the pinkie ring catching in the light.

'Show me, Rosie. Which button do I press?'

'Rhiannon.'

Behind me he stalled for a nanosecond. I pressed the green button. Concentrated on green, green for calm. He hovered as if he might lean forward, then moved sideways, back to ravaging the plans.

'This. This…Two of these…' Tierney lowered his voice as if he'd remembered he was in the library, '…second thoughts, can you do me three of everything so far?' He checked his expensive watch against the clock above the desk. 'I'll be back in an hour…oh and this, I forgot…This side elevation of the laundry block…Three again if you could Rosie…?'

'Roger.'

Tierney's eyes flared for a second, unsmiling. Then he was striding off, wheeling round a few steps later to tap at the watch. 'An hour.'

He was wearing odd socks. One green tweedy, the other black. I flipped up the lid and lined up the plans of the laundry block as Tierney's hands swooped into my hair, tilting my head up, and his mouth planted a showy kiss on my forehead.

'You're a star, Rodge.' And he was gone.

I was astonished when Mrs Atkinson materialised and asked if I would come down to the archive. I looked at her stupidly for a moment, stupidly enough for her face to register regret that she'd asked me. Then I recovered my momentum and before I knew it I was clacking across the lobby and heading down the stairs. I hadn't noticed the stone gargoyles until then, carved into the finial on the stone banisters. I noticed that as Mrs Atkinson moved down the stairs she touched the nose of the gargoyle, as if for luck. Surreptitious, a tweak of the nose as she reached for the banister.

Downstairs is not somewhere I've been before, except for the time when we had the builders in and we had to use the emergency toilet. We passed that room, filled to the ceiling just as I remembered with old manila folders. Mrs Atkinson isn't just the Senior County Archive Officer. She's a hoarder.

She turned sharp left into a side room, dark despite the long fluorescent bulb. You couldn't see where the walls were because the floor-to-ceiling steel shelving was packed with archive boxes, all shades of manila brown, faded and dusted with age. Some of the very oldest ones were creamy coloured, like parchment. The boxes with copperplated labels were the first, and then there were successive varieties of typewriting stretching forwards through the ages. I wondered who the archive officers had been back then, if they had thought about their handwriting outliving them.

'I need you to reorganise the photo library.' Mrs Atkinson's tone of voice was different down here and she had been talking for some moments before I realised it was reverence. She was outlining her plans.

'...alphabetical by place and then we can cross reference to specific town events and festivals, I've been making a list for a reference point. Not all of these festivities have survived. I thought we could collate the information and maybe pull in the museum curator on this. Have you met Winn?'

I looked blank. This should have been another moment

where Mrs Atkinson doubted her choice of assistant, but actually she wasn't aware of me. Here, this was her territory, she had descended to Wonderland.

'I'll go and ask Harvey to rig up the scanner in here and we can save them all to disk.' She turned in the doorway. The corridor light shone on her glasses but couldn't shine on the crack in her voice. 'We can't lose any of this Ruby, not one face.'

Not one face. Thousands. As I worked my way along the top shelf, the lids lifted on young men at the roller rink, prisoners of war digging potatoes at a local farm. They looked out at me from the past and I travelled. I liked the boot shop with all the hundreds of pairs hanging outside the windows. I liked the butchers standing outside their shop, the sheets of pork ribs like xylophones in the window.

The town was beautiful then, or so it seemed to me from my warm and well-fed twenty-first-century viewpoint. But looking closer, even the young men looked old somehow, behind their wiry moustaches. The women all pinched at the waist and pinched in the face. I thought of how life would be then, a life of childbirth and toil. A world without washing machines, your only detergent the sweat of your brow.

Mrs Atkinson did not give me her Lost Boys file that day.

Mrs Atkinson, who until about this time I had always considered to be a bit of a harridan, cold and reserved, did have some fellow feeling. I don't know why she handed it over in the end. I think it was that she couldn't stand to scan them in, she couldn't bear to look on all those faces and know that out of all the men at the station, all the hundreds of men trailing down Fore Street like some carnival parade, only twenty-seven of them came back.

It was much later that I learned that she knew all the names, had spent years sifting through electoral rolls and census returns and newspaper stories to find them all. She was supposed to be writing a book and she had all the information, had even made trips to France to assist with some identifications.

I didn't wonder that day, but I wondered later, what she found of herself in all that history, in all of that tragedy. That day, I sat in the ribbed room and scanned, the light on the scanner bed blinking and shining like the thousands of sunrises and sunsets between them and me.

HASHI O WATARU

Cross the bridge

———

The supermarket had only recently taken to opening late. Until then if you couldn't get there before eight o'clock you had to starve. And if you could get there before eight o'clock, most other people in town seemed to have had the same impulse. Now they're open twenty-four hours you can often go and find no one in there at all, apart from Jean on the tills.

I've always found the supermarket a kind of refuge. No one really notices you, so intent are they upon their sausage selection process and squidging fruit to see if it's ripe. You can hide behind your trolley.

Tonight there were balloons about, which should have made me suspicious. But it could have been Custard Awareness Week or a promotional tasting for the new cooked-meat deli selection. Last week there were skinny blonde women here, in skin tight hotpants and thigh-length white boots, promoting a new plastic bread. As if women who wear skin-tight hotpants ever eat anything as prosaic as bread, and certainly not plastic industrial bread. Blondes in skinny hotpants drink vodka and teeter through the world tempting you to reach out and topple them over.

And the background music didn't give me a clue either, although I did find myself thinking about things I shouldn't as I leaned into the freezer for the minted peas. It was a selection of eighties pop ballads about love and longing. Maria McKee demanding Show Me Heaven as if you might find it in aisle five with the baking foil. But that's normal. I didn't even notice that people were standing by half-empty trolleys talking to each other. I should have looked at the contents of the trolleys.

He wasn't tall, that was the first thing that struck me about him. He wasn't stooping to talk to me like some do. He was stocky, Celtic, and you knew that if you ran your hand across his back you would feel the broadness of his shoulders under his shirt. He was wearing a fancy coloured silk tie that he had changed into; the white shirt had come straight from work, from an office where he did something useful and everyday. Not a hero, not a fireman or a police officer. He looked like a salesman or a pen pusher.

He hadn't bothered with a trolley, or even picked up a basket. He was just standing there, with his dark raincoat on, looking soggy round the edges, but anticipatory. He was watching me lean into the freezer and I straightened quickly, moved on without looking at him.

It freaked me out that he was already by the cheese counter when I arrived there. Could he teleport himself? He did have a small package of cheddar—the woman at the till was sticking the label on it. He took it but didn't move away. So instead of asking for the Jarlsberg that I wanted, I looked the cheese over as if none of it interested me, and moved on.

He moved with me. The hairs on the back of my neck

23

rose. My heart seemed to be beating fit for two people.

'You look as if you're shopping,' he said then. I looked at him, and he smiled. A genuine smile, his nerves fraying it a little at the edges. 'You've actually got shopping in your trolley.' He eyed the minted peas. The toilet rolls. The box of tampons.

'This is a supermarket isn't it? Or have I pushed through the wrong door and ended up in the casino?' I could hear my own voice as if I was listening on the radio. It was brittle and it put him off. Slightly.

'I'm sorry. You really are shopping aren't you?' He looked puzzled, as if he was trying to save me from embarrass-ment. I nodded and was cruel enough to hold his gaze. I wanted to scare him; looking people right in the eyes, unblinking, generally does it. He made as if to turn away and then turned back, nonchalant. Just giving me directions for the ring road.

'Tonight is singles night, you know. If you happened to be shopping for something…not on the shelves.'

Then I noticed his badge, a traffic light with the amber light coloured in. A bright primary-school orange. A woman with nothing in her basket but a pair of black stockings pushed past then; she too bore a badge, a flashy green-for-go.

He stood there in my silence. 'Only if.' And he gave his edgy smile again. There was a heavy moment of silence broken by a shrill fuck-me laugh directed at the muscular teenage boy on the butcher's counter.

'Judd,' said amber-light man, and offered a hand for a formal handshake. I looked at it in silence. He managed a face-saving edgy smile before heading down the nearest aisle, past the washing powder. Then he took a couple of steps back and actually picked up a packet of washing powder.

I abandoned the trolley by the shampoo. Panic crowded me, my throat thick as the doors hissed open. Outside, the white carpark lighting seemed to cast a fog and I looked about, unable to find my bearings until I focused on the technical college, beacon bright at the end of the street. A redbrick palace clearly visible from the edge of the supermarket carpark. And then it seemed that as soon as I thought about it, I was standing in the doorway to the classroom.

Setsuke had already begun, and the Monday night strangers turned to look at me. Setsuke only smiled, her hand graceful as she gestured that my usual seat at the back had not been taken.

Later, I got off the bus two stops early. I like to walk in the dark, to be in the parallel universe of night. I don't really understand why we don't all walk around at night. The air smells better, as if all the scents of the day trap themselves, accumulate. Sound carries further too or perhaps there is just more room for it because all the cars are in their driveways and people are submerged in the babble of TV. I enjoyed the sound my boots made on the pavement, powering me forwards. My calves aching as the road climbed in front of me.

Inside the hallway I caught my skirt on that *bloody* bike again and went flying. The scrawny bloke from the third floor owns it. He's tall. And he stoops as if the world is just not the right size for him. The bike was taking up almost all the floorspace as usual, because he doesn't really care about whether anyone can get past, he's always more bothered about whether the derailleur is pushing against the gas meter cupboard. He's got an ironing board down here now too. What a minimalist palace he must live in. It must be bordering on Zen perfection.

Ambushed, I looked down at the red gash the bike had cut into me. The white rent of skin in the mound of my thumb. The snaggle teeth of that chain chewing me. Oil, like blood. My skirt tearing, as frayed as my temper. My leg prickled and stung as I hobbled towards my door. Trying to turn the key in the lock with my throbbing thumb. Nothing sticks out like a sore thumb, unless it's that bike. Scarred and battered, I moved into my living room and hitched up the hemline. *Sod* it, I was going to bruise. And I'd got oil on the skirt too.

So. I occupy the ground floor flat but I don't have the garden. The back of the house dips a level, so the garden belongs to the basement flat. Looking around, my own place is verging on a state of Zen, but I don't need coffee tables and rugs and stuff. Just the sofa and the TV, although I'd struggle to remember the last time I switched it on. Books? Well, I work in a library. I painted the place white when I first moved in but I regret it. The damp shows through on the front wall by the blinds.

The bedroom is a bedroom, therefore it contains a bed. There's a winter coat in the wardrobe but the chest of drawers is empty because all my underwear is drying on the radiator in the hallway.

I unloaded my shopping and put the kettle on, still feeling rattled from the supermarket. I ran the water for a bath, drew the curtains and the blinds and locked my door. I always wedge a chair under it. There have been a lot of break-ins nearby. And of course nowadays there's also the loon who's been stealing knickers.

I hoped the bath would settle me but it didn't. It got worse really, the thinking about things I shouldn't even be thinking about.

Music doesn't help either. Apart from the fact that the

woman in the basement, the one who owns the garden, complains if you so much as turn the radio on, there's the added aspect that music is evocative. Music and smells, the most powerful forces in the universe. So I mauled around the flat listening to the night, the creaking of the buildings, the wind in the trees outside. I sat in my aged bathrobe in the window of the kitchen with the blind up.

If you have the lights off no one can see you, and in the middle of the year when the trees are in leaf, the housing that runs at the back of this street is obscured. They can't see you, you can't see them. Gradually, as the year turns, the leaves fade and fall and this whole other landscape of strangers is revealed as you bear witness through bedroom and bathroom windows. I switch the lights out and I watch through the binoculars. We are altogether too careless with electric lighting.

It was about three in the morning when I decided I could go into the garden. She was asleep downstairs; I couldn't see the footprints of light from any of her windows. I opened the kitchen window and looked out over the new pergola. It butted up to my window and I'd been pleased when it went up few weekends ago. It formed a screen which meant I could look into the garden even when she was there. A bonus for me, because she is big on being nude, even in winter. She wanders around in big green wellies and leather gauntlets pruning the shrubs. And there was the memorable Sunday when she was masturbating in that hammock she's strung up. Didn't take the gauntlets off. She should have a website.

I stepped out onto the wooden framework, catlike, and felt the coolness of the night air sooth me. I crouched there with that feeling you have when you're a kid, that uncertain daring of knowing you shouldn't but doing it anyway. I breathed deeply, easily. It felt as if I hadn't breathed for years.

Later, I did not remember falling asleep at the kitchen table until someone's car alarm started to panic at about four and I uncreased my face from the cold melamine table top and wandered towards bed.

I was woken by a different alarm only a few hours later. Third Floor Biker Bloke clattering down the stairs. Every step echoed down to me, a countdown to the bellowing in fury as he saw his bike tyres.

Every day I will do it. I have decided. Every day until he realises it is a message. I am a very patient woman.

KOEN NI WA IROIRO NA TORI GA IMASU

In the park there are various kinds of birds

I was a week into the scanning process and it was as if Mrs Atkinson had taken her magic gloves and enchanted me. My day started earlier and earlier. I had been coming in at eight when I knew Mrs Atkinson arrived, but I had noticed that the doors were already open then, the lobby polished and smelling of lemon juice and beeswax and linseed.

The caretaker, Mr Machin, arrived at seven and now so did I. I think it perturbed him. The library, which he was proprietorial about at the best of times, had been his sole territory for an hour each day. But I was careful not to impinge. I took the five steps across his freshly buffed floor to the steps and I vanished. It was like a wormhole.

Then I spent just about all day down there. I moved through the townscape, consigning it all to the memory of the scanner and the CDs. The old views of the park when it still had railings, elaborate and curlicued. The railway arriving, everyone in their whitest Sunday shirt, their hat-shadowed faces. The ironwork of the construction of the railway footbridge, moustachioed men working braziers and metal.

Schoolchildren scowled from behind ranks of desks; one small boy at the back who had moved his head was blurred for eternity, his small hand, grubby, clutching chalk. The factories, the women standing arms akimbo by vast spinning and weaving machines.

I drank it all in, and at night I arrived back at the flat and fell into a shallow sleep, dreamed of the streets and carnivals, wandered the corridors and halls. Through the parks and gardens, past the fountains, where the leaves shimmered and rustled.

At last I reached the more domestic pictures and was forced to pause. My gaze lingered on the intricate lace of the weddings, the tight-angled bodices of brides, the stern bewhiskered jaws of grooms and grandfathers. The great army of bristles sweeping through history.

And then the laundresses of Kite House looked out at me. They were part way down a stack of portraits of domestic staff commissioned by Viscount Breck. Not for them the stiff formality. Instead, here was a quintet of women in a washhouse yard, bared forearms sinewed with work, the rubbed quality of their hands gripping soap, sheets bannered behind them.

I didn't know the history that first day I looked at it and then, somehow reluctantly, blinked it into the scanner. That's how it affected me; I held onto it, then I laid it face down on the desk and scanned in other images first, parks and gardens. The fish market off Wetherspoon Quay.

I just thought those women looked out at me. I'd been involved in other photos. I'd dreamed about walking the streets and buzzing round the roller rink, but this was different. The image spoke to me.

It was the girl at the far end, posed two or even three steps back from the others, by a washtub. Out of place. The girls in the forefront looked out with confidence, the middle girl, hand on hip, managing a hybrid of haughty and naughty. *Try me*, she seemed to challenge you. But the girl at the far end did not smile. Her face was turned to the camera as if at the last moment she had been instructed by the photographer to look up. She stood, arms at her sides, looking like a stranger, someone who had wandered in on an errand. Someone lost.

Mrs Atkinson found me. I had pushed the wheelie chair away from the desk because a thick splash of tear had fallen without me even realising it was going to. It so nearly splashed the laundresses. I was sitting stranded on the chair and the tears just flowed. Nothing wailing and dramatic, more like a persistently leaking tap where it's all wastage and you need to get it fixed.

'Ruby?' she said in a voice so unlike her Mrs Atkinson, Archivist voice that I was startled. I thought she was one of the laundresses, speaking to me across the space–time continuum.

'Ruby, whatever is the matter?' and she moved towards me. I whizzed the chair backward slightly and turned the tap on the tears. Turned it. The washer was clearly gone however, because I couldn't do it as instantly as I wanted. I used to be very good at that, at being able to turn it off so that I wouldn't be found out.

'Have you been down here all day?'

I tried to sound busy. 'I've found some good quality photographic images in the files for Kite House.' I had just about stopped it up now. I turned away from her and busied myself with the file, pulling out the few real beauties that I had found amongst all the work Viscount Breck commissioned. Most were standard set pieces, an interesting social record of the time and the people, but I found a few that had real merit. A different light to them, as if the photographer had taken the images at early morning or twilight, something it would have been quite hard to do in the days before modern lighting and cameras. He wouldn't have been able to snap away with a different aperture setting or fiddle about with a light meter. He would not have had a silver-lined umbrella to reflect flash back onto them. Even so, he had captured it. Time, snared, to be revisited.

'I was thinking that I could take them over to the print shop, see if we can have them printed up as posters. Or cards, perhaps. I've seen something like it in the museum shop, it would raise a bit of revenue for the library. Or, I don't know, some other good cause.'

I was relying heavily on Mrs Atkinson's English reserve now, on the fact that she wasn't going to push me, that I would be allowed privacy. I was also aware that she would head straight up to the staffroom for her tea break and tell them all about it.

Of course, I've already indicated that Mrs Atkinson is a surprising woman. Yes. She allowed me my privacy. Yes, she headed straight up to the staffroom. But she didn't speak to anyone, she made a cup of tea and brought it down to me. She placed it on the trolley table beside me so that it wouldn't be knocked over and spoil anything. She said not one word, not even, 'Do you take sugar?'

Is this kindness? I caught myself thinking that I was so far removed from kindnesses I couldn't tell.

Outside, when I surfaced for lunch, it was raining sheet steel. As I made my way through Queens Park the water was washing down my face and into my clothing despite my waterproofs. I thought about taking up my usual seat at the back of the rose garden but the weather drove me further round the curve of the path, past the curry plants and the elephant's ears to the stone pavilion. They had been repainting some of the benches in there for the winter and they were stacked neatly. I sat on the foremost. The wood warmed beneath me and I was happy to hear the rain pummelling down.

Rain makes me feel better. Or at least it did until I spotted Martha. She was dressed in her spectacular rain cape which is a waxy brown on the outside and a weathered and ancient shiny bronze on the inside. She had just come in through the side gate and I watched as she strode past the wide perennial border. She looked like a seed pod, tossed from one of the taller specimens there. She was moving away from me and I was, in any case, in a forgotten corner. I didn't wave because I didn't want company, but I watched to see where she would go.

And a voice inside my head warns, *Look away now*, but I don't look away. Instead, I take in the details because life is about the details. It's the small stuff that's going to count in the end. You won't care who was prime minister but you will care what colour her knickers were that day or how her breath smelled of liquorice. You will.

He was waiting for her in the orangery. I had not seen him. I wonder still if he had seen me, if perhaps his secret knowledge that I was there made her more delicious. She hurried in, Tierney holding the door for her and barely able to keep his hands off her long enough to shut it behind her. Then it seemed they were dancing, whirling round each other in perfect synchronisation as they moved further into the orangery. Actually that's only a couple of feet because the orangery is not exactly a cathedral of space.

Martha flapped up the rain cape then, its bronze lining flashing as if Zeus were transforming in there. Of course, the only thing that transformed was Tierney's face, burning with greediness, jaw clenching, as Martha was suddenly astride him.

I didn't finish my sandwich. But I stayed to the end.

Afterwards of course, back at the library, I couldn't look her in the face without thinking of the orgasmic O of Tierney's mouth, of the white marble of her thighs. She hadn't seen me, of that I was absolutely certain, but I had seen them and that was too much. I could hide in the archive but I couldn't stop my mind from wandering.

I hadn't felt that for a long time and I was terrified. That's how it had to be for me, because I could see the signs above it all, as if someone inside my head was pressing a buzzer, an alarm. You cannot know what you connect with when you plug into each other. It's the meeting of parts, not of minds. It shook my hands all that afternoon and my mind swirled with a strange brew of images of the laundresses and Martha and Tierney and other images, other memories. The last soggy photos in the bottom of my lifeboat.

I tried to think back to his face, smart and smirking by the photocopier. I wanted to think back and pick out the expression he might have had in his eyes. Not that I think I can decipher anything from that. Everyone, or at least the more philosophical everyones, tell you that the eyes are the window to the soul but I have to disagree. People can disguise themselves. There isn't anything useful written on flags hanging in the backs of their eyes.

KOTOWAZA: 'SARU MO KI KARA OCHIRU'

Japanese proverb: 'Even monkeys fall from trees'

As she stood beside me in the staffroom making a cup of tea, Mrs Milligan asked Martha about some university event she was supposed to be going to that evening. More cheese and wine and some arty exhibition at the new gallery they've just opened. I forgot the kettle was boiling. I could hear it rattling away but I forgot to switch it off.

My mind was distracted by Martha and the smells that came from her. Something of him was in there, not just his sperm donation. There was the prickling of sweat at the roots of his hair and that certain something, expensively flowery but masculine, that he'd slapped on his face after shaving. The cold damp cobweb whiff of the orangery had brushed off on her, not just on the cobwebs on her hem but something that had soaked itself into her skin. I don't know what is happening lately. I don't know why I can't keep the wrapper on it.

I wiped at my seeping eyes, giving an unconvincing pretence that some foreign body had lodged there. Neither of them said anything. Martha stirred her tea harder, talked about Mac Tierney and how Tripp Tierney Associates, his architecture practice and cultural hub of the town, is sponsoring this exhibition at the uni.

As that topic wound up, so too did Mrs Milligan's courage and she garbled out, in a nerve-strung squeak, 'You don't think you could wangle me a ticket to this Joan of Art event, do you Martha? Only I was at school with Joan.' The effort of asking for something nearly floored her; she was flushed with relief at having got the words out.

'Joan?' Martha's left eyebrow quizzed.

'The artist. It's her exhibition. Joan Twydall.' Mrs Milligan usually has that high-pitched voice on when she's put in charge of the story morning for the pre-school borrowers and their stressed out, verging-on-a-breakdown mums.

Martha didn't hesitate. 'There aren't any tickets as far as I know.'

A lie. The curve of her raised left eyebrow was the give-away. I couldn't work out why we wouldn't be allowed to go.

'Oh. Couldn't Mac pull a string or something?' Mrs Milligan queried, her voice wavering with the effort.

'I've been told it's a private show. Invitation only.'

And then I heard it, the high descant of doubt in Martha's voice. She, clearly, had not been invited and she, too, couldn't work out why. The scent of doubt, sappy and green, was what had soaked into her skin

In the end, all I had to do was phone up the university and find out. Setsuke, the Intermediate Japanese tutor, was on a half-term holiday in France this week and it seemed to me that the art show would shave a few hours off the evening, allowing for getting to and from the campus. I thought of telling Mrs Milligan but I assumed that she'd been feigning interest in the exhibition to avoid my spilling tears.

After a dodgy start I began to enjoy the day, thinking about the journey, possibly a meal in one of the campus cafes. It was a town in itself. It would be an adventure, I thought; but one that was safe and planned and within my limits. And then I caught sight of my reflection in the doors as I left. I had no time to head back to the flat and it would be a pointless trip anyway, there was nothing else there for me to wear. I had the clothes I stood up in and a couple of T-shirts, and the usual wash-through of underwear drying on the radiator in the kitchen.

I had not felt the tug of the shopping precinct for a very long time. It had been shoved under some dusty rug at the back of my head, and now it peeked out. Not frivolous retail therapy. Necessity: I needed new clothing. There was a shop called Norsk that I had walked past several times, stylised in white on a Gustavian blue background. I had always liked the headless dummies in the window, their calico covered torsos and elegant hatstand legs.

As I stood in the curtained cubicle and fumbled my way out of my work jumper, I was ashamed to see it was so worn in places that it looked as if it had been knitted by spiders. I realised that I hadn't bought anything new to wear for over a year.

Then, with a sudden rush of pleasure, it was dressing-up time. A bronze necklace against skintight bloodblack red top. Amber bangles. There was a rush of remembrance, more potent than heroin, as I pulled on a skirt that wasn't mine, something new, tight, purple, slinky, revealing.

Which I didn't buy. Burnt orange, cinnabar, peacock. Which I put back.

Black was what I reached for. Dark and dramatic. It was the only thing that didn't terrify me. I bought the long straight elegant black one. And a black cashmere top with a deep v. Black bra from next door to go under, because of that deep, revealing v. Make-up from the little pharmacy smelling of deodorant and hairspray. Next door to that the shoe shop and the new boots that took me less than five minutes to see in the window, try on in the shop, carry out in a bag. Those black leather boots took my breath away.

'Do you want me to bag these for you or bin them?' The assistant waved a cheery shoe-shop hand at my old boots; the appalling worn and mended, worn again and mended again state of them. They looked forlorn, abandoned on the countertop and I couldn't do it to them. They bore the imprints of my feet, they had moulded themselves to me and it just isn't that easy.

So I carried them with me in a bag. Plus the bag containing my old clothes. I boarded the bus that grinds up the hill to the university campus and I looked like a bag lady.

When I dropped my workaday rags at the cloakroom before entering the exhibition I felt suddenly naked in my new boots and my black clothes, until someone handed me a glass of sharp grassy wine and I felt myself stretch and uncoil like a waking cat.

It was all very civilised, people in good clothes standing around chatting over the grassy wine and the catered food, ignoring the hardworked art. My face was tired of smiling so I sipped more wine and took a look at the walls.

I had not expected the paintings to be good. I had anticipated an exhibition of someone's hobby paintings that would be at best decorative and at worst talentless. I had not expected to be moved or touched or slapped in the face by them. My heart raced and I couldn't work out whether it was simply that I was unused to the alcohol or the colours of the paintings and what they were doing to the inside of my head.

It was as if my memory flashed and blared on me, as if one moment I was there and the next I wasn't; I was revisiting some purple and amber tinted moment that should have been deleted. The squares and rectangles were like passages to me, places I had been, places I should never, never go again. And then the black clothes didn't seem such a haphazard choice. The black clothes cast their spell of invisibility.

I tried to cut a steady path through the room, drawn first to the huge rectangular daubing on the far wall that hummed at me with a deep teal blue splodged with a bright leaf green. It was a portrait. No, it was more. It was paint transformed into a woman. The hands reached out and slid themselves letterlike through the slats of my ribcage and tugged me towards it.

I drank more wine and as the room started to smudge around the edges and take on pastelly hues and broad strokes I thought that I was foolish. I had to get home on the bus, after all. In fact I was going to be a real Cinderella, not just because of the glass boots but because the last bus left campus at midnight and I had to be on it. Almost the moment I thought it, Tierney appeared. Charming. Alone.

Alcohol is a poison. This is how it works. That night, in the crisp white space of the University Gallery Mackenzie Tierney did not seem like a bad idea. In the miasma of pinot grigio he was handsome, desirable, dressed in a baggy and crumpled charcoal grey linen jacket with a black fine-knit sweater underneath. There was a suspicion of white T-shirt beneath the very slightly bristled chin. The granite-cliffed edge of jawline and the hand that reached up to smooth at the emerging bristle. A square hand; neat but not manicured nails. They were the nails of a man who gardens or cuts wood for fun.

His hair was the same salt and pepper it had been in the library when he had stood at the desk. But the alcohol had had enough time to steep itself into my blood. As I looked now at the well-clipped clean of his hair, the pepper was very black and the salting of white and grey gave it other hues, like slate.

The artist, Joan, swept up to him in a flowing linen outfit complete with big boots, soft and worn and making me feel homesick suddenly for my old boots in the cloakroom. I watched them as they spoke, thinking that either he was very tall or she was short because he had to stoop down, like a giraffe, towards her. His smile was warm. His lips brushed against her cheek and as her arms folded around him and they embraced, I couldn't breathe. I wanted that cheek to brush against my skin. I craved it. I wanted to know his smell. I wanted what Martha had had with him. My heart was racing as if it had legs and was running. Running. I couldn't stomach any more of the wine. I needed some water, my mouth had dried. I wanted his tongue to wet it.

I couldn't have been more obvious if I'd had a sign round my neck. I was all eyes, all greedy, all shot to hell.

Yes. He did lean towards me and he smelled the way heaven probably does, something sandalwood and cinnamon. I didn't dare put the glass to my lips, my teeth would have knocked against it. His eyes. Don't look in his eyes, I thought, but I couldn't turn away.

Well, what did I see? Because I've said there's nothing to be gleaned from them. They're as deceitful as the tongue. I turned my head in the direction of the painting on the far wall. I started to get a crick in my neck from looking away so I stepped once, twice, to turn my back to him. As if we were dancing an elegant tango he stepped once, twice, and was beside me. Tierney raised his glass, swilled the wine a little as he surveyed the painting on the far wall, *A Study in Three Greens*. Then I saw it, before it came, I saw it wheeling towards me.

'A Study in Black, she is dressed in the night.' He leaned, inclined his head, barely and purposefully brushing against my hair to speak directly into my ear. His voice a whisper, firing up every nerve ending in my neck and it seemed that my nipples were channelling electricity directly from the light fitting. The words so low I felt them spangling between my legs.

Only now, when he was so close I could lick him, I thought there might be an undernote to his smell, something bitter and unpleasant that I couldn't name. My hands began to shake so much it was all I could do not to drop the stupid wine. He was not anything I had imagined. I had taken a huge detour and it was in the wrong direction. I'd lost control of the steering wheel and the wheels were skidding out from under me. What was I doing? Why had I even come here? I had known what was possible. I was naked again, in the wrong boots. I wanted the painting to be a portal then, somewhere to jump through to find myself…

Anywhere but here. Get me out.

Tierney gave a shrug, chinked his glass against mine as if what he had said didn't matter, but it mattered. It mattered the way it matters if the sky falls on your head, the way it matters if you fall off a cliff and your grasping hands miss the seapinks by a mile as you plummet gracelessly to the waves below.

He hovered for a moment, like a cat picking over a mouse to see if there's life left. There wasn't. I averted my face, looking into the face of the nearest portrait. It stared disconcertingly back, as if it understood everything that was roiling in my head. Some sort of backslapping presentation began then, and I slunk out.

In the back of the cloakroom I took my real self out of the carrier bags and put it back on. I couldn't let Mrs Hyde out again. This was a lesson that I thought I had learned so long ago.

The Union Bar was almost empty. A birthday group of girls laughed and screeched and stubbed out cigarettes in the dregs of spent glasses. Against the neon flashing background of students playing slot machines and the metallic clatter of coin and electronic music, I sat. I was going to miss the bus but I didn't care by then. I needed to sit in a neutral zone and have a drink, even if it was only a ginger beer, to clear my head.

And I realised that my head has been too clear these last couple of years. It is filled with light; a harsh and blinding white light that illuminates everything.

NASURERU NA!

Don't forget!

———————

Mrs Milligan asked Martha how the evening went and Martha fudged it hopelessly. In the process she hurt Mrs Milligan's feelings. There was a sense sometimes that because Martha had the Affairs she was somehow a layer above us, 'us' being the spinsters and widows and divorcees.

'Ruby, you wouldn't like to go to the exhibition would you?' Mrs Milligan asked. This clearly was a measure of how desperate she was. At this comment, Martha gave out a huffy sound, glared at the back of Mrs Milligan's head and strode out.

'Erm.' I had no fudge. Mrs Milligan backtracked immediately.

'I'd like to go one evening, only I don't know if I can go on my own. I know it sounds silly, I am a grown up after all. Heavens, you probably go to lots of places on your own…' and then she thought about how that sounded. I didn't let her off the hook. I thought we would be even then. 'Oh, look Ruby, you wouldn't have to stay with me. Just get me there. You know, like the shuttle being piggybacked into space. You know what I mean? Once we got there you could just abandon me, you know, troll off and do your own thing.'

I looked at her with a thousand things to say, too cowardly to utter one of them. I have been here; I ought to draw her a detailed map of the ways out. And then the moment was gone and we were going to move forward and forget it.

'You're an independent young woman you see Ruby. I remember what it was like. Vaguely. You lose sight of it once you're a wife and then someone's mum. You get your life back eventually, but by then you've forgotten what you wanted to do with it.'

Mrs Milligan, clinging to her mug, managed an extremely jellified smile and turned to sit on the sofa. Her island refuge. I too gripped the lifebuoy that was my tea mug and sailed for the other island refuge, my seat by the window.

In the reflection on the glass I thought I saw something in Harvey's face as he stepped away from the table with his mug of tea. I thought he opened his mouth to speak to her, but instead of words coming out, a mouthful of tea washed in.

But I couldn't look out that day anyway. A couple were exhibition kissing by the war memorial.

I was in the archive later, tracking my laundresses through 1888–89. I had found an invoice in the household ledger that showed the domestic portraits were commissioned in the summer and autumn of 1889. I wandered through the blue marbled ledger for that year, my head filled with white linen snapping on strung out washing lines across the yard outside the laundry. I had walked there so often, picked my way round the buddleia and valerian that grew now between the thick cobblestones. I had found three of the laundresses. The first two, Maisie and Elsie, were local girls; another,

44

Alice, was from a farm on the border with the neighbouring county.

But the name that leapt out at me was Mary-Ann Penny. The housekeeper, Mrs Mason, had noted in her neat household journal that Mary-Ann had been born miles away from Kite House, in Totnes in Devon. I looked up Totnes online, found the neat streets rising from the River Dart, and took a virtual tour of the market town Mary-Ann had known before her washhouse and mangle.

I moved through the pages of the ledger, keeping my eye on the line that belonged to her, just below Maisie Arkwright and above Elsie Whitley. I saw the shillings and the stoppages that Mrs Mason had made and thought of all the days Mary-Ann had steamed away at the linens. Then, one week late in 1890, she was gone. No mention of reason, just a blank in the blue-marbled ledger where her name had been.

I felt a terrible panic for her. Where had she gone to? I noted the dates, flicked back and forth through the domestic ledgers, the household records for soap and raddlestones, finding anything and everything that could be chased up as a clue.

As I was scribbling down the details I heard a voice... *Lick*...a syllable punched out of the air. I listened...*Why not?*... It was Martha on the phone in the archive office. She was talking with...*Mac*...but half of their conversation was muffled, not just by distance but by the surreptitious way Martha was talking. She'd come down to the office specially while Mrs Atkinson was on her lunch break and had gone to the bank. Martha didn't want anyone to overhear. The few words I could tune into made no sense except for a sudden...*promise*.

They made some sort of date and I wanted to walk in there and slap her roundly. My palms itched. I didn't move as she hung up and moved off down the corridor. She probably thought I was on my lunchbreak too, that I had gone to the bank.

I followed her home after closing. It was easy to do. I just left earlier than her and made certain of my vantage point in the little side street that cuts down the side of the bank called Red Hat Lane. No one came through there so I could just lurk until Martha left the library and pick up her trail. She walked towards the centre of town, towards the new retail and luxury apartments development by Tripp Tierney Associates at the canalside. It's called Dry Dock because the canal doesn't go anywhere and no one from town could afford to live there.

Except, it turns out, for Mackenzie Tierney. I followed Martha until she slipped between the edges of the buildings. The early evening punters were arriving at the pubs and canal-side restaurants, a couple of hen parties getting an early start on the drinking and some corporate people, indistinguishable in their suits.

Their suits. I had forgotten the crispness of a good suit. I had forgotten what gentleman's grooming could be, the cedar tang of expensive aftershave, the hair cut in a salon by the style director. Men with all their edges knocked off, or rather their edges polished and honed, chins chiselled out of bristle and jawbone.

For just a moment I took my eye off Martha and nearly lost her amongst the charcoal flannel and moss-green wool. A glimmer of cufflink. The clean footprint of a leather soled shoe. They appeared like camouflage to distract and befuddle me. It was the suspension bridge that brought me back to earth. Just as she crossed it the floodlights came on, illumin-ating the glory of the spun-steel wires cobwebbing Martha's hurrying, scurrying figure.

Tierney was waiting at the other end of the bridge. He came striding to meet her, still in his lucky linen chat-up jacket, and I saw what he didn't. I saw her flinch as his arms enfolded her. There was no escaping the sight of that flinch. I saw her shoulders did not lose their tension as his linen-clad arm rested across them and they walked to a nearby doorway, glassy and lit. I could view them through the glass wall, making their way up the staircase as a woman with a great dane made her way down. They exchanged a greeting. It was like an ant farm.

I watched, standing in the darkness between the candlelit Italian restaurant and a smoky, rowdy pub. It was almost as if they sucked all the light out of the alleyway into themselves. There were tiny floor lights set into metal runners alongside the pavement that ran between the two buildings that should have illuminated me, the watcher. But they didn't.

Martha and Tierney moved all the way up to the top flat, to the roof terrace. To a tiny brushed-metal door in a wall of golden-hued wood cladding and the shelter of waving greenery. At the door she was hemmed in by his hands. On her face, in her hair. At her neck. I had seen what he had not; I had seen her flinch.

Sometimes we are in a web of our own spinning. We are the spider. When we're kids there's always the idea that our parents will pluck us free from the knots and strands. I know, it doesn't always work because they're spinning their own disasters into intricate design. But sometimes. Just sometimes. There should be someone for all of us, ready to catch us, should we fall.

I occupied no space at all in the farthest corner from the patio heater. I sipped at a Guinness and watched the cold autumn stars on the surface of the canal and did not look at the coin in my hand. I felt as if the world was all sharpened edges and there was nowhere to be at rest. All I could think of was the heat in the twenty pence piece turning between my fingers. The second the barman handed it to me, it had seemed to catch like a distress flare, a signal. *Flash*. I closed my eyes and—this is important, this is how *hard* I have tried—I stowed it in my pocket.

I zipped it. Metal teeth biting. Done.

Then I sat and waited. Who knew what for, I was grown up enough to know that she wasn't going home. She was there for the night, there for Tierney to make breakfast for in the morning. Except no, that was wrong. Tierney would expect her to make breakfast.

I waited because she had flinched, because there was something not quite right and I knew I wouldn't settle anywhere else. When the barman finally moved me out into the night and the lights started to click off all around the canalside, I realised I had missed the last bus home.

KOTOWAZA: 'UMA NO MIMI NI NENBUTSU'

**Japanese proverb:
'A prayer in the ears of a horse'**

There was, indeed there still is, a lot of time in the library to think. A library is everything hushed between the covers. If all the books were talking the noise would be horrendous, when you think about it. Not that I imagine people do, unless they happen to spend their time loafing behind the desk of the local library.

There is consequently a lot of space for brooding and torment. We aren't hustled or bustled, not even when the clock is ticking towards closing time and the last few Townswomen's Guild members are fighting over the latest Josephine Cox. If your life happens to be filled with angst then it can stew in the library. Thus it was that Mrs Milligan, mild-mannered librarian Mrs Milligan, was the one who spoke out against Martha.

Mrs Milligan had been on an emotional white-knuckle ride ever since her daughter-in-law Naomi had strayed. I have never had a child but it was plain to see that as time ticked on and the divorce proceedings soured, Mrs Milligan was struggling with the urge to do Naomi serious harm. Despite the fact that he was scorned, Mrs Milligan's son persisted in loving his errant wife and to be frank, that was all that saved her. Mrs Milligan's dreams might be filled with the fantasy of meeting Naomi in a back alley and ripping her face off, but saving Alex from further hurt prevented her from actually doing it.

Which meant that this rage had to find an outlet somewhere. No, this is not cod psychology. This is common sense. Everyone knew Mrs Milligan hungered for this, especially after the Tuesday evening when she was leaving work and Naomi was arriving, presumably to borrow a book, and Mrs Milligan trapped her in the revolving door.

She didn't say one word, didn't even look at her, she just made certain that as Naomi pushed to go in, she herself pushed to go out so that neither moved. She was utterly stilled, utterly patient until her soon-to-be-ex-daughter-in-law turned to face the street.

Mrs Milligan turned back into the library and they pushed in tandem, Naomi cast out into the street and Mrs Milligan thrown back under the carved gaze of Queen Victoria in the lobby. Mrs Milligan hurrying back to the staffroom for an umbrella she had not forgotten. Harvey trying to joke ('Does it have a wild goose on it?') as Mrs Milligan, voice squeaky with tears and fury, bent more than double to peer under the formica table.

It seemed Mrs Milligan had found out, rather as I had, that the art exhibition was not a private sell-out. What she had not found out was that the art exhibition was a raw nerve for Martha too.

'Did you enjoy going to the art exhibition with Mac, Martha?' was her opening salvo. And Martha knew it, it was squeaking out for all of us to hear. Harvey took four biscuits and ducked out into the office.

'Not much.' Which was, somehow, not even half a lie.

Something hissed in Mrs Milligan as she stiffened; it made a sound like steel cable being tensioned. As usual I was in my seat at the window and could pretend to be looking out whilst catching the whole show played out in reflection.

'Were there many *naked* people?' Mrs Milligan pursed her lips. Martha looked her over, trying to assess her. 'Well, were there? Nudes are something of a speciality for Joan.'

'It was all a bit colourful for me. Lots of purple.'

Martha was either exceptionally good at busking or she'd had a look at the catalogue.

'She has a fixation about penises you know.'

Mrs Atkinson walked in on this, as baffled as the rest of us as to whether Mrs Milligan was talking about Joan of Art, Martha or possibly the hated Naomi.

'Who has?' Mrs Atkinson, ever to the point.

'Joan. The artist, Joan Twydall. Always has had, ever since art college. If you ask me the show she should put on is her own very personal collection of penile portraits. She's very hands on, experimental. A suck-him-off-and-see sort of woman.' Her pursed lips lent the words a lemony tang. Mrs Atkinson's lips also pursed and I wondered at what memory.

'I should mention that to Mac. I don't think he knows about that side to Joan.'

'I think you'll find he does.' Mrs Milligan, horribly jolly. 'I think you might find Number 5 Violet looks familiar.'

Mrs Milligan didn't blink. She was offering information. A warning, warped slightly out of shape under the pressure of her anger.

Martha tried to sit down then, with a pleasant, peace-making smile and her mug of tea. Mrs Milligan took one graceful step, as if learning a dance, approaching Martha as her partner. They were almost touching, Mrs Milligan's small bosom just level with Martha's more ample breasts.

'You mention it to Mac Tierney. Perhaps he can have a laugh about it with Anita.'

'Anita?' Martha sat down, pulled a magazine from the side pocket of her bag.

'You know Anita don't you?'

It was obvious, even in the reversed world reflection, that Martha had no idea who Anita was.

'Professor Winstanley?'

Martha blew on her hot tea, shook her head vaguely; really not very interested.

'Tierney's wife.'

Pins dropped all over town and we heard each one of them in the silence. Mrs Milligan said it simply and sharply. No malice. No triumph. Just the bare fact. Then she walked out. Martha did not look up, but as she sipped at her tea the smallest drop splashed out onto the front of her top.

It was like waiting for the next episode of your favourite serial. Everyone was aware that Martha had shut herself into Harvey's office at around four o'clock and although there had been a sudden rush on and no one had the spare time to earwig on the conversation, we all knew that she had called Tierney. I was hoping she had a strategy, that her news about Mrs Tierney would give her a cast-iron reason to ditch him and she could live happily ever after, on her own or with anyone else.

But then, maybe Martha didn't want to live happily ever after. I began to wonder what she thought of bleeding hearts, pierced by the arrows of desire, dripping the O-positive of passion into your lungs until you suffocate on it.

It rained very hard after the phone call. It drummed on

the cobwebby chickenwired safety glass that they put into the cupola dome. Mrs Atkinson had to get a couple of buckets out for the leak in the corner of the staffroom. Call me over-dramatic if you will, but I felt all that day it was as if the sky was crying for Martha and her outright stupidity.

Mrs Milligan was red-eyed and if anyone pressed her too hard, for instance the man in the reference section who requested Keesings Archive, her voice cracked. She hid from Martha, trolleying up and down the shelves like a bibliophilic air steward to keep away from the desk. Shelving and reshelving and sorting out the Dewey numbers and God help anyone trying to take out a book.

I pushed out through the revolving doors into a street lit early with sulphurous orange. The sky was plum-like, bursting with the ripeness of rain, and the air had that clean smell that downpours always bring. How disheartening then to see a sleek and far-too-expensive sports car pull up next to the bank and Martha, skipping and hopping through the puddles near the zebra crossing before she skipped and hopped into the passenger seat.

I saw them. Tierney grabbing her neck, like someone throttling a rabbit, pulling her to him and kissing her, hands moving around her shoulders, encapsulating her. Then the windows steamed up and a big artic pulled up at the lights and blocked them from view.

O MI HARU

To keep watch

The next day the plum-ripe sky had not lifted and you could not tell where yesterday had ended and where today began. They ran into one another, like the paintings the kids do in the Arty Starty sessions that we hold on a Thursday.

Martha arrived late, smug and oversexed in a particularly textural outfit. A black embroidered skirt that looked as if it had done time at the Moulin Rouge swished beneath a persian lamb gem of a jacket, all foraged from the vintage place. She strode across the carpet in purple boots, laced, and with a striped-wood louis heel.

I'm unsure whether I felt shame that I ended up sobbing in the toilets over those boots. The freedom of the purple, the confidence of the shaped heel, as if everything I wasn't, right at that moment, was in that footwear. As if, in fact, someone else was wearing my shoes. Is this how Cinderella felt, I thought as I splashed my face with cold water, when she saw the ugly stepsisters trying to crush their bunions into that which was rightfully hers? Then I looked in the mirror and I knew who was the ugly stepsister.

The door creaked arthritically. Mrs Milligan slipped in, startled to see me and my eyes, a perfect red-for-red match for hers.

'I'm sorry Ruby, I didn't know anyone was in here. I'm sorry.' And she was slithering back out again, despite the fact that there are two cubicles in here. But of course only one sink. I stopped her leaving.

'That's all right Mrs Milligan. I'm on my way out.' And I pulled the door just slightly wider for her. She managed the wobbliest of smiles and it took such effort that I knew things had gone beyond her anger at Martha. I knew at that instant that everything about Martha was only the icing on the cake of Mrs Milligan's troubles. Something terrible was happening to Mrs Milligan. Her actions had seemed harsh but it was clear that Mrs Milligan had also seen some of the different angles in the Mac/Martha relationship, seen for herself that Martha needed to be helped. Assisted. Saved.

On my lunchbreak, I cheated the queue at the post office. I had put the letter together with those rub off letters that you can buy at the stationers and posted it on my way back to the library. I let it slip into the box marked 'all destinations', which seemed appropriate. I had no idea where it was going to take me. It would be a couple of days before it reached her but, as I have mentioned, I am a patient woman.

The very next morning, however, while Imogen the Arty Starty tutor was hanging out of the window having a post-Arty-Starty cigarette, Martha put the kettle on and smiled broadly at Mrs Milligan,

'Thanks for the advice by the way. You're entitled to your opinion.' And proffered her teacup as if toasting free will. Mrs Milligan looked up at Martha as though she were speaking Intermediate Japanese and said nothing.

Martha has a redeeming feature. That day, when she felt herself both cheated and vilified, when she felt like the Whore of Babylon, she had the courage to be brashly rebellious and devil-may-care, tossing her auburn hair and keeping up the pretence that she was proud to be her. She did not let go of her Self.

Who knows what Martha's reaction was on opening the letter but she had certainly thought about it. Why else would she comment to Mrs Milligan? *He is not for you* is what I had rubbed off onto the paper, and trusted that she would read the meaning properly.

Now I could see that she might misinterpret this. In the face of Mrs Milligan's comments she might be infuriated, see it as homewrecker censure instead of wisdom. I had my fingers crossed that the Martha underneath, the bronze, inner Martha, would hang onto the truth of the words and they would seep inwards. I had seen how she was that night at the canalside and the snatch-and-grab embrace in the car. Tierney was a classic, a married man taking his pleasure. Not giving, for he had nothing to give.

Make the leap, Martha, I thought, willing her onwards.

Therefore, I composed the next letter more thoughtfully. It needed more magic, I saw that now. I should have seen it before, woven into the raw silks and velvets and that persian lamb jacket. I chose a different set of letters from the whirligig display at the stationers, only just catching them open on my way to Intermediate Japanese.

I sat in my usual seat at the back like a miscreant school-girl, rubbing at the letters instead of listening as Setsuke took the class through the minefield of true adjectives. As the words *atarashii kutsu…new shoes* filtered into my head like music…

*atarashikunai kutsu...not new shoes...*I knew what had to be said.

> *Break from the false for you are true.*
> *He is a very bad idea.*
> *Trust me.*

I knew the day she'd got it even though she didn't mention one word, rubbed off or otherwise. I was in the archive again so I didn't see her myself, but I knew. I felt a draught at the back of my neck as I sifted through the census looking for the laundresses. It was as if Martha's temperature had dropped that day, you could stand at Books In as she manned Books Out and feel the chill. She fumbled. She dropped. In the staff-room she put the kettle on to boil and forgot to put the lid on. Then she went to cry in the toilets. If Mrs Milligan hadn't happened along, the wallpaper, such as it is, would have been peeling off. In the end Mrs Atkinson shouted.

'What on earth is the matter with you today Martha?' In a very tired and weary voice, like a schoolteacher after a long day with the learning-impaired having to come home to her own annoying offspring.

It had been a long day at County Hall for Mrs Atkinson. Every quarter, she found herself shoehorning her feet into her fancy shoes so that they'd take her seriously at the budgetary meetings in the Great Chamber at County Hall. The Councillors smacked their greedy lips over our stately sandstone building, and Mrs Atkinson fought to keep the library full of books instead of menus.

The day was stretching further into the evening as the book club ladies were due, in tandem with Harvey's *It's a Crime Not to Read These!* promotion on detective novels.

The book club meet once a month and I generally loiter

at the desk pretending to be working, but in fact I've usually got a copy of their latest read and I sit and listen. I can't decide whether I prefer an evening of Intermediate Japanese or the book club. Although that sobriquet doesn't nearly cover them, they are so much more than that, they are a coven. Wise with all their years.

As they sorted out their coffee mugs and opened up some of the cake tins that had been brought along they discussed the fact that Angharad (redhaired history teacher, recently traded in by husband for very much younger woman, a woman in fact, three years younger than the youngest of their four daughters) had spent an hour in the morning hiding under her kitchen table. She had been up as usual at six, and whilst brewing up a mug of peppermint tea had chanced to look out into the garden.

'There I am, expecting to see that woodpecker that's wrecking the apple tree and instead it's him. Five pairs he took. Five. And I wouldn't mind, but they're granny pants. There's no understanding it. Big cotton granny pants.'

The knicker thief, wearing a ski mask, had set her head as well as her rotary clothes line spinning.

'It's such an invasion. I haven't been able to unlock the back door all day. I just can't. And yet I know he's gone. I heard him going over the fence—which he's cracked. One foot on the fork of the plum tree and he's up and over, but that fence is only held together with paint. I keep telling Dinah next door we need to replace it. Cracked it like a twig.' She took a revitalising swig of the Australian shiraz Harvey had trawled from the internet. 'I hope the bastard hurt himself.' And they fussed and buzzed around her making a sound like a hive of bees.

As I turned to the computer, I hoped that somewhere the knicker thief was sweating with their curses. Then I noticed the movement in the lobby, an adjustment of shadows.

I tried not to crane forwards to see what was happening out there. Two figures partly obscured by the freestanding noticeboard pinned with Harvey's *It's a Crime Not to Read These!* promotional poster. And then Martha took a step back, edging into view beside Queen Victoria's fossilised petticoats.

I could see her shoes under her swirling turquoise hemline. Some 1920's Mary Janes with a stubby heel. The skirt swished again as Martha sidestepped Tierney's attempt to corner her. He seemed to have made himself much taller, looming over her, casting a shadow.

Martha's head shaking. Martha's eyes not looking at him. His eyes never moving from her face, his body filling all the available space and then, suddenly, the moment he had got what he wanted he stepped aside, his arm reaching out to the small of her back to shepherd her to the doors.

I was shaking, my fingers flabby on the keyboard, typing gibberish.

The book club ladies were taking their seats. Angharad came to the desk, looked over the top of the monitor at me.

'Ruby, have you seen Martha?'

'I found her.' We turned at Tierney's voice. 'Is there a prize?'

Martha stood beside him, expressionless as his hand smoothed down the curve of her bottom. 'Shall we join them?' he asked, increasing the intensity of charm in his smile. Martha moved ahead of him and his hand never left her back. He seemed attentive, gentlemanly. He turned to Harvey, pouring out wine beside the display of crime novels. Tierney looked up at the display with a sneering smile before he snaffled a bottle of New Zealand sauvignon blanc from the end of the table.

'It would be a crime not to drink this.' A patronising smirk at Harvey.

Taking his seat beside Martha, Tierney realised he did not have a glass. As he wandered back towards Harvey, Jill D'Eath swooped on Tierney's stolen bottle and began to pass it around. The book club have coffee as a rule, but now they topped up their mugs, earthenware ones made for them by Brid who does pottery at the Tech on Thursdays just before I turn up for Intermediate Japanese. They emptied the wine between them and then began to discuss *Garganey Watch* as Tierney returned, glass in hand, to wonder where his wine had vanished to. Ellen Freethy began to read a passage, and Tierney fumbled about, feeling for a wet and winey patch on the carpeting beside the empty bottle.

Abandoning the search he leaned back in his plastic chair, reached a relaxed arm around Martha's shoulders and let his hand—hairy, a heavy gold ring on the pinkie finger—drape so that it was at all times in contact with her breast.

Martha. She didn't squirm but her body began to close up, her leg casually crossed, her body turned just slightly away from him. She leant forwards to reach for her mug of wine, to disentangle his straying fingers from the fabric of herself. From the Books In desk I could see the patch of sweat on her back spread like a lake across the silk of her vintage blouse.

As Tierney sloped back to the crime promotion for more wine, Harvey made sure he received a bottle that contained a cocktail of dregs he'd funnelled from two bottles of sour sauvignon blanc and the book club ladies executed a neat and clever musical chairs manoeuvre. Ellen Freethy (tall and white haired; her son and daughter-in-law recently took over the Paintball Pandemonium combat zone out in the woodland) made as if to go to the loo then turned on her heel to take up

Tierney's place next to Martha. Returning with his vinegar drink, Tierney found himself ousted.

'There's a seat over here Mr Tierney,' smiled Angharad.

'This is my chair, I think.' His hairy hand rested on the moulded plastic chair back. Ellen, cut off mid-sentence in her theory that Esben Komstadius, hero of *Garganey Watch*, used boatmaking as an outlet for the masculine energy of his deep but unrequited love for the stubborn and independent Hannah, looked up at him, astonished.

'Your chair? What are you, seven?'

And it was as if a roman candle ignited in those eyes. Tierney held the silence for just long enough before he sat beside Angharad. He did not lounge now. He sat upright, shoulders broadened, powerful. His arm stretched across the back of Angharad's chair. Angharad leaned forward to talk, her legs crossed away from him too.

I couldn't hold *Garganey Watch* still. I turned it face down on the desk. I was struggling to hear the voices over the yomping of my heartbeat, struggling to fold my arms against myself, to still my shaking hands. I was going to be sick.

In the toilets I couldn't look at my face in the mirror, I could only swish at it with cold water. The coldest, letting the tap run and run.

'Ruby?' It was Martha; the book club ladies were leaving now. Mrs Atkinson was long gone. Thursdays were her yoga night. 'Ruby, it's time to close.'

Angharad and Ellen were standing at Books In. 'I've parked at the bank Martha…' Angharad fumbled for her keys in a leather bag the size of a small cow. She always gave Martha a lift home after book club. 'Fancy Giovanni's or do you want to try the new Thai Palace?'

'One vote for Thai Palace.' Ellen put her hand in the air.

Martha opened her mouth to speak but Tierney's voice came out.

'Oh, that's all right ladies, Martha's with me tonight.' He chinkled his car keys in a gesture that resembled nothing more than a gaoler taunting a prisoner.

Ellen glared at Tierney. 'Martha?'

'Let me know what the Thai Palace is like,' Martha said quietly. Tierney was tracing the line of her vertebrae with his ignition key. Angharad and Ellen left, talking conspiratorially past the chickenwired doors. I saw the look between them, the look of anxiety and puzzlement.

I did not reach for my belongings. Instead I reached for the trolley, began stacking returns from the counter. 'I should just do this…'

'I think we've finished for today. I'll see you tomorrow, Ruby.' Martha moved to shut down the computer terminals. I saw her hand was shaking as she reached for the mouse. Tierney hitched himself up onto the desk. Marlon Brando in *The Wild One*.

He reached down for my handbag, which I had carefully left under the desk so that I could come back in a moment.

'Goodnight Ruby,' Tierney said, unwinking. His eyes gave me a direct alpha-male look but there was not one flicker of recognition in his face, only contempt.

I stepped out into the lobby. The lights were already off in here and the heating had shut down so it was very cold, very stony. Queen Victoria looked very disapproving.

'Do not leave,' she seemed to say. 'We are going to regret this.' I looked at her for a long time. It seemed the blanked out stones of eyes followed me. I thought of the sculptor, presented with a block of stone and seeing Queen Victoria squatting inside it. I wondered how many other fragments of the same cliff face were scattered across the landscape, the other stone dead eyes looking out from library niches and elaborate pigeon-perch plinths.

I moved to touch her. At full stretch I could only reach her hem and I found myself tucking my body into the gap between the statue and the niche wall. I let the coolness of stone filter up into my fingertips. I felt the stone before it was stone, when it was mud and clay and sea creatures, before it was crushed and compacted beneath the prehistoric seas. I have been crumpled and bent and twisted into this and then at last, I have been chiselled and chipped away and become something not me.

Outside, the eight o'clock bus rumbled and sighed and then the lights switched off in the main library.

There was the sound of a cup or glass falling off the desk. I slung my bag across myself, shoulder to chest and, sinking to all fours, I sneaked back in. In through the chickenwired door and a very sharp left into fiction. I had a notion of movement by the desk. Martha sitting on the desk, Tierney before her pinning her legs, his hands gripping her wrists.

'Let me down Mac,' she was whispering. 'No. Let me down...'

He was laughing, low and dark and not loosening his grip. By now I was standing tall in the far corner, shielded from their view by the stacked shelf of sale books, REMOVED FROM CIRCULATION stamped all over them.

'Mac, I'm serious let me...'

'*I'm serious. Let me.*' He was snaffling at her like a truffle pig and she was squirming backwards, which I wanted to yell out to her not to do but it was too late. She slithered on the countertop and with her hands gripped in his she couldn't save herself. Legs sliding, feet scrabbling, she was under him.

Cold sweat seemed to spring out of every pore I possessed. She didn't have words now, just grunts and barks. Tierney's kisses were hard, his body a wall. Then with a carpeted crump he was all over the floor. Unable to decide which to clutch first, his broken coccyx or his bruised cock. Martha moved to help him up and he shoved her aside.

'If you weren't playing so fucking hard to get,' he hissed at her. 'Christ.'

'Mac.'

'What the fuck are you playing at Martha?'

'I don't want to play. Mac, we're done with. Believe me this time. I've said. Time and again…' Clear and without any waver in her voice. 'I mean it. We're done with. No more.'

'What?' he was on his feet now and was leaning on her for support, his arm around her, his frame towering over her, his voice sharpened with sarcasm. 'Didn't catch that Martha, what did you say?'

'It's over. You know it.'

His low, dark laugh came again and his gold-ringed paw clamped around her face and tilted it towards him. His lips brushed her face, her cheek, her forehead, her lips, her neck. I remembered the sexual charge I had felt at the exhibition, only now it was the superfuelled panic of adrenaline. He pulled her towards him and kissed her on the mouth. Martha was struggling but he had lifted her too high, she was beyond tiptoe now.

'I'm not done.'

Martha pushed at him. His hands lifting her skirt up over her hips.

'No…Mac, no.'

'This is about Anita isn't it? Fuck Anita. She doesn't care.'

64

'I don't want you.'

The sound of his hand slapping at her bottom. His low rumbled laugh. 'Stop misbehaving.'

'No. Stop…I don't…want…to…' Martha's toes touched the carpet briefly before he slung her back up onto the countertop. The computer keyboard skittered off, dangled by its curly wire. For too many moments I could see only a churning, flailing mass of darker darkness and the restrained grunts of Martha and the tear of clothing as she pulled free. His grunt as one hand let her slip so the other could grasp her. Martha was panting. Again, his low dark laugh as he picked her off the counter. A rending of fabric that ripped through me. A flash of whiteness, of her torn underwear, as he cast it aside. Martha scrabbling backwards, his hairy hand feeling its way spider-like into her left bra cup as she did so.

Which is when I switched the lights on. Five switches set into a shiny brushed steel plate just by the Baroness Orczy shelf. *Click.*

Click. Click. Click. Click. They flickered on in ranks, starting at the back over the reference section and chasing forwards.

'Shit.' Tierney, belt unstrapped, leapt back from the desk. Spooked. Suddenly released, Martha slid too far backwards, falling with an awkward thud over the counter. I was negotiating my route under cover of crime fiction, science fiction and fantasy, making that last doubled-over-keep-out-of-sight leap towards occult and spiritual before darting, cat-like, under the counter. Martha was picking herself up with a nasty bruise starting under her eye.

'Who's there? Who the fuck is that?' Tierney's voice struggled not to squeak at the ends. He was re-strapping his buckle now, tugging the belt tight as if it was holding up a pair of six-shooters instead of his designer trousers. 'Come out you bastard!'

So I did. 'Martha, I forgot, we were supposed to pick up the archive boxes from County Hall at nine-thirty. Remember? Mrs Atkinson had to reschedule because of the conference.'

Martha, grey lipped, avoided my eye. Tierney spun to face me, aghast.

'WHAT?...HOW THE FU...?'

'Sorry, I was at the bus stop and then I remembered. It's the census stuff she's collating for that Moving Forwards conference next week. The conservator's coming in in the morning. I've got a taxi waiting and I've called Maureen to tell her we're running late. I'm so sorry Martha. I'd completely forgotten...'

I couldn't look at Tierney. Only at torn Martha, the red flare of carpet burn angry across her face. I clutched up her bag and coat, carried them like a shield as I moved towards her.

'You're kidding me? Right? This is a wind-up?' Tierney tried to sneer. I shoved Martha towards the door, really shoved her, like someone herding educationally subnormal sheep. He took a step towards us and I lashed around.

'*I mean it*,' I quoted, and he got the message. He snatched up his jacket and I could smell the scorn wafting off him like burnt biscuits, distinct and tangible. I kept myself between him and Martha as we got through the chickenwire door.

'Keys, Martha.' She looked benumbed but she handed them to me.

'The lights,' she said, turning backwards. It was like dancing as I stepped myself into her and moved her again towards the doors. Tierney outside the circle as if I had cast magic, a silver net to protect us. 'What about the lights?' she repeated.

'What about them?' I kept my voice low, calm; didn't look at her as I pushed her into the safe circle of the revolving doors.

Out in the street there was no taxi. I improvised, cursing the impatient driver, and started to hurry her off in the vague direction of County Hall. Tierney, it seemed, had a silver net all his own to cast. His parting shot was not goodbye.

'This isn't done with. I'll see you again.' Before he turned and walked towards his flashy car, parked in the corner of the bank carpark. It made a delighted squeal as he kerchunked the alarm. At least someone was pleased to see him.

KASA WA NANBON NOKOTTE IRU KA WAKARIMASEN

I don't know how many umbrellas are left

Would Tierney scare that easily? No. But I wasn't aiming for scared. I was satisfied with shamed. I was content with embarrassed. All of these were personal attacks of the deepest violence, because these were the punishments he would inflict upon himself. You can recover from a severed arm or the loss of an eye. You can move forwards and arrive at terms. A wound to your pride never heals. It festers. It seeps.

Martha and I had walked further and further, saying nothing. The Thai Palace was bright and sparkling and so were Angharad and Ellen Freethy. I was cold and red and shaking but clear: Martha was not to go home. No one asked why, Angharad simply offered accommodation at her place. She would drop Martha in at the library on her way to school. No trouble, no trouble at all, she drove past the library every morning.

I had missed the last bus again. Last buses and I are destined never to meet. Now I walked back to the flat, my brain ticking over. I was scared, but there was also the adrenaline surge of what I had done. Of what I had managed to do. I had not run away.

As I started up the hill I knew it was time to stop picking over it all like some leftover chicken carcass. If I could start to slough it from my head now I might manage to fall into some sort of sleep back at the flat.

I let down the tyres on the bike, still blocking the hallway. The hem of my coat now bore the oily teethmarks of the chain. Inside, my hands were shaking as I put the kettle on. I didn't need to switch on the light. Miss Nudey downstairs had her garden lighting on.

A soft rain began to patter at the window as I stood at the table, looking out. She was in the garden, clothed tonight, taking a pair of frothy silk knickers from the line. Except, as I watched, she moved indoors leaving the knickers stranded on the line in the mizzling rain. A moment later and the lights blinked out.

I stood in the darkness, sipping hot tea and watching the ghostly underwear begin to flap and panic in the building wind. Why bother hanging them out when a storm is coming?

Bait. Miss Nudey was trying to lure the knicker thief.

But surely she was missing the point. The point was he liked knickers that had been worn. Stained and bleached out, fraying elastic. He desired full briefs that covered belly buttons, not for him your high-cuts or your thong. 100% cotton and the gift of a stray pubic hair curled into the elastic. He wanted comfort and control, not danger.

Are scanties empowered? Is all that tarting about really a woman at home with her sexuality? Or are the 100% granny pants the ones genuinely imbued with the freedom of choice, the rebellious non-conforming to the myth of knickers?

Next morning in the staffroom I put the kettle on and stood looking out across the park. I heard the door go behind me and instantly I saw her reflection. I tried not to spin round, not to react in any way. There was a tinny sound.

'You forgot to put the lid on again Ruby.' It was all Martha said to me that day.

She looked tired. She didn't speak much, only answering borrower queries, hardly looking up from the computers all day. Not answering the phone.

'Martha, you were sitting right beside it, how could you not hear it ringing?' Mrs Atkinson quizzed.

But we were sitting right beside Mrs Milligan later and no one heard the doorbell of doom ringing in her head. I had already noted that Mrs Milligan too was struggling today. She had had a protracted hushed conversation with Joachim the French student in the lobby as she headed out for her lunch-break. He had been reassuring her about something, had even reached out one of his big, square hands and patted at her shoulder from his great height. He was wearing a heavy sheepskin jacket in a pale golden colour that matched his wild hair and tinted up the ruddy skin of his face. It looked like something he had caught, skinned and eaten only that day. But for all the savage edges to him, there was something wise in that gesture.

Now she was standing near to the window and staring out. She had been standing like that for some minutes and suddenly something seemed to give in her. I looked out, beyond. There were some playgroup kids in the park dressed in fluorescent green tabards. Their playgroup leader was helping them collect autumn leaves. Overhead a plane winked white in the bitter autumn sunshine.

A shiver went through her, a spasm. Martha spotted

that, and saw too that Mrs Milligan had gone way beyond clinging to the sofa for safety. Martha was the first to spot that Mrs Milligan was going under, and it was Martha's hand that reached out and saved her. I was busy rifling the biscuit tin.

'Mrs Milligan?' No response. Martha told me much later that looking into Mrs Milligan's eyes was very scary at that moment. Martha said it was like looking into the darkest part of the night sky. You could see the tears falling inwards like imploding stars.

'Mrs Milligan, what's happened?'

I dropped the biscuit tin then, as Mrs Milligan's entire body seemed to flex. She lifted the armchair closest to the window and threw it straight at the glass with a scream that seemed to come from her feet and reverberate through every bone in all our bodies. I leapt and saved the chair, falling awkwardly by the washing-up cupboard.

It made no difference to the window. It looked as if the metal studded end of the left leg had caught it, but I think we all knew better. It was the resonant raw grief of that scream that shattered it. Martha caught Mrs Milligan as she started to crumple, folding up as if she had expelled her Self with that scream.

Martha held her, stroked her hair as Mrs Milligan sobbed into her fifties print shirt, ruining the nap on her vintage velvet maxi skirt. We sat there, amongst the diamonds of glass.

Her son Alex was leaving the country. Was on a plane at that moment, heading for the other side of the world, for New Zealand and a new life away from his divorce. She had been at the airport the night before to let him go.

Harvey gave her a lift home, with an open offer to trawl the supermarket if she needed anything. I thought that what

Mrs Milligan needed could not be found on the supermarket shelves.

Much later, after dark, I emerged from the library and made my way across town to the redbrick Technical College. I moved down the corridor to Room 47A and sat at the far back, next to the bookcase.

When I started Intermediate Japanese, for the first few sessions or so, Setsuke didn't ask me any questions and I laboured for a while under the delusion that my skill at invisibility knew no bounds. Then the more logical part of my brain told me that the real reason was she knew I had never attended Beginners' Japanese.

Until the first time I answered a question. A question directed at the tall suited man at the front who always thought a cheery smile would cover for his lack of diligence in doing homework.

'*Dochira no tatemono ga toshokan desu ka?*'—Which building is the library?

Of course he was unable to answer, for it was my question. Formed for me. A tumbleweed silence fell and then the words came out of me like a spell.

'*Ano tatemono ga toshokan desu.*'

That building is the library.

Setsuke's gaze shifted towards me. A smile glimmered in her eyes and she gave a nod before moving on to see if anyone else could locate the fishmonger.

I liked to be at the class. It wasn't just that if I left the library and headed back to the flat it seemed like a lot of evening to cover. I liked the school smells of the building, the bright lights, the wrought ironwork of the old staircases. Most of all, I liked to hear Setsuke speak Japanese. She had a beautiful smile that shimmered with feeling. It made me wonder what she was thinking as she tried to twist her mother tongue around us.

Have you noticed that when you are in a foreign country you imagine the conversations around you are all important, eloquent, intellectual? Once you understand, you can hear that it is all the same wherever you are, the football, the price of shoes, the location of the bus station and the as-yet-unapprehended knicker thief.

Japan was not here. What had led her to this classroom and these people? I know that I liked to be there because I felt she might be someone who would understand me, someone I would not have to explain things to in Broken English or Intermediate Japanese. Mythology, of course.

I didn't put the lights on again when I arrived home. I walked from college in the end because the stars were out and the frost was coming. I liked the sharpness, the cold clean of my breathing as I moved through the streets. I made a pot of tea and opened the window to sit out on the top of the pergola below. I had some scanned documents in my bag, a few pictures and a couple of the original work ledgers I wanted to really go over.

I knew there were stories of doom and drudgery waiting there for me, the lost history of the laundresses, but I didn't feel like an unhappy ending that night. I left my coat on and dug out an old pair of gloves from the back of a kitchen drawer, some hideous fleecy things I bought last winter. As I sat out there, my tea cooling fast, I realised that I might not be able to do this once the real hard frosts arrived. The wooden struts might be slippery. I didn't want to skid off the end of the construction and land headfirst in the hammock. I would have to sit in the window, possibly on the sill.

I thought about Martha on the roof terrace and the night in the library and wondered what memories she would have that she might wish to erase. I thought of Mrs Milligan and the memories she would archive forever.

I thought, a very clear thought, one complete and crisp idea. 'Something has to be done about all this.'

But, at that point, I did not know what.

Rusu Desu

Nobody is home

It was a grey week grinding towards Halloween. I had expected some backlash from the thwarted Tierney but all was silence. I had been hard at work on several projects that I wasn't, strictly speaking, paid to pursue.

I was paid to stack books and smile beneficently at Mrs Wild as she ordered large print soft porn. It was due solely to Mrs Atkinson's kindness that I was allowed to uncover the hidden history of the laundresses of Kite House. I had expected woe. But as the pieces began to fall into place, those places were more nuanced.

Tragedy: a fatal brawl between two of the grooms at a harvest home over the favours of a housemaid. Vice: the kitchen maid stealing the silverware to finance a new life with the footman, and ultimately abandoned and shamed in the local newspaper. Evil (class motivated and socially sanctioned): another girl, separated from her bastard child and put into the laundry to pull herself together had stolen a baby from the village and been sent to the asylum.

You would not have thought they had time enough away

from the starching of napkins.

I had been sifting through the Kite House photographs and the ledger, trying to put names to the faces. The gardeners, grouped by a greenhouse with their wheelbarrows, had been easy as they were listed by rank in the payroll. The laundresses proved more difficult. They were equal, none stood above another in the ledger except alphabetically. Then I uncovered a portrait of the entire Kite House domestic staff, done up in best bib and whitest tucker, posed in sombre ranks in front of the house.

I scanned it, sectioned it, enlarged the laundresses. Now familiar faces looked out. Miss Haughty but Naughty with the hint of a smirk and the rest of her sisters in starch; but the woman from the far left of the laundresses portrait was not there. I scanned and enlarged the original image of the lost girl's face and picked my way back over the staff portrait with the magnifying lens. She was not hidden in another row of servants. She had not worked her way through the ranks of housemaids. She had not been blurred or faded out of the edges by sun or time. She was simply not there.

The date was clear on the back, stuck on a tiny label in browned-off ink; *Kite House, Domestic Staff – Christmas 1891*. A light flicked on red in my head, even as I flicked back through the ledger. The name jumped out at me from July 1889, Mary-Ann Penny from Totnes. I checked and double checked. Early December in 1890 she vanished from Mrs Mason's household ledger. I riffled through the red box to find another portrait. *Christmas 1889*, spotted with mildew, the edges fading out so that the figures placed there looked like ghosts.

Yes. There at the back on the right, the last laundress standing beside…It was Henry, the first of the gardeners.

The face. She was Mary-Ann Penny, looking out from the portrait at the far left, standing by the dolly tub, the line sheets a billowed blur behind her where the wind and the camera had clashed in capturing the scene. Mary-Ann Penny. It felt as if she gazed out and knew that one day, far into the future, I would pull her from the darkness and look back at her. She would tell me more than all the other laundresses put together.

I began with a three-week search of the register of births and deaths and the burial records, starting from the date she vanished from the ledger. Nothing. If she was dead by 1891, she had not died locally. There was a possibility that she had left and travelled home to Totnes, so I ran up a phone bill chatting with and emailing their archivist. I travelled down there on two consecutive weekends to sift through their records, drink tea from their staffroom and scoff their biscuits. Whirring my way around their microfiche collection, I called up the census taken in 1891 and although there were still Pennys in Totnes then, a couple of younger brothers and her father, there was no-sign of Mary-Ann. But I knew she was there somewhere. I just needed to find the lines to read between.

Back in my basement hideout at the library there didn't seem to be enough hours in the day to do this. I trawled the internet for information whenever I could, anxious that the path I had been following was going to close up on me if I didn't keep with it. I could see me having to cut myself off later and losing the way.

As the weeks chugged on I stayed later and later, pulling out more and more documents and hogging all the computer terminal time in the archive. Mrs Atkinson always seemed to come, coat on, to throw me out just when it felt I was on the verge of finding Mary-Ann, and the next morning I could never seem to find my place. The loophole in time eluded me; it did not feel the same.

Eventually I found some relatives of Mary-Ann working at a big house near Totnes prior to 1889 and amongst that information I unearthed a house party attended by Viscount Breck of Kite House and his wife, Beatrice.

The house, Brakers Meet, sat above the town and was owned by a man called Hazard. Clearly a man of hedonistic and epicurean taste, he had kept records of handwritten programmes drawn up for the evening entertainments at his house parties. They were part of a permanent exhibition in the house, which was now open to the public.

I ought to have missed them entirely, not thinking that Mary-Ann Penny might be hidden amongst them but there she was, her name Googled to the surface on a site illustrating the Brakers Meet exhibits:

– A MidSummer Night's June at Brakers Meet –
To feature for your enlightenment and entertainment:
– The Lady Lily at the pianoforte with a cacophony of
Clementi –
– Colonel Whitside and his Prestidigitation –
– Readings from the Golden Lectern –
– a –
– Selection from Persuasion –
– by Miss Jane Austen –
– the latter to be read by Mary-Ann Penny –

Was this my laundress? A well-bred young lady seen fit to read Austen in polite company? I scrolled around some of the online selections of the Hazard artefacts. Other evenings listed her again, reading Dickens and Eliot from her Golden Lectern alongside the more exalted-sounding pianists and prestidigitators.

Then, just as swiftly, she vanished again.

ISSHO NI IKIMASHO O KA?

Shall we go together?

The next day Mrs Atkinson was tied up in a conference being held in County Hall. They were going to discuss the way forward for County Information Systems, which is what the Powers That Be call the library now. Mrs Atkinson didn't tell us then, but the only idea they had was to close up all the picturesque old sandstone library buildings and sell them off to developers—a contract supposedly to be put out for tender but in reality neatly folded into Tripp Tierney Associates' back pocket. Then they were going to build a state of the art library, or to give it its official title, 'County Information Systems Centre', in the city.

It was the kind of idea the council often had, ideas full of grandeur and hot air. Knock this down and build that. Sell this. Redevelop that. They weren't so much interested in the 'centralisation of resources' (I read the mission statement later) as they were in playing Lego with the locals. That's how we ended up with the new migraine-inducing shopping centre and the leisure complex that turns swimming into an orienteering exercise.

Mrs Atkinson was rallying her forces to show them that her library and its fellows in the other small satellite towns were a vital community network. She was putting together what amounted to the defence in a murder trial, and she knew if she didn't get it right she'd be doomed. Divorced and out of the job she loved. Divorced, in fact, from the library.

I was married or at least engaged to the archive by then. I began the day scanning a more informal series of photos I'd unearthed of the Travellers who visited town. We had an extensive collection because at the *fin de siècle*, Viscount Breck's wife Beatrice had formed a penchant for photography, with a particular interest in what she called 'the Romani'. The little hobby she'd taken up to fill in the gaps between house parties and charity work became a document of the Travellers' history.

After an hour I began to be able to trace the faces as they aged through the photographs. By half past ten I was putting together the family groups, the Kirchers, Pikes and Herons, and beginning to wonder about them. I saw the different family homes, the wagons and trailers and hard work. I loved the accident of it, that Lady Breck in her genteel pursuit had accidentally captured the truth.

Going back over the stacks and folders from recent days, I riffled out the images that had fixed themselves into my mind. I placed them together but the arrangement didn't fit. I shuffled, switched, and suddenly it seemed I was standing in their light. An old woman watched me from a Kircher family campfire and the boundaries of the photos blurred into each other, girls dancing, men beside a fire working metal. Yes; it was the same stylistic sense I'd noticed before. The use of light, the informal poses. It was Lady Breck who'd been chronicling the town.

A clang resounded, startled me into the present.

'Sorry.' Harvey, apologising from the corridor, picking up the folded legs of the collapsible display board.

It felt as if I had drawn back the curtain of time and stood on the edge of their lives. Now I had to know more—which Kircher, which Pike—and by one-thirty I was rifling Mrs Atkinson's desk for the key to the written archives.

There's a room at the far end of the corridor that shakes when the buses pass. If you could look up through the ceiling you'd see the edge of Massey Street where they've just started redeveloping some rundown Victorian terraces. As I stood, doing my fingertip search of the archives I could feel the vibration from the machinery, feel the changes being wrought. It was three o'clock when I found Lady Breck's journals.

She had a lot of time for writing journals, Lady Breck. After all, she had teams of people carrying out the everyday duties of life. The first one I unearthed that day was a collection of menus and place cards. They seemed interesting enough from a culinary viewpoint. Aspic and potages and all that copper-kettled palaver; hot-house peaches, custards and blancmange for the high-ups. Wild duck, no doubt shot on their estate, unless the cook happened to frequent the newly opened Queens Park and bumped a few of them off around the boating lake.

Since I was hiding and in no hurry I was also neglectful. I put each menu to one side, sifted through the beautifully written place cards. *Lord Buttermere...Mrs Lionel Irving... Capt. Thom. Whitside...Lady Lily Strand-Fforbes*. Names that meant nothing to me, names that had eaten cold roast pheasant and country fruit cake at a shooting party in 1885.

I put them to one side without turning them over. It was only when a draught fluttered them to the floor that I was shown the other side, the not-quite-so-correct handwriting, the abbreviations, the personal code of who was who at the dinner table. *Plays violin as if the guts were still extant in the cat!!!!!!!* she had written beside Lord Buttermere. Capt. Thom. Whitside was 'dashing', as only a captain could be.

I spent the latter part of the afternoon schmoozing my way through the autumn 1885–88 dinners and 'at homes' of Lady Beatrice Breck. It was not hard to measure the perimeter of their social circle. A few names, such as Capt. Whitside, cropped up regularly and others were bussed in, to be judged on the back of a menu and never heard of again.

Brays like a donkey she said of one. *Ate the leg of lamb entire to himself.* With a row of exclamation marks.

After 1888 the notes began to spill into marbled notebooks.

Have become adept at the brewing of tea, much to Courtley's chagrin. He considers it an affront that I have decided to take an active hand in the garden, and resented my ascent of the stepladder this morning to oil the mechanism that opens the windows in the pineapple house. Rather enjoyed his bottled fury and fuelled it further by brewing the eleven o'clock tea in the Bothy. He arrived to find me already stirring the leaves and setting out the pot beakers. He drank the tea, chewing at his pipe between mouthfuls, uncertain whether manners dictate that it was wrong for the lady of the house to be brewing tea for a servant or more wrong still that in order for the social situation to be righted, a man should brew said tea for a woman. Courtley may puff his cheeks all he likes. It is my garden and I shall dig in it.

Evening—
Courtley laughs the longest in his blessed bothy. He has

complained to Breck and henceforth I am banished.

Boring dinner with Whitside lingering forever like old smoke and kippers. He mentioned to Breck that he has his sights set on some pink and white debutante. The man is like a pike prowling for minnow.

I thought of the laundresses cleaning all the table linen and everyone's smalls. I wondered what secrets they could see in the stains and the dirt they were faced with. Of course they would not have had much time to think, with the copper boiling endlessly, the steam, the sweat, the hard work before them.

I thought of them all the way back to the flat that night. I thought about them again as I filled my own washing machine, did my own ironing. By then it was late and I was tired and fell into bed.

And didn't escape them. In the dream I felt grass underfoot; opened my dream eyes to see them all busy just beyond me. The men metal-working, the children being herded to tasks, a girl struggling to carry an infant sibling across the camp. Laughter. Shouts. A woman singing. I was searching, I knew it, each face looking back at me as if I wasn't a stranger and then at last I found her, but the camera flashed, the powder igniting and I raised my hand against the white light of it. Woke up.

It was early and springlike as I headed to work. It had been less than twenty-four hours since I'd delved into the first of Lady Breck's journals and already, as the sun rose over the town, I felt I was heading to meet up with an old friend. Lady Breck had a title and privilege but she'd taken time and care to step away from the enforced idleness of her class. She was curious about the Romany community. She was interested in how people lived. In her journals, private, intimate, not for public consumption, she was unswervingly honest, not only about the people she met but about herself. She was a woman at home with her failings; her notes, respectful and observant, giving tantalising views of the Roma clans. The feuding Kirchers versus the battling Pikes, the politics of the Herons marrying into the Keets.

Lady Breck's passion and curiosity made me want to know more, to use her eyes to look back through time, and that is why I surprised Mrs Atkinson.

I had thought I was early but it seemed Mrs Atkinson had been earlier still. She was slumped on her desk. She didn't have her white gloves on. Her arms were flung out, all angles, elbows and shoulders as if perhaps she'd fallen from the ceiling and landed there. There was a scent in the air, something fragrant but woody, as if in stepping into the room I had crushed pine cones under foot. Mrs Atkinson was silent until suddenly a weary sigh escaped. I stepped back from the doorway in case she moved, in case she saw me.

My vision saw two slices. One through the gap between door and jamb, the other, at the farthest edge where the door angled open. I saw her hands reach upwards towards her face but I could not see her face, only the way her bottom curved into the back of the creaky swivel seat. I saw her foot as it slid off its shoe and curled itself around the splayed spindles of the chair, the toes furling and unfurling, catlike. Creak of chair, unzipping of handbag. The foot slid back into the shoe and the chair creaked forwards, into business. Slithering papers, the tilt of the back of her neck, a hand reaching up to grapple and fiddle with the hairline there. The clackle of her glasses as she put them on. She looked over them at me as I made my presence known in the doorway.

'Ruby?' she didn't give away the fact that she wanted to

know how long I had been there and what had I seen. I did my best to look oblivious. In the past, I have interfered so perhaps you'll call me hypocritical, but there is a difference between interfering in an underhanded and possibly criminal way and standing in a doorway with a sympathetic look waiting for someone to humiliate themselves before you. I vote for underhanded and criminal every time.

'I've been going over Lady Breck's journals and the Traveller photos she took...I wonder if there's any room for us to do an exhibition...in time for the October Fair, perhaps...I don't know how the council feels about Travellers...'

Mrs Atkinson wasn't listening, she was reaching into her bag, digging out her big bunch of keys.

'Yes you do, Ruby. They come second only to pigeons on the council's list of nuisances. Anyway, what the council feels about anything is not our concern. We're...an information system...' Her voice was scornful but steady. '...We're in the information business...and...if...I can...just...' She lost patience with herself and tipped out the contents, picked out the elusive keys from under a pair of spare knickers. She handed them to me, a silver Yale one between her finger and thumb.

'You might find some "information" of use upstairs. In the store rooms. The one at the end of the corridor is packed with more of the Brecks' belongings. All sorts of documents and personal effects they brought from Kite House when it was sold off...boxes of it...I've never had the time to get all the way through. Feel free, Ruby.'

I took the key and she gave a wistful smile. 'Save whatever you can from redevelopment.'

She dropped her eyes back to the paperwork, adjusting her glasses further down the bridge of her nose. I turned away, towards the stairs and smelled the piney smell again, as if I had disturbed a forest carpet of needles. It was heady, dizzying, melting the basement into woodland, and as soon as I stepped back into the corridor it was wafted away. Instead I breathed the papery dustiness, the polished wax of the parquet flooring.

Her worry about the council was just the surface, there was something more. It was something I recognised the way you recognise yourself suddenly reflected in a window or a mirror when you aren't expecting it. She was hiding in the archive too.

MEGANE O KAKENAI TO MIRU KOTO GA DEKIMASEN

I can't see if I don't wear glasses

'You want to get yourself webbed up,' Harvey suggested to Mrs Milligan, shovelling battenberg cake into his mouth during a rainy Friday lunch break. Harvey could eat an entire battenberg, just as if it was a KitKat. You'd have said that might account for his portly shape, but Harvey was not, is not, a fat man. Solid. Stocky. But nothing wobbles anywhere and he doesn't have man boobs. He has a strong defined chest and in the summer, when he wears short-sleeved shirts, you can see his arms, his biceps and triceps sculpted, flexing and stretching as he loads up the mobile library. What he reminds me of is a gorilla.

'Get yourself a PC and a modem. New Zealand's as good as next door on line. Get emailing him. You could even get a webcam.' Harvey moved to the wastepaper basket to tip crumbs from the well he'd made in his jumper. Underneath, his T-shirt was trapped and lifted. Mrs Milligan's eyes flittered over the brief view of the curling dark hairs of his belly and she visibly brightened, as if the cartoon lightbulb of thought had popped on over her head. In all her distress and confusion of feeling email simply hadn't occurred to her.

Mrs Milligan had mourned her son's decision to abandon the country, but in a round-the-world way it gave her the freedom to abandon her own country, to take steps. That first month she had been hiding in the staff tea room. The cut sides of Alex's departure had not yet healed over. Taking a look at her, clinging to that sofa clutching those cups of tea, you might have thought they never would. But they were scabbing up, the wounds were repairing and she knew it. We all know it when it comes upon us. It is the process we fear most. Letting go.

'I've never had anyone to email before,' she confessed later, smiling over a fresh cup of tea brewed by Harvey in the little china pot from the back of the cupboard. Before lunch was over and the exchanged French teenagers arrived to wreak havoc amongst the periodicals, Mrs Milligan was on a sure thing at PC World with Harvey.

You wouldn't automatically associate an out-of-town computer superstore with a den of romance but Harvey told me later that it was home territory for him. He knew where he was amongst the modems and scart plugs. He could talk to her easily; he was not worried and so he could concentrate on doing something for her instead of impressing her with a wine list or a flashy car. Harvey, it is now clear to everyone, has his head screwed on straight.

Once the computer was purchased and in the back of his car he could extend their companionship into the supermarket. They'd already visited there together, it was an easy move. They didn't even spend the time in the supermarket together, just armed themselves with their separate baskets and headed off for their individual shop. It was only as they stood side by side at the checkouts that each looked in the other's basket and noticed the similarities. The same cheese, the same bread, the same chocolate biscuits. The same saying nothing about it.

It is a coming-to-rely-on that happens. It's that thrill of knowing that there will be hours in the day spent with that person, the glimpses of the back of their head, the sound of their footfall on a stair. Sometimes I think maybe we shouldn't move any further than those petty minutes. Keep safe behind the barrier of not knowing. But Harvey and Mrs Milligan weren't going to be warned. And the first I knew, I could smell it.

It was just a citrussy tang in the air at first. I had come in early and was already making a start trying to match Lady Breck's journals with another stash of photographs I found shoved in a shoebox labelled *Sundries*. The second I turned them over the light shone out of them. They could only be Lady Breck's work. I was unpicking two strands of her life woven tightly between the pages of her marbled notebooks.

The new finds included a sequence of not-quite-formal portraits of the hunting shooting and fishing that went on at Kite House. She had captured smirks and a flash of ankle; shut eyes, a smudged Earl. For years the archivists and collectors had assumed they were simply taken by a servant, or by the local photographer who was often on hand to record the antics of the gentry. But I found the journal that matched up. I could recognise her eye and the way it looked out on her world.

And I was so delighted with my detective work, I decided to emerge from my burrow for a cup of tea. As I moved up the stairs from the basement I was thinking of a triangle or two of the genuine scotch shortbread Mrs Atkinson had brought in the day before in its tartan tin. I didn't tune in immediately to the voices I could hear above me. What pulled me into focus was the hint of a smell of vanilla and rosewater. A true distillation with all the clarity, the decoction of pod and petal. And then the voices were distinct.

'…they'll be starting to arrive at about seven so we need to have the chairs out by half six. What do you think, Harvey?'

'Yep. Sounds organised.'

Harvey was erecting the events easel, a cork board on a flip chart stand, as Mrs Milligan was pulling out the flier for tonight's Romance and Ruination event from her events calendar file. This time Devlin Kennedy, clearly a jack of all trades, was coming to give a talk on romantic novel writing to a group of dedicated creative writers and other interested parties. There was going to be wine and cakes, and some anxiety about whether Kennedy, flying in on a cheapy charter ticket from a book signing in York, was going to make it back in time.

I watched from between the stone banisters of the steps to the archive. I had only a back view of Harvey and a slice of Mrs Milligan, her right hand side as she sorted her publicity items, the author photo, the banner that declared, excitedly TONIGHT!

'Be a tight squeeze if you want to grab something to eat,' Harvey mentioned, as offhand as he could manage, but I saw how he snagged the soft skin between his thumb and fore-finger snapping down the easel support. His face pinched tight with a grunt of pain. They were like scissors, those easel struts, ever ready to snip into you.

'I brought sandwiches. I remember the rush last time.' Mrs Milligan was making last-minute poster adjustments with one of Mrs Atkinson's permanent markers.

There was a sudden squally gust as one of our borrowers shushed through the chickenwired doors into the lobby and swizzed out through the revolving doors. The concussion of air ruffled and flittered the papers Mrs Milligan had laid out and my slice of her danced slightly out of view as she dipped to retrieve them from the floor. She bent from the middle and I caught the hungering and delicious glance that lit Harvey's face. The parabolic curve of her arse illuminating him, exactly like a full moon.

'So I couldn't persuade you to a pizza at the art gallery café then?' You could hear the pent-up courage, the daring that breathed through every word.

Mrs Milligan missed it. 'Sorry? What'd you say Harvey?' she dodged back into view then, reloading the staple gun. I held my breath. I held Harvey in my gaze. Willing him.

'I was just saying…'

Do it.

'…just saying that I don't like sandwiches. Much.'

Do it. Don't blink. Don't move. Breathe through. Do it.

'Nor me. Bloody hate them in fact, but needs must. I got beyond it last time and I can't be bothered cooking when I get home. Does that look all right Harvey?'

She was faffing about arranging the author picture. Harvey only had eyes for her.

'Perfect.'

He had not blinked. I maintained my gaze, imagining it was a tractor beam, holding him in orbit around her. Do it. Now, Harvey. Harvey went one better. As Mrs Milligan stapled the author picture at a jaunty angle Harvey took one step to move behind her. Then, his muscled arms reaching out over her shoulders, his face not quite touching her hair, he unfurled the TONIGHT! banner. She took a step back to examine her handiwork, a step back into Harvey.

'You. Me. And a pizza?'

There was a terrible Einstein second of silence before her voice came like a whisper, the tiniest nod of her head, a scent of toasted cinnamon.

'That would be lovely. I would love to.'

And she stapled TONIGHT! into place.

Eventually I arrived in the staffroom to find it was Mrs Atkinson's turn to boil the kettle dry. She was standing by the window looking over some papers, something a couple of pages long stapled together. I popped the lid back on the kettle and refilled it through the spout. It made a vicious hissing sound but even that didn't bring her round. She was stooped over the two pages, flicking back and forth. I had to crane slightly to see that it was the schedule for fixtures and fittings for a house sale. The telephone began to ring, a harsh bleating sound. She took a deep breath then, surfacing to pick it up.

'Central Library, Mrs Atkinson speaking...oh...hello. Yes...yes...they came this morning in the post...yes...not a problem...'

I wanted to escape and yet bolting for the door would break cover. So I took careful slow-moving steps backwards until I felt the wall. I leaned into it, as if it might meld me into itself. The hem of the curtain seemed to tap at my fingers, 'Hey, here I am, take cover,' and I rolled myself into the fabric.

'...I've not made any problems about this. If you think about it I've done all the donkey work for you Grae. You've not had to deal with any of this...Well if I've been obstructive how come the house is sold?...No. I only said I didn't really want the sign up...Because some half-cocked idiot will trash it over a weekend. You remember when the Hargreaves sold up and their sign showed up in everyone's garden at at some point...I'm not exagger...Oh think what you like.' And she hung up the receiver.

I could see her through the weave of the curtain, so that she was standing behind a cloud of stylised sixties dandelion heads in a field of murky green and sulphurous yellow. Harvey had already commented that the curtains were a vintage print. Too precious for eBay, but he had a friend who was into vintage textiles and made handbags and hats who had already made him an offer if he'd steal them for her.

Standing behind them, watching Mrs Atkinson salt her tea with tears, I thought they'd need dry-cleaning first. They reeked of forty years of librarian book-breath.

TOSHOKAN WA SHIZUKA NA HAZU DESU

The library is supposed to be quiet

I was prepared for the sleeplessness. It had been that sort of day. No doubt there are psychologists somewhere who say that my expectation of insomnia guaranteed it would happen. My view is if you're going to be awake all night, face up to it. Get comfy.

I enjoyed my perch on my improvised roof terrace. It was very cold that evening and I fished out the old gloves again from where I'd left them on the top of the fridge. Miss Nudey Gardener downstairs was at her yoga class but I was still careful not to make a noise. It felt good to perch up there, cat-like. I had a tray of tea resting on the kitchen windowsill so that all I had to do was reach in for a refill. Possibly I should have had a saucer of milk, although I haven't ever seen a cat lap at a saucer of milk. The cats I have encountered have generally preferred tearing the heads off sparrows.

I reached for the binoculars, pulled focus on the backsides of the other homes, jigsaw-pieced through the branches of the trees and shrubs. The lean-tos, the decking. The man in the workshop planing wood, making a frame like ribs and a spine. I watched him for a while, lost in his work, and felt guilty that he was oblivious.

Sometimes I think that perhaps we can handle the past better. That's why most of us live there. We know what's happened. We've got the pictures and, most of all, we know we are safely out of it. The future is infinitely dodgier, like one of those games when you stick your hand in a bag and it has been hinted to you that there is, at the very least, a tarantula in there. That's it, my philosophy based on experience. The future is hairy and black and possibly venomous.

I headed back to the library at about three a.m. It seemed pointless to while away the night time bloating myself with endless pots of tea when I could be in the sanctuary of the archive keeping company with Lady Breck. I let myself in with the key, and took a torch so that I wouldn't have to turn the lights on and give myself away.

'...is too pompous, too stuffed a shirt,' she was bemoaning when I opened the pages. Her Traveller observations were crashing into her daily life.

...rigid in his petty and snobbish insistence that the Roma are wastrels and hobbledehoys casting curses and telling fortunes. I have seen their culture first hand throughout this last year. Their strong held beliefs and traditions are as worthy as anything Breck holds dear. Our own Dr Hamer would do well to consult the women and their wide ranging knowledge of herbalism and healing.

Vancy Kircher, a matriarch of our local Roma camp at Gabriel's Hundred has questioned my lack of offspring. At first, I know, it was an attempt to wrongfoot me, possibly frighten me off but now it has become something more. It is a bridge between us. Mrs Kircher has an eagle's eye and has seen what I am about, that I mean neither disrespect nor harm to her or her kinfolk. That eagle's eye has seen how I too question why I have not been with child. Vancy Kircher has offered healing. In her society, as in mine, the arrival of a baby is a vital and celebrated event, the continuation of the bloodline into posterity. It is clear after this difficult evening that Breck will hear naught about it, will not countenance such measures.

Of course, some matters cannot be healed with herbs.

Breck has declared that my visits to the Roma camp at Gabriel's Hundred should be curtailed and a visit to the October Horse Fair is similarly forbidden.

Is it conceivable that he has lived all this time with me and does not know that such a phrase is but a gauntlet thrown down? Or that I will always accept the challenge?…

It seemed to me that just as Lady Breck prepared for her Horse Fair Rebellion I heard the bull grunt in the corridor. My eyes didn't leave the graceful slopes of her copperplate handwriting, only my ears tuned harder. A lorry drove past, clanging over the manhole so it tolled like a bell. Nothing. Nothing? No. There it was again. Low, reverberant, close by. Animal.

I used to be afraid of the dark. Not now. If it is a monster it will be careful not to be seen. No one has ever yet taken a photo of the creature under the bed, have they? It was coming from one of the side rooms facing me. I took a quiet step, kept my torch beam down low.

The first room revealed the stationery store. The second revealed Mrs Atkinson in a sleeping bag on a lilo. As my torch beam skittered away from her face she shifted slightly, rolled over, caterpillar like in the sleeping bag and stopped snoring.

I was quick and quiet gathering my things. I did not even need the torch as the security light's steely glow lit the way for me. It was past four now. Outside, the bitter cold was as welcome as the sun. Every breath I took in seemed to clean me. Orion the Hunter strode across the black sky and the usual yellow fug of street light seemed bronzed now in the iced air.

I walked vaguely homeward. I was in no hurry, for I was no longer tired. It was as I passed the small park with its benches, the tiny bucket-sized duck pond and the couple of swings that I scented the air. It was something synthetic, the afternote of something that had been there. A soap or cologne leaving its trail.

I stopped, glanced into the darkness of the playground for a moment. The swing at the far end was in motion, jagging and tipping as if someone had just knocked past it.

I was at the desk the next morning. Martha had called in sick for the second time that week. Mrs Atkinson had 'arrived' wet-haired, having been to the leisure centre for a shower. She was heading off to County Hall for a meeting with Heather and some councillors, so I had to abandon my time travel for the day and man the desk. There was an air of battening down hatches against a couple of nasty viruses rumoured to be making their way around the schools. It was clear Martha had fallen prey first because she'd been busy the previous week with Welcome to Words and spent three days being breathed on by battalions of snotty-nosed, nit-haired brats from the local primary schools.

At one, Harvey and Mrs Milligan returned from their joint lunch break and I burrowed down into the archive to take mine. I was still trawling the church registers from time to time looking for Mary-Ann Penny. If any new records arrived to be catalogued or preserved I was first on them but she had not appeared. She was huddled in the darkest corner of my mind, some feeble tallow candle guttering on a cheap table as she breastfed the child I imagined had been her downfall, the illegitimate heir to Viscount Breck.

Not that I had ever found a child either. I had worked on dates from six months after Mary-Ann's disappearance from the ledgers but there were no babies registered to a mother by the name of Mary-Ann Penny. That lunchtime I stopped trawling for them and it seemed to me that the candle guttered out. I couldn't look. I had to leave them in the dark.

Lady Breck let me out into the chemically captured sunlight of her photographic passions. The journal showed not only how she worked around the restrictions placed on a woman of her status but also how keenly she felt the need not to intrude too much, not to make the Travellers seem like dolls for a well-bred lady with no children of her own.

My interest in the children is accepted. After all, are not women supposed to be delighted by babies in much the same way as they are delighted by a basket of kittens or a barrel of monkeys? Am I not a 'gorjer' with no child of my own and therefore to be pitied? This role works to my advantage. As I stage the tableaux of Roma children, so the background scenes are revealed openly to me and no one thinks to tidy away the campfire or to shirk from their tasks Not all are successful but there was a splendid one of a group of the women peeling vegetables and preparing a meal. I hover for as long as I can flitting about the camp trying not to be noticed, trying not to get in the way but grasping the smallest opportunity. If I could only paint, I might be able to put down the pictures

*that are saved in my head, and oh for a manufactory that
might bottle the smells!*

The portraits of the children would be the ones we could use for an exhibition. Lady Breck had captured them, grubby and suspicious. In order to show that I was still busy with my project I took the journal and the relevant photographs to Mrs Atkinson in her office.

She didn't mention how her County Hall meeting had gone and it was impossible to tell whether the stress that vibrated out of her was down to County Hall or Mr Atkinson and their dastardly divorce proceedings.

She took a long time over each image, examining the faces. 'These are perfect. This exhibition is going to be larger than you think, Ruby. We'll need to tackle all the aspects of life that Lady Breck caught on camera, not just the Travellers. The domestic staff are going to be of interest and these…these are just…perfect in their imperfection.'

She handed them back. I mentioned the other finds I'd made, the informal photos of the upper class, Lady Breck's guests and visitors. Mrs Atkinson nodded.

'Tradesmen?' was her only comment. I promised to look around once I'd finished scanning in the children and the journal entries.

It was down in the basement, as I turned the book over to sit the relevant pages on the lightbed of the scanner, that I saw the imprinted gold lettering on the back of the journal.

Chas. Goodrich and Daughters
Stationer and Paper Merchant Totnes Devon.

I took out the box and began to look over all the journals. Some were plainly marbled with black and grey and white but others were thicker, the paper more a clotted cream golden yellow. These were all marked Chas. Goodrich and the covers were stouter, marbled elaborately with a leafy green and a deep purple the colour of Advent robes. I ran my hand across the pages where the journal I was scanning had fallen open and it was creamy beneath my fingers. Cool, breathing. I riffled through, letting the paper cascade and release its old scents. There was something captured in there. I riffled again and woodsmoke breathed out at me.

I checked over the journal I had been scanning and found no mention of a trip to Totnes but I felt sure that somewhere here there would be a strand of Mary-Ann Penny's life. Her history was hidden somewhere in these pages. I moved over to the boxes and sorted the Chas. Goodrich journals from amongst the others. Nothing was in date order here. Mrs Atkinson had told me that she hadn't had time to go through it all. I took the Totnes notebooks and began to put them into chronological order. They began in 1888. April. But they did not begin with any mention of Devon.

So we are still in Wiltshire on the pretence of chasing duck. Monty is a bewhiskered buffoon who rules over his estate like an Ottoman Despot, and in that description I am including his wives—do, Dearest Diary, note the plural! Monty was put out of humour shortly before our arrival over a spate of poaching. Consequently instead of hunting duck we found ourselves on the trail of a poacher! I am almost certain that I glimpsed someone in the wood and was thankful he outwitted us and evaded capture.

Evening:
GHASTLY. Monty and Breck and the other dullards ensconced

with the brandy and cigars after dinner, the ladies, myself, part of the company, retiring to the drawing room. Here, perched upon an uncomfortable chaise I was left to the mercies of wife Edie and mistress Miranda. Spite reigned. Their situation is unenviable, Monty's good favours are bestowed turn and turn about. Each aired the most personal resentments towards the other with no regard for my presence in the room. I was forced to sit, a blank-faced witness to all their domestic torment, managing, in the uncomfortable final silence, a feeble compliment regarding the roast lamb at dinner.

How I would love to sit in the kitchen and hear what the servants make of this trio!

Something was beginning to tug at the edge of my memory. Some of the names were familiar to me now, they were part of the social circle, but I felt there was some tiny detail I'd overlooked. It was important, and I knew it would come to me. I headed downstairs to steal yet another cup of library tea and let my thoughts sift and surface.

The book club were still talking together. As I walked through the library it was like hearing a familiar tune that I couldn't quite place. Their voices were lowered, concerned, not the usual banter and disagreement and literary passion at all.

I had my hand on the door to the staffroom when Angharad spoke, her voice almost a whisper, 'Is it true?'

My brain, fuddled and time-travelled as it was, snapped back into reality. I looked round. The book club were all turned towards me.

'Is it true, Ruby?' White haired Deirdra, the small black rectangles of her spectacles perched elegantly on her roman nose, stood up. 'We thought you might know.'

Know what? Ellen Freethy read my baffled face.

'About Tierney's wife.'

Mrs Atkinson, keys clipped to her belt, spoke decisively, a rhetorical question. 'Tea anyone?'

I let them all move past me into the staffroom.

Angharad brewed tea in the huge steel pot she dug from the very back of the cupboard under the sink. There were spiders in it which she chucked out of the window into the darkness of the flowerbed outside. Mrs Atkinson revealed a secret hoard of biscuits concealed in one of the old tin lockers in the far corner.

I did not sit down, I could sense that if I did I might not be able to get back up again. I needed to stand, to lock my knees out against disaster. Mrs Atkinson seemed to sense this, and handed me the unopened packets of biscuits. 'Plate them up, Ruby.'

In the more confined surroundings of the staffroom everyone relaxed and spoke more easily. It seemed that Deirdra's daughter, on a ceramics course at the college where Tierney's wife taught, heard that Anita Winstanley had been offered a university teaching job in Stockholm. She had taken most of their savings and put their house on the market, but left Tierney the keys to the car and his 'shag-pad' at Dry Dock.

As they talked about why a woman of Anita Winstanley's intelligence would link up with a man like Mac Tierney, Mrs Atkinson kept her face almost hidden by her mug. Her eyes glazed as if contemplating how a woman of *her* intelligence could have hooked up with someone like Mr Atkinson and ended up camped out at the library.

Amid the background noises of their reasoning (the lure of masculinity, its deceits and disappointments, power, strength, disillusion) my mind was going over the fact that

Martha had been absent since the day Anita Winstanley abandoned post and husband and flew off to new opportunities in Sverige.

Possibilities began to riffle and shuffle through my head. She might genuinely have been laid low by the bug going around. Instantly I had a terrible mental image of a vulnerable Martha puking into the toilet whilst being taken from behind by the recently freed/bereft/emasculated Mac Tierney.

What if he'd arrived on her doorstep, homeless and single, eyes raffish with charm. Would she let him over the threshold?

'No.' Angharad did not even have to consider her answer. She shook her head and the others all agreed. 'She wouldn't get back with him. There is no way on God's green earth that she wants *anything* to do with Tierney. Not after the Thai Palace evening. Not after that.'

But the decision might not be hers. The words whispered in my mind. I daren't say them aloud. Mrs Atkinson had tried calling her flat several times in the last couple of days but the answerphone was permanently on and her mobile was switched off. 'I just put it down to the bug. When you're laid low with that kind of thing, you don't want to talk to anyone do you?'

My sweat was now liquid nitrogen trying to supercool the scared heat of panic. Just as it seemed my breathing was going to shut down, I had a thought.

'Has anyone called her sister?'

Iris's number was in Martha's file. Angharad called from the front desk. At first it was the answerphone and then as Angharad was part way through her message Iris picked up. Angharad listened for a moment and said her farewells. She put down the phone and gave us all a triumphant smile.

There had been a run-in with Tierney the night his wife left. She had fled to Iris's flat, Tierney kerb crawling beside her in his sleek Audi. Iris had helped her to send him on his way and thought it best that Martha stay with her. The lease was up on Martha's own flat at the end of the month and they had decided that when Iris moved to her new house next month, Martha would move there too. They had already lugged her stuff out to Iris's storage unit.

It was cold when I finally stepped out of the library. The night was clear and the light from the streetlamps glittered the frost so eerily that you could be convinced that there were faeries. I thought about the first time I had ever seen Iris. After the first day that Queen Victoria set her stony gaze upon me and I landed the library job.

I had found myself walking past the Galleon coffee shop more times than I now care to remember. I couldn't muster the courage to push open the glass door. There was always a reason not to. The woman with red nails seated in the window. The bad weather. Excuses.

When I did finally push open the door, the masts on the etched image of the galleon seemed to creak as it gave inwards. There was the sound of the ocean, only later, sitting down, I realised it was just the rushing of panicked blood in my ears.

The panic. A tsunami of unstoppable magnitude. The money in my purse that seemed like foreign currency, my brain unable to cope with the mathematics of a pot of tea plus a round of toast, already the black stars imploding in my sightline. It had been a mistake. A terrible mistake. Then, an elegant white hand reached forward, the only colour an amber stone set into a chunky silver ring.

'Let me.' And her coins fell like glitter.

I looked up. Her face, the white skin and dark eyes beneath sculpted brows. The dark tint she had painted her lips, not blood, not plums. She smiled and as I fumbled my purse back into my bag she took my tea and toast and settled me at a corner table. An arrangement of stark twigs spangled with fairy lights beside me.

Her hair, past her waist, was drawn behind her head to drape down one shoulder. Like a scarf, only not like. There was a shiny blackness to her, like patent leather. I had never seen hair like that, the sheen to it. I watched the drape of her coat as she reached for a napkin, the boots beneath her long, lean, black skirt, buttery leathered and chunky soled.

I had breakfast every day there after that. Just to be in the same room with so much sheen and self-assurance. A few weeks later she came into the library one evening to pick up Martha and the connection was made. We exchanged greetings and niceties about the weather each morning after that, until she got her new job at the university. That was Iris.

She lived towards the other side of town in a Victorian conversion, past Queens Park. It was a huge old detached house, complete with sympathetically done conservatory. There was a turret-style room, a Lutyens knock-off, first floor front. I could imagine Martha up there sitting at the breakfast table with her hair pinned awry, looking out over town. I approached very carefully, trying to stay close to the walls and fences and hedges as I made my way up the hill from town.

There were odd lights on here and there, a copse of trees lurked behind a sooty black wall, carrying with them a deeper darkness as if, if you happened in there you might be blotted out. In a kitchen window a woman in a dressing gown cradled a yawling baby. A man, revealing himself naked in an upstairs room before the light blinked off in embarrassment.

As I approached the house I noticed there were three cars parked nearby. The nearest to me, a black BMW, had headrests that made me stand, hesitating, for some minutes thinking it was occupied. In front of that, a silver Honda pulled out suddenly, a woman in a supermarket uniform at the wheel. That left just the red Mitsubishi on the far side, much further up, the chestnut trees overhanging the pavement making it darker, more difficult to see if anyone might be inside. I edged onwards, keeping to the darker shadows.

No one. No sign of the silver Audi. Tierney was not staking out Iris's flat.

Later, I stood on the spun steel bridge at Dry Dock, the rain soaking me. The lights were on in Tierney's canalside apartment. I could see him slumped in the chair the light from the TV playing across his face as he sipped at a beer can. And in the window, in primary colours, a square sign:

MILTON AND DUFREY
FOR SALE.

FUSEN WA AGAIMASHITA

The balloon ascended

Next afternoon, it was muggily hot in the basement archive, the old-style radiators blasting out heat you could have founded iron with. I hadn't realised I'd fallen asleep beside the photocopier. I was sitting in my chair, sitting very still as Lady Breck lifted the camera's cover and the sun shone through the lens in a whiteout of burnished light. In the real world it was a paper jam.

Later I was called upon for a stint on the desk. Martha had been late in the morning and was looking grey and peaky. Her final task of the day was the secondary school history group. Harvey and Mrs Milligan were preparing for Story Time. They were talking in low voices, conspiratorial. No one else took any interest but I kept them in the periphery of my vision. It is not hard to see what is in front of you. They kept close, they were happy invading each other's space. Something was happening between them. I waited, listening, almost certain that I would hear them clicking together like Lego.

But the sound was obliterated by the unholy racket surging in with the party of secondary school children arriving for their

'History is Our Future' presentation from Martha. Thirteen-year-old schoolboys shouting 'QUIET' and 'SILENCE' over the high-pitched drone and whine of thirteen-year-old girls, bored and boring in equal measure. 'FUCK!' someone shouted, and the teacher, thick-set and powerful in his shirt and tie, pounced on the culprit like an educated bouncer.

Which was when Martha fainted and all hell broke loose.

The girls divided into the ones who cried hysterically and the others who stood resolutely smug. The teacher was attempting to struggle through the boys who had taken on the herd mentality of bullocks, milling and bellowing, punches and kicks flying. A trio of losers up at the front, began shoving the tallest of their number, a bumfluffed bruiser of lad, towards the floored Martha, their feet kicking and scuffing. 'Go on Beggsy…' they jeered.

'Kiss of Life, Beggsy.' 'She's gagging for it Beggs…' 'No tongues.'

'That's ENOUGH.' The teacher barked at them and a thick, claggy silence fell as Harvey, knight in woolly pullover that he is, strode quickly over to Martha's prone body and lifted her up. Mrs Milligan opened the door to the staffroom and they all vanished behind it. I looked at the grain of the door for a moment or two and then the teacher cleared his throat. I looked at him. He smiled and seemed familiar.

'Would you care to step into the breach?'

I felt as if the contents of my brain had suddenly been flushed down a toilet.

'Could you give the talk? Or would that not be allowed?' He was glancing at his watch. 'Or we could busk something.'

His smile again, familiar and kind. Probably he looked just like some other teacher I had once known; it was a neat, authoritative teacher smile. Wasn't it?

I had heard Martha give the talk several times and she'd already spent the last half an hour setting up the overhead projector and the flip chart. It had to be done, there was just me and a slide presentation to stave off mayhem. There was a group at the back still talking, sitting turned away from me. How did Martha grab their attention?

'You. At the back.' One boy turned, a sly smile on his face, a surreptitious glance to the teacher to see what he could get away with. 'You're history.'

And that was the way to do it, to pretend to be Martha. I stepped into her shoes in my head, the victoriana boots she was wearing that morning with a deep purplish bronzed sheen to the leather and the small stubby heel. There was one desperate moment when I envisioned myself wearing only the boots and my mouth went dry. I thought that I might faint too, but Harvey materialised before me with a mug of tea.

'Where you are sitting is Geography. Who you are, that's Anthropology, or even Psychology...So, perhaps it's time to introduce you to Mr Melvil Dewey, the man who cut us a set of golden keys to libraries all around the world...'

It seemed to go as well as any attempt at education ever does. The ones who are interested listen, the rest pick their noses and smirk. It was the most wearying hour I have spent in the library. A sullen girl at the back kept drawing my eye, but rather than wonder what black secrets might be in her head I concentrated on holding them in thrall until the time was up and the minibus would arrive to take them away.

It was almost closing time. As the teenagers filed out they seemed keen to be released early for good behaviour. I saw the smiling arrogance of Beggsy and I wondered if he had the foggiest notion of what heat-seeking missiles life was going to throw at him.

'Don't you think?' The teacher said, reiterating something I hadn't heard.

'I'm sorry?'

'It went okay? I thought you did very well under the circumstances.'

His smile was more nervous now.

'Yes. Well, I've heard Martha's version enough times.'

There was a silence then, broken only by the noise of Beggsy trapping one of the girls in the revolving doors. She squealed like a culled seal and two other girls set upon Beggsy from the street side of the door. The teacher seemed unaware. It was as if we were in a bubble running on extra slow speed as they whirred and spun around us.

'You don't remember me do you?'

I struggled with the controls of my face, veering suddenly away from the terror I felt, aiming vaguely for stupid, careless; hoping that at the very least I could manage bored. For just one second I flashed back to the lecture and saw the vision of me wearing only Martha's victoriana boots and my skin.

'In the supermarket. A while ago. Singles night?' He did not try to make his voice sound encouraging or fakely upbeat. He simply stated the facts. I didn't remember him. In the supermarket. And then of course I did.

'I'm Judd. Mr Pennington to the students, at least within earshot.'

I could feel all the nerve endings in my face beginning to spasm as if I was going to be felled by a stroke at any second. My breathing was too shallow, some internal refrigeration unit was overcooling my sweat again. I could see Judd Pennington's mouth moving but I wasn't translating the words. I should have taken his face as a focus and concentrated on that. The scrapy, mown-bristle quality of his skin, the well-ordered cut of his hair, could have anchored me properly, let me breathe.

But this is my problem. I can't see his face. I can't see the every-morning shower cleanliness of his hair or the school-boyish nervousness that lights his smile.

What I saw was that I was hemmed in. My back was to the wall, cornered in the worst possible way and each second that I stood there more people seemed to be leaving the library, abandoning their keyword catalogue searches and their reference tomes. Abandoning me. I couldn't see why he was here, why he was doing this. *I don't know you. Go away.* My spasming face muscles unable to form the words.

I struggled to keep my face a bored blank. A woman was trying to move through the tide of teenagers, trying to get into the library. I stepped forward.

'The library is closing,' I said, hoping that when I stepped back he would be gone, cuffing Beggsy into the minibus and setting homework.

'If you're finishing here, you know…perhaps we could meet up later…' And then Beggsy set off the fire alarm and we had to evacuate the building.

Outside on the pavement I avoided looking at him. When all the fire alarm protocols had been gone through I was first up the stone steps. As I turned back into the library to collect my things I saw Judd Pennington glance my way before turning to deal with Beggsy and the wrath of Mrs Atkinson.

I had set off towards the Tech before I remembered there was no Intermediate Japanese tonight. Rattled, I stood at the bus stop.

I let three buses go then adjourned to the coffee shop across the road. I say road, it is more like a square, the parish church, a Victorian Gothic edifice, firmly plonked between the road into town and the road out of town. Seated in the far left edge of the window, I had a decent view of the doors of the library but anyone caring to look in would probably not notice me. Mrs Milligan and Harvey left together, turning into the gates to the park. As they moved along the tarmacked path past the council gardener and his barrow of winter prunings Harvey put out his hand and Mrs Milligan, without hesitation, took it.

Winter prunings. I had to look down into the surface of the cappuccino and remember where I was. I curled my finger tightly round the cup and lifted it, scalded my lips. Safe.

Martha left next. She revolved out of the doors, shrugging into an ultramarine blue velvet forties-style swing jacket with three round black buttons like coffee cup saucers. It had a stand-up collar and big turned-back cuffs. She was wearing a long, thin black wool skirt and those victoriana boots, all laces and heels. Her hair was coming a bit adrift. She had pinned it up that day but it wanted to be free. I had ambition to be Martha's hair, wild and free, an undomesticated creature.

Tierney seemed to peel himself from the bark of the tree in the concrete shrubbery that landscaped the taxi rank. I saw him, as slinky and evil as a satyr, and then he and she were obscured from view by the church.

I was out of that coffee shop like a gust of wind.

Martha was a trusting fool in that she made her way home via a small hedged-in ginnel that cut between the back of the old red brick technical college and the carpark to the civic centre. The ginnel is marked on all the maps as Darley Cut but is known locally as Harm's Way. It is a muggers' paradise. The raincoated flashers all favour it.

Darley Cut ran for a dangerous and narrow half a mile before coming out on Harper Road. If you looked at it with other eyes, it didn't seem dangerous at all. It was mysterious and magical, a leafy, fragrant slot in the red brick and concrete maze of town. It was literally no more than shoulder width and to enter into it was to disappear from view. It was a beech-lined wormhole where you could imagine you were somewhere else, somewhere greenified and distant.

I didn't catch her. She had already moved through into the walkway, down into Harm's Way, the burnished bronze of the beech hedging, and who knew what thoughts were in her head. No thoughts of Tierney in pursuit. I felt the paving pound against my feet as I sped towards them, trying to fly and always finding I had to push against the tug of gravity. Always finding that gravity won.

Tierney was about to slither into the pathway. His stride was long and I estimated that he would have caught up with her somewhere in the centre, too far for her to run out. Too hidden for anyone to hear or help her. The streetlights were blinking on. It seemed they lit before me as I ran, like torches marking my way. I skidded on wet leaves at the corner of the civic centre and scraped my knee across the rough brickwork. It only made me faster. Then I almost slammed into the back of him as he halted, a brewery lorry making a delivery, nearly backing over him.

I darted back the way I had come, skirted the building, grazing my hands along the bricks as I careened around the far corner. Ahead of me I could hear the delivery lorry's reversing warning beeping out like a robotic chicken. And Tierney was suddenly nowhere to be seen. My heart was thick and meaty in my mouth as I saw the upturned sole darting through into the walkway. There was only one way to catch him now.

He did not see me. The light had faded into the gloaming. I scuttled out of range of the lorry headlights as they winked on. I was moving so fast my bag strap snagged on the shrubs as I cut through the children's park, but I was determined and yanked it hard enough to break the branch. The boughs of the bare shrubs clabbered and clawed at me as I ran onwards towards the side gate that led into the special needs primary school. I could see the padlock but I didn't care. I made an almost vertical take off, up onto the bench, jab foot into loop of plastic coated chain, swing right and onto the metal frame, grab the top of the gate and swing over onto the dumpsters at the back of the school kitchens. My landing echoed down into the body of the dumpster with an empty *pbom* sound. I was level with the hedged walkway, could see some movement through the crisped leaves.

A flash of blue like a kingfisher. Martha. Still going. Still safe.

I was crossing the school playground now, heading towards the climbing frame that looked over into the walkway. I was up and over, crouching at the top as I waited for Tierney. He was dressed in earth tones and as the light faded and the yellow streetlamps blinked on I almost missed him. He was striding, not hurried but horribly graceful. And he was catching her up.

I launched myself off the climbing frame, over the hedging, nothing in my head that connected me to Martha or the crunching reality of where I might land. I saw only those thoughts that connected to Tierney. To bringing him down. Flying. Invisible. I was of a piece with the darkness. I skimmed the top of the hedging, felt the harsh winter of the branches scratch at me as this time gravity lent her hands for me and plunged me earthwards. Hard. It was a confusion of bronzed leaves, yellow streetlights, brown moleskin jacket. My head connected with his head as I dived and yawed against him. Floored him.

There was a scrapping snarling tussle, a brutish wrestling, before my hand curled into a grenade that exploded at his face. My mouth watered, salty, as the pain rivered through my hand. Tierney stumbled, the hedging bouncing him back into the fray. As my hand snapped back in readiness to meet him, all I aimed was instinct and he toppled, treelike. A moment stretched until he breathed, groaned; did not get up.

The sky was clear as I walked the long way back to town. I had left Tierney on the narrow, broken and mossy tarmac path and turned towards Martha. As I cleared the hedging at Darley Cut I saw her reach the corner. A battered VW Beetle was parked across the way and as I looked Martha picked up her step and Iris flashed the headlights.

The battered green car drove off and I made my way up Harper Road. It led back towards town in a long, gracefully curving route of Edwardian villas and pollarded trees. They looked like fists, raised in defiance, gnarled and knuckled against the darkening sky.

Back at the coffee shop they had chucked out my almost untouched cappuccino. That seemed to be a last straw somehow. I found I was shaking so hard I could hardly open the door to let myself out. The world seemed to glint, very sharp, very metallic. I twitched and burned inside as if I had been struck by lightning. I had. I had let go of something in myself.

CHIZU O KAITE KUDASAIMASEN KA?

Won't you please draw me a map?

I couldn't go back to the library. I couldn't go back to the flat. I could only walk.

The cold damp of twilight became mizzle and then a slow but steady rain. It seemed everyone had deserted town except for me. I was alone with my footsteps and then I could hear it. The metallic chink. I looked round, afraid. Blinded briefly by headlights passing, refracting and distorting in the rain. But no, there was no one behind me.

As I took a step the metallic sound pinked again. Something, tapping against the zip of my pocket as I walked. What was it? And then the universe contracted down to the bright star of the coin. The twenty pence piece still safe in my pocket.

It had been so long, so long. I felt as if the world had emptied and I just couldn't bear it. I couldn't move through it. It had rained about seven times since I imprisoned the coin there. Each time I had pulled the jacket on I had felt the zip's closedness. The forbidden zone.

Now I was cutting quickly through the shopping centre, a concrete blocked walkway of shops that they tried to revamp last year by putting on a glazed roof and fitting lighting so dazzling it scorched your retina. If you cut up and through you come out at a little back street. It's beginning a renaissance. Where it was a closed up Post Office and a furniture store, now there are some Bohemian arty cafes and a craft studio and the small boutique, Norsk, with their temptations.

But I did not care about that. What was important to me that night, has always been important, is that at the end of the street stands the last phone box.

The door was stiff, rusted over with urine. The rain whipped in now under the sides and door. I stood there for an age listening to the rain and let the tinny metal urine smell sting my nose and I knew I wouldn't be able to stop myself this time.

The receiver was very cold and it made an echoey click as I lifted it. I was so close, just a few numbers. My heart was in overtime, using up all the beats of my life it seemed, as the chirrup sounded at the other end. I could see the room where it would be ringing out. The view through the window. The angled, open door. The sofa. The piano.

'Hello?' He sounded normal, everyday. I felt the world tilting suddenly, blurring me.

'Hello?' A tinge of uncertainty. 'Hello?' I couldn't speak because I didn't exist.

'Hello?' one last try. Then a silence to match my own. Then a moment or so later, the click as the phone hung up.

I listened to the dial tone until the recorded woman said, 'The other person has cleared. The other person has cleared.'

I began to cry then. Raining inside the phone box.

I used my key to get into the library building, clicking on my torch so I wouldn't have to use the lighting. I stood at the top of the stairs leading down to the archive rooms, and as I did I knew she wasn't there anymore. It wasn't a great absence of snoring—after all, it was only early evening—it was absence itself.

In the little storeroom I saw the gap in the shelving where she'd been holed up these last few weeks had been carefully filled with stationery boxes and cartons of toner cartridges. There was no sign of her sleeping bag or her bed roll. What I should have felt was a lifting of weight, a sense that I wouldn't have to be quiet now, I had the run of the library. But that is not what I felt. I felt the old panic make a butterfly of my heart.

In the staffroom I could see by the light from the memorial gardens beyond the window. Everything was suffused with the pale sulphurous orange, bitter and bright. I made myself a pot of tea and sat down on Mrs Milligan's sofa. It was lower than my usual spot at the window and I couldn't see out from there. Equally, no one would see in.

I sipped at the tea in the dark, only now aware of the sharpness in my chest, the scoured feeling of breathing too hard and too fast. I took a couple of long deep breaths, the first deep breaths for years, as if tonight, on this sofa, I was suddenly safe. It was just me. I gave a shudder, my eyes aching after the tears. If I could just close them for a moment, just lean back in the dark. Beatrice, Lady Breck, put a gentle hand on my shoulder.

'Ruby?' she said softly and there was a green, dank scent of water and weed. Cooling. Soothing.

'Ruby?'

Only it wasn't Lady Breck. It was Mrs Atkinson. I was slumped over on the sofa. The greenish winter morning light was streaming in through the staffroom window. I sat up feeling crumpled and caught. My left eye hurt. I'd slept awkwardly and clearly that side of my face had borne the brunt of the bouclé.

'What happened?' Mrs Atkinson's brow furrowed as she looked at me. I looked blankly back, my mouth still full of dream marshmallows.

'Here.' She touched my arm gently, I looked down at a hot cup of tea.

'Drink this. Give yourself a couple of minutes.'

She hoiked herself up from her kneeling position beside me and moved to fetch her own cup. She came to rest on one side of the sofa, her eyes still anxious, regarding my face intently.

'I must've…must've fallen asleep…I'm sorry.'

I mumbled an apology as I struggled to get up, impeded by the bundled layers of coat and cagoule I was wearing and the sagging springs of the aged sofa. Mrs Atkinson touched my arm again, shaking her head,

'No, it's fine. You're not in trouble Ruby. Just tell me what happened.'

Where to begin? I sat there struggling with the fraying edges of my face much as Mrs Milligan had done once upon a time. I could feel how weary my nerve endings were becoming, constantly defying fear and guilt and bone weariness. Mrs Atkinson said nothing. She moved to fetch the first-aid box out of the cupboard. Then she tugged gently on my arm, steadied me to my feet.

'Let's sort you out.'

Mr Machin was mopping the cubicles as we entered the ladies' toilets. With a nod from Mrs Atkinson he cleared out, giving me an odd wincing look as he moved past with his galvanised bucket. It was the look you might give a boxer after they'd lost a fight.

It had not occurred to me that there might be anything untoward about me. Peeling myself out of the claggy cagoule, I turned and caught sight in the mirror of a scarecrow wearing my coat. Mrs Atkinson turned to fumble about in the first aid box and I had a moment to take in the view.

My hair was whorled and twisted in places with broken bits of twig, bark and leaves, alternately crispy and slimy bronzed, from the hedging at Harm's Way. The top left shoulder of my coat was torn away and the jumper underneath crusted with an armour plating of mud. The front of my coat was muddied and there were long grazes, the fabric fraying and snagged where I had landed heavily and skinned across the tarmac of the alleyway.

But the clothes and the hair were nothing to the purple and slate blue of my left eye. It had nearly closed up on itself, which explained why I felt so half asleep and bleary. It was as if Joan of Art had painted me while I slept. I had been scraped and grazed. Blood was crusted and smeared from forehead to neck. Mrs Atkinson ran some hot water into the lone sink and soaked a handful of cotton wool.

Cleaning and patching the scrapes and cuts only highlighted the riot of colour swamping my eye. With clean skin as a backdrop the colours pulsed and hummed.

'Ready to talk about it?' Mrs Atkinson put away the first-aid box. I shook my head. What could I say? I beat up Professor Tierney in an alleyway? I wondered what he looked like—if, indeed, anyone had discovered him yet.

'Anything in your make-up bag you can use to disguise that?'

She checked out my eyeball as she spoke. It was bloodshot.

'No.' I don't wear make-up. Not any more.

She handed me another wad of cotton wool, steeped in cold water this time. 'Hold that against it for a few minutes. You should see someone, Ruby…I could get Harvey to run you down to the sur…'

I was shaking my head slowly as she spoke. She took in a deep breath. 'All right. I'll see if Martha's in. She'll have something in her magic handbag I'm sure.'

'No. Please. Don't.'

It was my turn to touch her arm, only I wasn't gentle, I clutched at her. Please don't tell. Mrs Atkinson's hand reached to cover mine.

'Just to get you some cover-up. I won't say anything. I understand, even if I don't agree. Let's see what Martha's got and we'll do our best.'

I saw the sense of it.

'Do you want to go home Ruby? Harvey could…'

I was shaking my head again, it was beginning to look like a nervous tic, a side-effect of my set-to.

'There's no one waiting? No one worried? No one I can call?'

I thought of the phone box and I wanted to run there. To run and keep running. I felt lightheaded with the thought of it and the edge of the sink was cold under my fingers.

'Do you need somewhere to stay?'

Don't crack now Ruby, you've come such a long way to be here. So I shook my head and stood up straight.

'I'm fine. At the flat.'

Mrs Atkinson borrowed some cover-up foundation from Martha and left me to do the best I could. Only a paper bag would have done the job.

I emerged to take up my wand at the desk. Clearly Mrs Atkinson had primed them all to say nothing. Martha, wearing a bronze-coloured mohair wrap cardigan over a deep green velvet vintage dress, was engaged in an uncharacteristic bout of librarianship. She stole a quick glance through the books as she reshelved.

Seated at the computer, Mrs Milligan managed to not even look at my face as she confessed, 'I've buggered something up, Ruby. It's frozen on me.' She looked intently at the screen as I tapped at the keyboard ineffectually. Harvey wandered over.

'I can sort it, Vanessa. Ruby, can you help Mrs Longden find what she wants in the newspaper archive?'

Harvey had addressed her as Vanessa. The name seemed to transform her into a different person, someone not Mrs Milligan. And as I looked back at her I realised that her haircut was new.

Other than that, it was all business as usual.

'What happened to you?' Mrs Longden, seated in front of the microfiche reader, peered over the tiny windscreens of her reading glasses.

'I fell off the bus.' My swollen eye giving the impression of a cheeky wink.

SHIRANAI UCHI NI, INU GA HEYA NI HAITTE KIMASHITA

While I was unaware,
the dog came into the room

For most of the morning I was able to hide behind the display boards Mrs Atkinson and I were erecting in the exhibition space next to the media library. It's a light room, a deep curved bay shape. Once that was under way, I was despatched to the print shop to drop off the text and photos that we were having enlarged and put onto display boards.

As I looked into the now-familiar faces I couldn't shake the feeling that someone was missing. Had I brought all the selections from the archive? Had I left some image on the scanner bed? Something, someone important? Who was missing? And then I realised that I didn't have any photos of Lady Breck. I had no idea, except in my own imagination, what she looked like.

Upstairs, Mrs Atkinson and I began to trawl through the myriad boxes that I hadn't got to yet, with no success. It seemed she had photographed almost everyone in the town, her house parties, her Traveller portraits, her domestic staff were catalogued and captured in time. Only Lady Breck herself was absent.

After lunch Mrs Atkinson waylaid me.

'I've had a word with Winn at the museum. She says you can come over and she'll take you through their collection. She's got a few ideas for you, and doubtless you can tie up some of her loose ends too. There are a few paintings that came from Kite House that they've had a struggle identifying.'

I had always enjoyed the pictures in the museum, a huge collection assembled in the auction houses of Europe by Viscount Breck, and his father and grandfather before him. They had taste similar to my own. Others might find the choice dismal but I don't care. I like to wander through *Winter Landscape in Brittany* and marvel at the glare of *Sun on the Water*. I know that as I climb the staircase that rises up beside the Bronze Age gallery there is a familiar face awaiting me at the turn of the stair.

She hangs on the wall beside a gypsy wagon bearing the sign No Entry. To some the portrait is probably garish; to me it is vibrant. I have always liked the palette of purples, umber and ochre. The old woman is posed in a mannish great-coat beside a fire. There is a cauldron suspended over the flame and the woman is smoking a pipe, looking directly out at us through the thin gauzy haze of woodsmoke and pipe smoke from her small, white, clay pipe. The frame declares: '*A Pipe of Baccy* by Virginia Brett 1921'.

Each time I turn on the stair she seems to greet me. 'Back, are you? Where've you been then?' And the sky above her opens out, cerulean and ultramarine.

Now, following Winn through the card-swipe security system into the museum storehouse, I could glimpse other treasures that had not seen the light of exhibition. There were portals and doorways here, where just one look could transport you through time and landscape. I wasn't paying any attention which is why Winn had to backtrack to find me.

The pictures she had for me had been salvaged from the sale of Kite House after the end of the First World War. They had been dumped at the museum and put away and no one had paid them much attention. As Winn tried to research their origin she'd discovered a few had been commissioned by Viscount Breck from a local artist, one Blaise Godwin, who had shown early talent until he travelled to Paris and vanished from view. It was rumoured that he found whores and gambling in lieu of inspiration.

'Of course,' sighed Winn as she set out the first few portraits and groups, 'no one has any interest in him except me. I'm becoming a bit of an expert, a bit of an obsessive compulsive about our Blaise. I'm trying to blag some cash to go to Paris, follow a few leads.'

I looked at the pictures. One stood out instantly, a five foot by six foot canvas of a shooting party. On the back, in the artist's hand were painted the words *Hares and Hounds*. The painting was set in the grounds of Kite House, the windows of the conservatory a blur of silver and titanium white in the background. The gentlemen were grouped standing, their shotguns all broken, except for one at the back whose gun aimed rebelliously skywards. They all wore serviceable tweeds and every variety of fashionable moustache, but there was something odd about it. Something other.

Winn clearly knew the secret and stood, waiting for me to see the magic. Suddenly it sprang out. Hares. Hidden. Amongst the earthen browns and greens of the tweeds, in the shapes and contortions of the shrubbery, in the knees and elbows of the hunters. Hares everywhere, woven into the fabric of the painting. I gasped. Winn grinned.

'Every picture tells a story.' And she began to slide out other paintings.

Lady Breck did not emerge from the stacks. Captain Whitside was there in a wedding portrait with his pink-and-white debutante bride. And there was a busy port seascape. A tall boat loomed into the sky. It was strange the way he had painted the crowds milling around, the porters and baggage. The traders and cabs.

In all of that melée two women stood out on deck. He had picked them out in different tones to the rest. One woman standing at the rail waving frantically at us. Another beside her, more restrained and dignified. Less self-assured. I looked at her for a long time. Her face was not clear, rather it was an impression of a face. It seemed familiar. I had that sense of déjà vu, of having viewed this scene before. And then I knew that she was not dignified or restrained. These were things she was pretending to be. What her face held was trepidation.

There were a few landscapes of Kite House and another of a house I didn't recognise dated June 1889. It was titled *A Luncheon* and a well-to-do party were taking lunch in a lush and verdant garden. Maidservants carried trays from the background. Surely one of these seated ladies was Lady Breck? That one, at the far left, the shade of a cream coloured parasol obscuring half her face, a face turned towards the artist as others fussed over the food and the wine. Winn's magnifying glass showed up the dark and light blotches of paint that made up the illusion of a face. At the other side, a tall thin young man was turned towards the maidservants in their black and white. I made a note to look in the journals and see if I could place the Brecks in June 1889.

In another portrait a man sat in a wing chair dressed in evening attire. He was smoking a cigar and looking directly out at us as if to say, 'Damned cheek'. The cigar and the extravagant moustache seemed to tag him as Monty, he of the duck hunting and poacher baiting. But no definite sighting of Lady Breck.

I took my leave of Winn and wandered out, across the footbridge and over the walkway, reading the information boards and biding my time. Then I could see Queen Victoria, looking out through the fanlight above the library doors. I reflected, not for the first time, that whoever put her there seemed to have thought about her outlook. She's looking for him, isn't she? Albert.

She held me in her gaze as there was shunt at the traffic lights, a grunch and screel of broken brake light and bent bumper. Horns beeped, like panic-stricken elephants. The chill breeze caught at my swollen eye and soothed it. I could go on. It would be fine.

I was on the verge of smiling by half past six. I had gone to the archives and sorted through the journal for a link to June 1889. It was missing from the ones I had already sifted, I would need to go back upstairs and dredge out some more of the journals and papers up there. I moved back to desk duties, picking up my computer wand, anticipating the search ahead, knowing that there would be some adventure of discovery waiting for me in the cardboard archive boxes.

I had it all planned. I would leave at seven when we closed. I would eat somewhere special and different, although possibly not the Thai Palace. Then, refreshed, I'd return with my keys and spend the rest of the evening time travelling. I could fall asleep over the boxes because even if everyone decided to come in early tomorrow, they would never think to look in that small roof room. I would fall asleep there and dreams would open the doorway, would let me find out what and who and how and where. I could visit.

I didn't hear that the news was in. I hadn't seen Heather come in with Mrs Atkinson. I was busy sorting out some reservations for a student who'd found that the university library copies of her books were always on loan to some other student. I was deep in a paper trail of specialised academic literature. I was enjoying myself. I remembered how to, it seemed. I was useful and helpful. I was a librarian. I was a System of Information.

What I did hear was the sound of ears pricking up and a whisper that began to run from the chicken-wire doorway over to the reference section. *Tierney* the whisper whispered. A whisper that was picked up and echoed by Mrs Milligan and then Joachim and then Harvey. I felt eyes turn upon me, not just the staff but one or two of the borrowers. *Floored. Mugged. Down in Darley Cut. Don't know. No one's sure what happened...* One or two had looked at my battered face although none had been as bold as Mrs Longden that morning.

Martha was in the office, a door between her and the whisper. *Tierney. Have you heard about Tierney?* Except that somewhere a telephone was beeping out. It matched the beep-beep of my wand as I despatched books. It matched the beep-beep of my heart, steady and measured for once.

But, as the last few pairs of eyes turned towards the desk, as the door to the office opened because Martha had had the news and had done the geography, as these things fell into their slots, I was not there.

I was three, four, five strides into the whiteout of the winter sunlight.

TEGAMI O KAKNAKUTE, DENWA O SHIMASHITA

I didn't write a letter; I telephoned

I was like a sad old druggie in the newsagent because she wouldn't simply give me change. I heard the words 'float' 'change' 'no' but my brain was struggling to stop my hands from scrabbling into the till.

'I just want to change the fiver. Not anything small. Pound coins will do.' But it was pointless. She was not in the habit of giving change. She pointed to a sign. NO CHANGE GIVEN FOR CARPARK.

'It's not for the carpark.'

I was almost weeping as I bought some chewing gum. Now, at last, she could give me change. I turned blindly, knocking into a beer belly behind me.

'Hey! You forgot your gum,' I heard as the door clumped shut and the street noise took over. Cars. Buses. The heartbeat beeping of the road sweeper buffing the kerb.

I didn't look left or right. I knew exactly where I was going and the quickest way to get there. I was not going through the precinct with its bright commercial glare and its nosing CCTV. I crossed quickly, dodging the cars rather than waiting for spaces. I cut down the side lane where the delivery trucks pulled in.

Picking my way past the colour-coded dumpsters for the video shop, the bakery, the hideous home interiors shop with its black and brown furniture that looked as if someone had stapled pallets together. Past sodden cardboard, plastic sheeting, a flurry of pigeons. Down the thin straight passageway where the concrete of the sixties shopping precinct met with the rough red brick of the eighties multi-storey carpark. A smell of urine as if all the drunks in town had marked this out as their territory.

The phone box was a pocket of space and it seemed as I shut the door that all time and noise stopped. I thought that if I looked along to the street there would be coloured blurs where the people and the traffic had been halted in their tracks. As long as it seemed that way I would be safe so I didn't look anywhere except at my fingers putting the money into the slot, the coins falling into the void and my fingers, working autonomously, tapping in the number.

It began to chirrup out and I was there instantly. The ochre coloured carpet and the draught from the front door because the postman or the milkman might be there handing over the post or a pint of milk and the gossip. The front garden through the window. The long rectangle of window. Behind me, not the urine sticky doors of the phone box but the French doors that led out into the garden. The French doors that he never seemed to shut until winter. The back garden beyond, green and forest-like. The Corsican pines that had been growing across the back boundary for nearly as long as he'd been there.

He might be outside now, raking through the pond with one of the old fishing nets. Or sitting in the shed with his binoculars watching the heron steal his fish. The heron, the only reason he puts fish in that pond.

'Hello?' he had let it ring for a long time. Ten rings. Maybe twenty. Now I was startled to hear his voice in my ear. He was not uncertain this time. Just listening. My silence. My money ticking down.

'Hello?' and the words I wanted to say came battering at the back of my lips but I couldn't let them out.

'Hello?' the tone altered, there was something there that was subtly different. I can see his face at the piano and he's intent on some music, some notes. *It's a pentatonic scale...and this is where it modulates and...there...hear it...just a semitone lower but very beautiful...amazing what can be done in just five notes.*

'Hello again.' There is no question in his voice this time, just patience. The tears are washing down my face and I make a stupid hiccup sound. I clamp my hand over my mouth, trying to get a grip but the snot is sliding and sliming. I wipe at my face with my sleeve. I am rustling and crackling.

'I'm already double-glazed. I internet bank. Am I getting warmer?'

No. But I am, just by the sound of his voice. The major third of it modulating in my head, moving around the semitones and demisemiquavers and semibreves of speech, reaching down the phone line to touch me. Amazing what can be done in just five notes.

And then he really reached. I could see his hand very clearly as it landed softly on my shoulder. 'The heron's not been around for a while.'

I stopped crying. He listened. I made a terrible snottling sound as I tried to stifle my noises. He spoke again, gentle, quiet.

'There are so many fish in the damn thing.'

The tears that fell now felt cleansing against my face. My sleeve, soaked with snot and tears and relief.

'I'll have to use the net to clear a few.'

Another pause. No hurry.

'I'm not sure if you can eat koi.'

He was listening again and I knew that even though I was silent, he heard me. He knew. He knows who it is.

'Have to browse Amazon, see if I can find an eclectic Japanese cookbook.'

And the phone beeped in panic *moremoneymoremoneymoremoney* and I didn't have any more. I looked out.

The street beyond was moving. Time began again.

The keys to the flat were in my handbag, under the desk at the library. There was nothing for it but to go round to the back, a gap in the Leylandii where the dogs and cats and badgers cut through. I lingered a while, checking that Miss Nudey Gardener wasn't mooning at me as she clipped the weigela. On all fours I cut in through the gap, keeping low as if I was in a spy film, and scooted across the garden. Onto the plant trough, reaching up into the pergola. I hung there, monkey-like, for a moment, unable to hitch myself through the gap. My arms began to ache. There was a plastic water butt. I swung towards it, the toe of my shoe missed, I swung, caught. Levered at last, I pulled upwards through the squared slatting of the pergola. The bedroom window was jammed shut I knew, but the kitchen window was easily opened.

Shaking, I found myself, coat on still, stuffing my clean black clothes into a carrier bag. What else was there? I could call in and collect my handbag from the library on my way.

On my way. Where? Never mind. There was safety in readiness. I stuffed the bag under the bed.

The doorbell seemed to switch on an electric current in my bones. No one called here, not even Jehovah's Witnesses. I moved to the window, to the far left so that I had an angled view of the doorway. I couldn't see who it was, just a movement of coat. And then I saw that Iris's old green VW was parked at the kerb.

Out in the hallway the bike's pedal renewed its attempts to break my shin. I stumbled towards the door and opened it. Martha was there in full Astrakhan glory. Heavy black biker boots, a long drapy dress in a deep vermillion and a startling silver pendant. She was accompanied by my handbag.

'We thought you might need this.' She offered the bag. I nodded thanks, and took it. Martha didn't move away and I didn't make a move to close the door.

'You heard about Tierney?' she asked, trying to look into my face, which I was stubbornly not letting her do. I managed a nod but no words.

'I was there yesterday. In Darley Cut.' Her voice was quite small now. I nodded again and she matched it with one of her own. Her lips wobbled and she didn't dare blink.

'Don't.' I murmured in my head, only to find it had sneaked out through my mouth. Martha looked down, looked about to turn away. Then with a sudden flurry of arms she grabbed me, hugged me to the textured front of that Astrakhan coat. I felt the softness, the warmth, the smell of her. A rich scent of rosemary and a cooling overtone of black peppermint. Something beneath that, something oniony and savoury. Her hair brushing my face, coarser and thicker than it seemed. Strong.

'See you tomorrow,' she said, matter of fact, as she pulled away. In the car, she wound down the window. Her last look over the top of the glass. Her uncertain question, 'We will, won't we?'

I nodded.

Back in the hallway the bike spun its vicious front wheel round and winded me with its curled rams-horn handlebars. I shoved at it, reached down and yanked the chain off, the oil like blood on my hands.

KOTOWAZA:
'NAKITSURA NI HACHI'

Japanese proverb: 'A bee to a crying face'

I stood at the staffroom window watching the police officers fingertip search the Memorial Gardens. Behind me, the kettle steamed on and on. This time, Mrs Milligan had forgotten to put the lid on. We all stood watching the search. Mrs Atkinson with her arms folded across her front, Mrs Milligan chewing at her thumbnail. Martha, elbow resting on forearm, one fist curled, her face obscured by her other palm, her fingers tapping anxiously at her nose. Eyes wide. Eyes narrowed. I found the sunlight too bright. Dust motes seemed to suffocate the air.

The knicker-thief had ceased to be a joke. He had progressed from the slightly comic hobby of filching pants from washing lines and poorly attended service washes to become a sex offence genius overnight. The details were blurred, but the fact was he had attacked a woman in the street last evening. He had approached her from behind, brutal hands rammed up under her skirt. He had taken her knickers hot from her body, tearing them down, ripping clothes, grazing flesh, tripping and pushing and, once the victim was floored, trampling over her to get away.

The underwear had been found in the Memorial Gardens by the Parks and Gardens man on his way to clear the beds. He had told Mr Machin that the fabric was stained with knicker-thief jism, now being analysed. In these days of DNA sampling it is as good as a calling card. Now they were looking for more, plaster-casting a footprint under the far shrubbery that backed onto the bank carpark. Through the chainlink fence and the gaps and patches of the thick hedging we could see the glimmers of fluorescent police vests as they scoured the tarmac of the carpark, and the kettle began to scorch itself with thirst.

May 1889. It was a Chas. Goodrich journal that had been deposited under a creased pile of drawings for a new Orangery, dated 1914. All sorts of ideas that never came to pass. As Viscount Breck was scrawling *V. Good. Best yet.* on a set of the drawings, Archduke Franz Ferdinand was being assassinated and setting in train a different set of plans.

But that concealed May 1889. This journal was damp and mouldy. It had not been kept with the others and it looked battered and weatherbeaten, as if it had travelled through tempests in attempting to rejoin them. Some of the pages were stuck together and couldn't be unstuck without tearing. I made a mental note to buy razor blades in my lunch hour and opened what pages I could. But I was thick-fingered, unable to concentrate. It seemed that every creak of every floorboard made me leap out of my skin. Was it likely that a knicker thief, newly promoted to the rank of sexual offender, would frequent the library? I knew, of course, that anything is possible.

I found I wasn't reading Lady Breck's sloping handwriting. The words were swimming and curling before me but my head was going through the male faces I met in the course of a day. The man on trolley duty in the supermarket carpark. The white van that picked up the team of plasterers from the newly developed two-storey block of flats at the corner. The parcels delivery man who called in at the computer store each afternoon. I thought of the faces at Intermediate Japanese. That tall chap at the back who always yawned. The balding man in the suit who never did the homework.

Who were these people? Mr Machin. Harvey. Mr 'History-Teacher' Pennington. What did I know about them?

'...without so much as a by your leave,' Lady Breck fumed across the page.

By the time we return the Travellers will have moved on, not to return until September. I have half a mind to stow away to the horse fairs with Vancy Kircher. All my rebellions are imagined and at the last, I know, duty will call and I shall answer.

Several pages were stuck together.

...journey to hell with bad weather and clattering trains. Hazard's brougham awaited us at Kingswear. How wonderful to glimpse the sky and the sea and the castle on the little outcrop and to breathe air. I don't care for the train, that miserable iron box. Complain, complain, complain. But, the house is magnificent. Breck quite jealous of the Japanese Garden...

The journal pages were stuck fast. I turned over, missing maybe ten or twelve pages out.

...not prizes to be won, nor beasts to be tamed. To overhear them after dinner fills me with shame. They are beasts. I would not have believed it even of Breck but there he sits, puffing Hazard's cigars, every...

Empty pages. Another five or so stuck together in a wedge. I turned it over. I was already thinking that the house in the landscape was probably Hazard's house, the house

Lady Breck was writing about with the Japanese garden. Most likely the men at dinner were those of their acquaintance, Whitside and Monty. They milled about between country houses being fed, watered and entertained. Well-dressed tramps some of them, with nowhere to go but to the hospitality of their friends.

...local girls. The latest is his favourite pet, a thin girl of no more than fifteen who is capable of reading. He calls her into the library and she is made to read passages from Austen until he tires. Monty is, for the moment, utterly rapt by Austen. Mary-Ann Penny reads very well, better, it must be offered, than Monty. She has expression and understanding notwithstanding that she is employed in the Laundry. As her fellow laundresses fall into their beds to dream of mangles and coppers rolling to the boil her attendance is requested at the Golden Lectern in the drawing room. Each evening she appears more tired and draggled than the last, the dark circles under her eyes deepening. Breck is taken with her and wonders where she has gleaned her small education.

I dislike Hazard. He is a slow poison of a man.

Now the fluorescent bulb of memory juddered into life. The names I had seen before, not just familiar from Kite House. Familiar from the Brakers Meet entertainment programmes. The social circle.

I took the journal down to Mrs Atkinson's office. I needed some air. I needed to keep moving so that I didn't think about knicker thieves and violent hands and slow poison.

As I moved to the first step on the Tech stairwell I waited for my usual sense of uplift, of moving not just physically up the stairs but mentally upwards. Lightening. Letting go.

Tonight it didn't come. As I topped the stairs the corridor seemed quieter than usual. At the far end Ceramics students were donning aprons, but no one seemed to be swotting for their vocab test. The door was shut to me, a small typed notice sticky-taped to the chickenwired square of window.

DUE TO CIRCUMSTANCES
BEYOND OUR CONTROL
THERE WILL BE NO SESSION
OF INTERMEDIATE JAPANESE
THIS EVENING

It didn't occur to me to wonder why. I assumed flu or a babysitting crisis and then pondered what else I could do with my evening. Ceramics? No, that would require some skill, not just the donning of an apron. Discouraged, I continued on down the corridor, and as I reached the foot of the stairs the frosted glass door to the reception office opened. I halted at the murmured voices of the receptionist and the Tarot tutor, heard Setsuke's name float out of the hushed cloud of gossip. I learned how the knicker thief was the circumstance over which they had no control.

All the things I had not known about Setsuke.

That she had come from Japan five years before to work in some faceless shiny-windowed building in the nearby city. That she had married someone she had worked with there and now love marooned her in this alien, Western place. That she had taken a career break to bring up her two small children and had been delighted to be asked to teach Japanese at the college a few evenings a week and be part of a community-wide cross-cultural initiative, an idea to get us all speaking new languages and engaging with people from other cultures.

That after all of that, it was Setsuke who had engaged with the knicker thief. That besides love there was indignity, fear, humiliation.

All these things were now common knowledge, splattered greedily all over the front page of the local paper. Which I did not buy. Which I did not read. I listened at the foot of the stairs and I walked away.

Back at the flat, Third Floor's bike had fallen across the doorway and blocked the door. No amount of shoving and pushing would shift it. I buckled the wheel trampling over it and it took revenge by twisting my ankle down into its spokes. Locked out yet again, I hiked back over the bike's carcass and headed around the back to break in again via the pergola.

Inside I was restless, churning around like a caged zoo cat. The walls seemed to blank me at every turn. I glanced through the kitchen window and saw not a light. Not a one.

Blinds down. Curtains drawn. No lights. The neighbourhood was on watch.

At last, as if a magnesium flash exploded in my head, I knew there was only one thing to do. In the bedroom I rummaged the carrier bag of belongings out from under the bed and took off my clothes. The worn and baggy grey jumper, my slim and seated cord skirt. I shed them like skin. I pulled on the black skirt and deep v sweater. I zipped up the soft high-heeled leather boots. I didn't think my cagoule would cut it so I opened the wardrobe, where my old charcoal coloured coat was slumped in the furthest corner. I dragged it up like a pelt and slung myself into it. It smelled of rain and buses and lemony wood polish. And piled deep within the fibres was that other smell, a smell of long ago and not quite far away enough. But needs must, and the devil always seems to be driving.

It was unlikely that he would strike again given the fact that the town was on red alert. However, if cheap detective novels and amateur psychology were to be believed he might have got an unquenchable taste for the deed. Brutality and power are probably more addictive than heroin, although I haven't done the research. Imagine the laboratory. A box of brutal thugs being asked to pummel and rape, up against a box of other thugs being injected with opiate narcotics. And no one looking at the men in the white coats brandishing the clipboards, who have more power and more brutality and more addiction than anyone else there.

You see I was rambling. Not rational. My head was seething and boiling as I began to walk the streets.

I had the map of town in my head; I had walked most of the streets in my two-year stay. Where had the attack on Setsuke taken place? On a side street at eveningtide. An extraordinary moment in an ordinary place. I walked to the parish church and, keeping the library to my left, I took in the townscape. There were the streets but also there was Queens Park, the quiet Victorian area surrounding it, leafy with big front gardens that secluded and excluded. It would be daring to attack there, under their noses. My own part of town, the oldest part where the rows and terraces backed up against each other, squaring off back gardens, creating little behind-the-scenes towns of sheds, back lanes and garages. Would he dare go there? Wasn't that just trap territory, the windows all watching? And there was Darley Cut and the school...

What the hell. There was no point second guessing, so I walked. Come and get me.

If you asked me now I would say I was reckless. Delusional, all the thoughts in my head convinced that only

I could do this, and if I did, I could save them all. Setsuke and Martha and Vanessa Milligan and Georgia Atkinson and red-headed Angharad and Ellen Freethy, all the women who ever came through the library doors, who ever pushed their trolleys round the supermarket, who gardened naked, who sat on the bus.

I was a beacon, burning. Come and Get Me. You'll see. I am dressed in the night for a reason.

I am slow poison.

I did not find him. I walked the outer edges of town finding nothing but residential streets and rowed houses. Only parked cars for company, lining the streets and growling along the motorway in the distance.

In wintertime everyone abandons the streets in this town. Further up the dual carriageway there is an industrial estate with a nightclub that has a record of a murder a month and the drunks and sluts draggle around the maze of units trying to find their coach or their bus or their vandalised car. But in town, there are a couple of pubs that run quiz nights and bingo and that's it. Everything is finished by ten o'clock. There are takeaways of course, busy into the night, people reading the local paper and watching the fish tank, waiting peaceably for their midnight kung pao chicken.

It was nearly two o'clock in the morning when I shut the door on the phone box. The coins flashed like comets in the moonlight and each titanium white beam of light seemed to slow time. Down and down. The tinny sparkling sound as they fell down and down and my fingers, like highly trained creatures picking out the numbers. It rang out at the other end. He would be awake, at the piano possibly, going over the Beethoven, working his way through the Bach.

'Hello?' as his voice answered I crowded myself closer to the phone and let the tears come. I was utterly silent.

'I was just thinking about you,' he said, matter of fact. It was what he had always said before, those several spooky times when I had picked up the phone to call him and found him already on the other end, waiting for his call to me to ring through. We always laughed. About a hundred years ago.

'Just wondering. That was all. You know. Things.'

A sound escaped from me, a hybrid sniff and sob and after it an echo of silence.

'She's doing very well, by the way. Keeps me up to date with it all, but she's captaining the ship superbly. And Irene is still doing the teas. Just in case you were wondering. You know.'

Time slowed further. We're like the centre of an orrery, an utterly still point in the night, in the universe and everything spins around us.

'I've abandoned Beethoven for a while. Wrestling with Freddie Chopin instead. That yellow book of preludes. For a while.'

I'm listening to the words and I'm not in the phone box. I'm back there, my legs curled round the legs of the music stool and we're trying to play 'Arrival of the Queen of Sheba' but I can't manage it because I keep laughing. The frantic pomp not matched by my fingers blundering and clashing. The stool wasn't wide enough for two, he used to pull up one of the dining chairs and sit, just slightly too high.

I hear a clomp on the end of the line then, the floorboards creaking under the carpet as he moves. And he starts to play. Sparkling and bright, a burst of stars. It isn't Chopin. It is a message. Clear. Written down by Schubert as an Impromptu. Number 4, A flat major. *Allegretto*.

All regretto. Music is powerful, reaching down the telephone wires to clasp me tight. To let me know, before my money runs out.

ASHIMOTO NI KI O TSUKETE KUDASAI

Watch your step

The next day I knocked on Mrs Atkinson's door and retrieved the spoiled journal. I took it down to the archive to try and separate the pages with no skill at all, just desperation. The pages tore of course, layered into each other, inseparable. Still it was possible to make out words and start to put some sense to them. The trouble was that once I started to pick out the words and the sense hovered into view I wished I had left them stuck together.

...could not be found for luncheon. Yelland organised a search whi   not   uccess. I joined the ladies in the   merhouse and we said not a word   inously silent. There was a   ment, just a second of time when Miranda   ied to speak   ceived a kick in the shin   der the table from Edi   I could not disguise my shock at   eemed not to   hey all hold some secret knowl...

Which would never be revealed to me as the pages were fused together. The next in a broader stroke, as if she hurried. *...Monty! Oh, unex   cted knight,   rth for her. His rage*

is   ail, and his protests hav en him   harried   ouse.
oices raise   calling up the fo men to arm th   pokers...

Further on. Calm. Stark.

...Now it is revealed the   ave   eed the p   chase as if
were livestock. We return to Kite House on the morrow.

The surgical steel blade slivered on. To blank pages. On. On. Blank upon blank until I thought the water must have washed away the years, and then, centred onto the endpaper of the last Chas. Goodrich notebook, blotched and spotted by mould and twisted with time, one final furious, broadstroked, entry.

Who am I if I cannot regard my own image in the glass? What stranger is this, hanging her head before me? Evil only prospers if good men do nothing. All that remain to me are Shame and Fury. Let them embolden me. Let them end this <u>*punishment*</u>.

There was a twisting in my gut that was not the knicker thief. This twist was for Mary-Ann. This was the beginning. Whatever was going on at Hazard's house was the beginning and the end for Mary-Ann. I looked at the art knife I'd been using to slice between the damaged pages. It was not a time to be around knives.

No, I was not afraid of what I might do to myself. I am not a suicide. I have been to that edge, taken there by someone else and I'm telling you, it seems a long way down.

I had not yet completed the task of scanning the photographs and only this week we had received another ten archive boxes from the University. The faces and landscapes were piling up around me. It seemed that afternoon that they all looked out at me very precisely. They all knew. These strangers and ghosts. I wandered amongst them, those who were company but could not be touched, biding my time amidst the scan and flash and hum.

Scan. Flash. Hum.

Out on the streets again that night, I left nothing to chance. I had brought my clothes to work and changed before leaving the library. Mr Machin did not appear to see me as I crossed the lobby in my black garb. I hesitated in the revolving door. Mrs Atkinson could be seen crossing the road, loaded with grocery shopping. I watched her move along the street towards the bridge. And then, suddenly she seemed to vanish. The bus had passed her and she was gone. Not on the bridge. Not turned back. Not over the bridge. Gone. My gasp steamed up the window of the revolving door.

Out I spun like a roulette ball, rolling into the street. I headed straight for the bridge, scanned the stonework. There, at the edge was a gap and a twisting flight of steps. I dodged the bendy bus as it tried not to ground itself on the arch of the roadway. As the bus passed, a woman was cutting down the flight of steps with a scottie dog on a retractable lead. Peering over the stonework I was surprised to find the canal. I picked my way down the steps onto the dirt track towpath.

It was quieter down there. If I looked backwards, under the bridge, I could see, just beginning at the curve of the canal, where the new Canalside development took up the floorspace. But here, this was old and overgrown, the path not tarmacked or gravelled, just worn through. There were others there with dogs, the scottie woman passing the time of day with another red-haired woman with a red setter. On the other side of the water abandoned warehousing waited. Ivy had grown over and around it all, and Russian Vine was making swift progress through the broken windows. Pigeons flew from the roof-space. There was an abandoned dock, rotted and bending into the water. I could just make out Mrs Atkinson and the back end of a narrowboat.

I began to walk. It was more deserted here, more left to the wild, the steep banking at my side was thickly overgrown with bramble and ivy. Up above were the edges of town. The backs of the shops, the ends of the long thin yards, piled high with boxes and vats for vegetable oil, pallets stacked, workshops crumbling. In one the building had come to the edge of the banking, the wall sprawled at by ivy, a ventilation unit blasting out noise and hot air and the sound of clanking dishes and water. It was the back of the pub. The Saracen's. Beside it a breezeblock shed, the windows blocked out with cracked and peeling whitewash.

Mrs Atkinson had vanished again, a magic property of her white conservator gloves.

But no, the light came on through the cabin doors of the nearest moored narrowboat. Mrs Atkinson, at the sink, unloading her shopping. She moved to the kettle, reached for an earthenware mug, one of the ones Brid had made for the book club. Then she reached up and shut the small slatted wooden blind.

I kept walking. It was cool and shadowed by the water and, let's face it, I had nothing better to do. I had walked through the streets over the last two years. On daring days I had tested out the boundaries, finding my way to the new canalside development, drawn by the brightness and the water and the vertebraic bridges cutting and dashing across the water. The boats moored there. The people together by candlelight checking over menus and the four-storey warehouses redeveloped, their doors torn out and windows put in. The evenings I had spent watching the boxed up, stacked up lives.

I had not crossed this bridge. I'd stood in the bus stop sometimes on the opposite side of the road from the library, my back to the green bank of lawn beside the church and the noticeboard advertising God's services and wares. I had watched the traffic pull over the hunched back of the bridge and drive down through the buildings. There was nothing much at that end of town, the bones of industry waiting to be picked over. The signs were up. To LET, FOR SALE, PRIME LOCATION in all the broken windows. Clinging to all the chainlinked security fencing.

I had walked a couple of miles and now it was crossed by a wide concrete bridge. Beneath, in the abandoned canalscape, a pair of teenagers snogged earnestly. I was the lone spectator, everyone else it seemed was trundling above us, on their way in their cars and lorries. I couldn't have moved past the bridge anyway, teenagers or not. It was a boundary.

I felt ravenously hungry suddenly and I struggled to think when I'd last eaten. I had thought of eating out the other evening and been distracted. Now I was determined. I could go to the American style place that had opened at the furthest lighted edge of the canalside development. It was brown leather and cosy looking, with neat booths where I could be private. All I'd have to do was walk back the way I had come, continue on and I would wash up, canalside.

Before the first of the moored narrowboats I was aware of a sudden scorch in my senses. Something. Someone. I didn't stop but I swivelled my eyes into the back of my head. It's easy to do, as you're going forwards you think about all that you have just passed. The path. The patch of weed. The moorhen scuttling out of the way. Scuttling. Before I had reached it. The banking. A rough scuffed escarpment through. Into the hedging at the top. Into the hawthorn.

There was someone in the hawthorn above me. What was beyond that? I tried to orientate myself again. It was derelict land, where they had cleared the old supermarket to build a multiplex cinema and the money had fallen through. Whoever-it-was moved at the boundary of the hawthorn and the wasteland.

Where was I? There was something up ahead I knew I had to be aware of. What was it? What had I seen on the way, on the edge of my sight?

Steps. Wooden steps and a rickety white peeling-paint handrail cutting up into the hawthorn, up into the narrow short cut of a path. A miniature and more dangerous version of Darley Cut, another path to Harm's Way. Of course. I knew who it was by now. There was not much time between me and the first of the narrowboats. And I thought, *You do it. I dare you. Come and get me.*

As I reached them the steps were nearly in darkness. Aware of my own black clothing, I thought it was going to be difficult for him to spot me. I could pass by unmolested and invisible. If I wanted.

I didn't alter my pace but I altered my heartbeat. The pounding in my head muffled his steps behind me so that instead of hearing him, instead of sensing the vibration of him through the packed dirt of the pathway, I found my face crumped against a wall of dirt before I was even aware I had been felled. There was no falling. Just the full stop of my body against the earth. As my face stung and my front teeth rattled in their sockets I was briefly dazed, and then horribly aware of his hands, coarse hands, hot, clammy, pushing my hips into the dirt. His nails scratching, catching in my tights and the laddering nylon rippling as it ran up against my skin. It felt as if I was coming apart. I tried to breathe in underneath the weight of him. The dirt and the panic clogged my throat.

No. Not this, not now Ruby. *Now is the moment, now Ruby, do something now.*

His nails digging into my skin as he curled his fingers around the elastic of my underwear. I tried kicking out but, oh for christ's sake laugh out loud, my knickers were twisted around his hands and my legs. *Don't, don't get your knickers in a twist Rube. Don't.* My own underwear the weapon of my destruction.

In a confusion of grunts and manic laughter I arched and reared against him. I was like some oversized tench he had landed, flippering and slippering beneath him. He was a human clamp pinning me to the damp ground. Small pieces of stone embedding themselves into my skin, dirt in one of my nostrils. I heard low animal grunting that I thought was him. It was me. I could feel all the anger and courage starting to drain into the earth. I was cold. I was afraid. He was tugging at my underwear and his nails caught my skin. I could feel his breath against my neck as he wrestled against me. *Now* Ruby. *NOOOOOWWWWWWWW.*

He was heavy as a fallen tree, crushing down on me, my legs unable to move beneath him. As he yanked and yawed at my underwear my legs were yanked and yawed and tangled. I could taste nothing but dirt and blood. He rolled and shifted, leaning his knees into the backs of my legs to pin me as he righted himself. No. I could see the firmament of black stars imploding inside me.

Panic. No. *Never.* Fury. Fury. Say it Ruby. *Never again. Never again.*

I arched backwards, fighting not to be beached on that towpath and as I did his balance faltered. Now we were both flailing and the blood seemed to flood into my mouth. Hot and bronze. This time I made a spear of my elbow. Launched it at him. The pain shimmered through me and lit all my nerve endings like tapers. I became a wild creature. Not caring which pain was his and which was mine. Pushing against the mass that was him, digging my own nails deep into his flesh until he yelped and tried to pull away, but I was not letting go. Battering at me. But I was not letting go. Standing upright to shake me off. But I was not letting go. Reaching round me, punching at my back until my breath stopped. But I was not letting go. Punch me. Punch me. Punch me. Punch me. There is *nothing* you can do to me. *I am not letting go.* Not this time. *Never again.* My legs rigid with fury, now curled around his legs making him stagger. *This is the last time. The last time, now and forever.*

And the index finger and thumb of my left hand reached up and pinched into his eyeball. His arms flailed upwards, as if signalling. He gasped agony.

This is the last time, I thought, as he jaggered backwards a step, a step and down into the waiting daggers of the brambles. I felt the thorns hook into me as I was hooked into him. Thorns taking charge of me. And then there were lights. Moving lights. Glow worms. Faeries. I fell deeply downwards.

I was freaked out to wake in the subdued lighting and soft pillows of the incident centre. I opened my eyes to see an Ikea sofa in the corner and a woman police officer waiting with a victim-support face on. It was as if the last two and a half years had been rewound. I had not been a librarian. I was still there and it had all been a dream. I shot off the lounge sofa I was draped over, knocking over a side table. A glass jug of water splattered all over the neutral rug and Martha jumped up to catch me. I heard her voice first, even before I felt her strong reassuring hand on my shoulder.

'Ruby. Ruby it's okay. Ruby, it's me. It's Martha. You're safe now.'

KOTO NI NARU, YO NI NARU

Come about, come to pass

It was an predictable headline. LOCAL WOMAN GETS KNICKER THIEF IN A TWIST. I did not want to brag it up, I preferred to run away from it but this is a small town and I had become 'heroic'. If they only knew. I was purposely obtuse in posing for the photographer. I did not want to be in the paper; however I was also going to have to be in court at some point so I thought it the better part of valour to scowl at the camera and bear it.

Charges, of course, would be brought. It had not occurred to me in my quest for vengeance that I was putting myself into danger. There had not been danger, somehow, in the fumbled wrestling match on the towpath. There had only been my vision of retribution and justice, and Retribution and Justice were, indeed, on their way. Let's face it, they were always headed for me. I had known all along that the two years at the library were borrowed. Now, just like all the books, it was time to return them.

That morning, as I walked into work after a sleepless night at the flat I had seen a flight of geese in arrow formation above me. They flapped steadily onward, going, I knew where. Where I could not.

Home.

It seemed to me the library was stone cold that morning. Martha peeled off her chunky wool cardigan, her face flushed. Mrs Milligan joked that her flush was the hot flush of being too flipping far over forty. I was the only person to shiver that morning. I had spent half the night squatting on the pergola trying to inhale all I could of the night garden. In the end I had not been soothed or eased, I had only become bone cold.

I looked at the vibrant burnt orange of Martha's cardigan as it draped sloth-like over the back of her chair, daydreaming, thinking that if I could just slither myself into the sleeves of it the world would somehow snap into colour again. As if the world was as easy as Oz. My mind was a piece of paper caught in a draught, unable to settle. So I loaded up the returns on the trolley and started to shelve.

I did not see him enter. It was more that I scented him, the old and everyday aroma jolting me as it breathed into my nostrils. The undertone of olive oil soap, layered with cotton shirt and the sappy green of sweat, beaded, caught in his chest hair. I looked up. I could see a couple of the French teenagers in the reference section, busy together with a project. Joaquim was busy at the computer. He was wearing a white shirt, the sleeves rolled to his elbows. There seemed to be explanations all around. I took a deep breath. Because, of course, it wasn't possible, was it.

'Hello, can I hel…?'

Martha wasn't allowed to reach the end of the greeting.

The click of a photo onto the counter.

'I'm looking for this woman.' He cleared his throat and my heart paused, took in and held a breath. As if it had to remember…something that it used to do at a signal from this voice. What was it?

Ah. Yes. Panic.

I knew. I did not have to look, I knew. But my head turned, I stooped slightly so that I would have the slim letter-box view of the desk from behind the shelves. I saw the back of his head. The hair neatly shaved. The collar of a white shirt just visible above his dark raincoat.

I expected to see all my blood soaking into the carpet as it drained out of me, leaving a white hot molten metal of adrenaline.

'This was taken about four years ago. She might well have changed her hair.'

Martha is leaning forwards to look at the photo. What will she see there? I am not breathing now; my heart has halted. So I am, if anyone cares at this point, clinically dead. Only my brain is functioning.

'No…I don't think…I can't remember seeing her here.'

He doesn't respond, except to nod. A nod of gravitas and authority, his eyes half closing. Martha steps to one side.

'Harvey?'

As Harvey turns around I am lowering myself to the floor, crawling, movements as slow and controlled as I can make them without the benefit of synapses. Except where is there to go?

If I try for the staffroom door it is visible from the desk. I can smell him. The musk of him. I lean against the bookcase. Above me, the sky unzips.

'Is there a problem then?' Harvey asks outright.

'I'm a detective.' I hear the slick plastic flip of ID. 'I'm looking for this woman.'

Harvey is studying the photo and looking puzzled. Shaking his head. He would do that. The photo isn't of me, Ruby. It is of a much thinner, much blonder woman wearing shoes that look good but pinch. She is standing by a bay race-horse, for those were the days of colour, of blonde and bay. She is wearing a linen suit that cost almost as much as Ruby the librarian gets paid in a quarter. The blouse underneath it is silk, smooth and cool as lake water over her bare skin. She smiles out at the world, thinking whatever she was thinking on that day.

Mrs Milligan looks vaguely at the photo of this stranger as Martha informs her that the gentleman is a police officer. Mrs Atkinson is coming out of her office. I hear, from my hiding place, the door click shut. Exactly like a gun, cocking.

Mrs Atkinson takes a long look at the photo. Makes a face over it. Puzzled. Shrugging.

'I'm sorry. She doesn't look familiar. My colleague said you are a detective…can I ask what this is to do with?'

'She's missing. She's an out-of-hours favour I'm trying to do for an old family friend. Any help you can offer would be appreciated.'

'Yes. I understand. Well, we might have her in our borrower register if that would be…'

'Jeannie Gaffney,' he says in his rumbling voice, crisp and enunciated. Like a Roman senator. Or God. Martha moves now and stands beside Mrs Atkinson.

He speaks again as they tap at the keyboard. Polite but magisterial.

'She might be listed as Jeannie Flynn. Or possibly Ryan or Rideout.'

Martha and Mrs Atkinson come up blank on all counts.

'Double check. If you would. Please.' An order.

Mrs Atkinson puts on her brightest and best customer service voice. 'Certainly I can. Could you spell Rideout for me?'

I hear the plastic creak as she turns the monitor towards him so that he may see for himself. He spells out the name.

'No, I'm sorry, nothing coming up. We don't have any Gaffneys listed. No Rideout. There are a couple of Flynns although I don't think you're looking for Dave or Bernadette. I don't know what else to suggest, Mr…?'

'Did you check under Ryan?'

'Yes. Three Ryans…no Jeannie Ryans I'm afraid, Mr… Ryan, is it?'

He doesn't volunteer his name. There are more clicks on the mouse.

'Electoral roll perhaps?' Mrs Atkinson suggests brightly, 'Harvey could…'

'No. Thank you.' Authoritative, in charge. Mrs Atkinson has a sudden thought.

'Ruby might know. Where's Ruby?'

My heart suddenly begins again and decides to rumba around my ribcage to make up for lost time. I stand very still. Make myself as thin and bookish as possible.

'Think she's in the archive,' Martha states.

'No. I saw her with the trolley earlier…Ruby?' Mrs Milligan spots me. I have no choice. Nathan has turned, is looking towards the shelving now, patient. I step out from my hiding place and approach the desk. I can't look at him. I can't gauge whether he knows or not. It seems that the library is about a hundred miles long, each footstep I take as slow as a moon landing. My breath as heavy as moon breath captured

159

in the bubble of a helmet. I reach the desk.

'What is it?' I manage, my voice thin. Actually I sound like a very conscientiously quiet librarian.

'Take a look at this photo?' Mrs Atkinson turns. Martha doesn't notice that I lift her glasses from her desk space, put them on as if they are my own, squint out through them at the picture. I daren't take the picture from her because every nerve I have is jangling and sparking. It is the photo I knew it would be. The day at the races. Nathan owned that horse, with Liam, until it fell in the National and he shot it.

'No one I know, sorry.' A casual shrug.

'The name? Does it ring a bell perhaps?' he asks. This Roman senator. This God. I glance at the monitor and make a shrugging face. Keeping it as simple as I can. Trying to be convincing. But he has spoken to me. I think he knows.

As I turn I'm relieved that Mrs Longden is waiting to check her books out. I turn away from Nathan, from Mrs Atkinson. Mrs Milligan moves over to the information desk now. Martha is tappity-tapping. Harvey is hovering ready to go for the sandwich run.

'I'm sorry we couldn't be more helpful,' Mrs Atkinson says. I can see him reflected in the computer screen. I can see that he isn't looking at Mrs Atkinson. He is checking out Ruby.

'Is there anything else we could help with?'

Nothing. A silence. The chickenwired doors to the lobby fab open, fob closed.

It is hard to know which burns fiercer, the tears scorching down my face or my pee as it wends and weaves its way down my leg, drips onto the carpeting. Drip. Drip-drip. Drip. The wand beeps on Mrs Longden's books and it is the last sound I hear.

KOTOWAZU: 'YABU SO TSUT-SUITE HEBI WO DASU'

Japanese proverb: 'Let sleeping dogs lie'

'Who is he, Ruby?'

Half carried into Mrs Atkinson's office by Harvey, I feel their eyes upon me. Mrs Milligan has propped me up on the chaise sofa thing that Mrs Atkinson, I now learn, brought here from her house. It is the only thing she didn't cut in two for her husband. Everything else was divided up, as Mrs Atkinson put it later, 'the furniture, the kitchen utensils, my heart'. Everything split down the middle.

Not that the errant Mr Atkinson ever had much use for the kitchen utensils, it seems; nor that utensils are on anyone's mind right now. It's like chinese whispers beyond the door, 'Is she all right? What's going on, Georgia?' They all know it can't be good. A detective has come looking for me so at the very least I am an axe murderer or an internationally renowned jewel thief. Mrs Atkinson is smoothing her hand over my forehead, I realise. She is not wearing her white gloves but her hand is very cooling, very soothing.

'Who is he?'

But I can't answer. Mrs Atkinson leans forward, folding

her arms around me as the tears come, and before I've finished sobbing she looks as if she's been caught in a squall.

'Sandwich run. D'you want anything Ruby?' Harvey pops his head round the door, terribly matter of fact. That is Harvey all over, he will do the sandwich run for the end of the world. The suicide bombers are here, anyone fancy an avocado and chicken mayonnaise baguette? Mrs Atkinson gives a *what do you think Harvey?* sigh.

'Cake,' she says simply. 'Bring cake.'

Harvey nods. Cake is his specialist subject. Martha brings tea and Panadol.

'Who is he Ruby?' Mrs Atkinson asks in a very quiet voice.

'Is he a detective?' Martha asks. I nod. He is, isn't that funny? A guardian. A protector. He is the law. I feel so exhausted. I can't seem to keep my eyes open as Mrs Atkinson asks again, still quiet, her eyes looking anxious, her brow furrowing.

I have put a lot of lines into that brow lately. But I'm slipping under now, every part of me has let go of itself and not even the hiccups of my sobs are going to keep me awake. I see Nathan standing in the door. Not this door of course. That door. Then.

'My husband,' I whisper.

There was nowhere I could go without wiping myself out again. Without beginning another beginning and never ending. Who could I be next time? No one. I was me. I had come to like Ruby, Ruby was all right. Ruby wanted a home to go to.

It was dark when I woke up. I was under a blanket and the anglepoise lamp was on on the desk. Everywhere seemed quiet and I could hear a bus pulling away from the stop opposite. I sat up with a jolt.

A claggy fug of my own smell puffed up at me as I moved. As I stood up to head out to the ladies and try to wash up I noticed that a washbag had been left, along with a hairbrush and toothbrush. Beside that were clean clothes. One of Martha's velvet vintage numbers and a big intricately cabled purple sweater. Someone had been to the supermarket and bought fresh knickers in my size. I gathered it all up and made my way out to the ladies'.

Looking at my reflection in the rather manky mirror, I wondered how Nathan had found me. I didn't look like me anymore. Or possibly I did look like me, I had been an impostor before, pretending to be the lovely, lively, blondie Jeannie. I hadn't thought back in a very long time, it was far too dangerous to start sifting through memories. Now, as I swished cold water over Jeannie's face, I thought back. I thought long and hard. He couldn't find Jeannie. Jeannie was dead. Couldn't I just hide? Please, just let me. Just this once.

Begging again. This, from the woman who felled Tierney and brought down the knicker thief. Ha.

When I pushed through the doors into the staffroom, they were waiting.

The evening sun was shining in through the window and they all seemed to be in glorious Technicolor. Angharad, her red hair crackling and flaming as she made teas and coffees, Ellen Freethy with her precision cut white hair, slicing cake. Iris, in her customary sleek black, washing out mugs at the sink. Mrs Atkinson and Vanessa Milligan and Martha. They said nothing. At least not with their mouths. Eyes and breathing and a plate of cake spoke volumes.

'It's a long story,' I said. They had left my favourite chair, my window chair, free on purpose, that was easy to see. Martha was standing beside my chair, one hand on the polished wooden back.

'Well, we've got time,' Vanessa Milligan volunteered.

'Story time.' Martha's voice was very low. There were smiles. I hesitated, for effect more than anything. Because I, out of all the women in that room, knew that it was indeed story time.

I took the five steps towards the chair and sat down. They were all waiting.

'Once, upon, a time…'

PART 2

A game called Hunter

Urtica dioica

stinging nettle

---

*carry it in your pocket to give protection
from lightning strikes*

Once upon a time there was just Jeannie Gaffney and her dad. Ted. A music teacher.

Once upon a time there had been Jeannie Gaffney and her dad and her mum. But those were the days before Mr Greenhalgh. So, while Jeannie Gaffney and her dad lived in a nice enough, middle-class enough semi with a big enough garden in a leafy enough suburb, the ex-Mrs Gaffney lived in France somewhere with Mr Greenhalgh. Mr Ted Gaffney never spoke of them although there was a secret joke in his head where he called them 'Les Gites' because that was what they had gone to France to do. To run away together and run a gites complex. What a pair of gites, Mr Ted Gaffney thought.

But he kept his thoughts to himself and concentrated on bringing up his daughter alone. He was forever shocked at the way that his wife had discarded their daughter. He could puzzle out why she might have left him, in fact when she first absconded he made a long and comprehensive list on the *Don't Forget...* shopping-list pad that hung on the back of the kitchen door.

Mr Greenhalgh had taste in clothes. Mr Greenhalgh didn't play chess. Mr Greenhalgh didn't find himself vanishing into the space-time continuum of a Bach prelude. Mr Greenhalgh had more money and more body hair. Mr Greenhalgh laughed with an expansive freeness of spirit. Mr Greenhalgh was (hazard a guess) better at sex, possibly Olympian in both skill and endowment. An Olympic-size penis.

So it was easy for him to work that one out and each day, depending on his mood, he was more certain that one particular reason as opposed to another was The Reason. He never, *never* could work out why she didn't contact Jeannie.

Mr Ted Gaffney also took to annoying Mr Greenhalgh's ex-wife and ex-daughter by asking if they would forward photos of Jeannie to France. The ex-Mrs had left no contact numbers or forwarding address and Mr Greenhalgh's ex-family, although they were in on the conspiracy, were not forthcoming.

'She has her reasons and it's nothing to do with me,' the ex-Mrs Greenhalgh would snap. 'Stop bloody bothering, you'll get nowhere.'

Mr Ted Gaffney bothered them because he was bothered. He felt like a burglar throwing a grappling hook up a sheer wall only to find it clanging down on his head each time. In the end he gave up. Not on Jeannie. He never did give up on Jeannie.

They played piano together and when Mr Ted Gaffney was appointed to the music college in the nearby city, Jeannie often found herself hanging around the rehearsal rooms and concert hall and her life was filled with music and the idea that she and her dad were a team, working together.

She used to make lists too. But Jeannie's lists were in her

head instead of scribbled on the *Don't Forget...* shopping list. She dropped off to sleep at night cataloguing reasons why her mother would leave her without one backward glance. If things had gone wrong during the day, awkward and ugly moments at school, small father–daughter arguments, Jeannie would go over and over them finding the faults and the cracks and being certain that these were the things that had made her mother go. Her lateness. Her dislike of peas. Contributory factors.

So by the time she reached secondary school, Jeannie Gaffney was on a mission of self-improvement. She was not brilliantly academic but she was bright enough and as all her school reports bleated year after year she was, above all things, diligent.

They didn't clear the dishes. It was a lovely evening, warmed by a rosy pink light and the sun bronzing the horizon. Even though it was September it was still warm enough for Dad to have left the doors to the garden open. There was the first tang of autumn in the air, the slightly sweet chill that came as the garden started to go over. Jeannie had made a trifle and the kettle was on.

Dad had donned wellies and now she was watching him through the kitchen window as she waited for the kettle to boil. The garden stretched for a long way, all the way down to the railway line at the very bottom, screened by a vast hedge of Corsican pines. She could just make Dad out as he made his way down the lawn towards the pond.

The fishing net she used to go rockpooling with was leaning up against the apple tree and he picked it up as he passed. He was going to clear the weed. There would still be a lot of frogs and Dad was always careful to tip the netted weed onto the edges of the pond so that anything that needed to could crawl back to the water. Jeannie watched him. As he stood up at last and began his soggy welly trek back to the house, Jeannie gasped. She had not noticed how grey his hair had become.

Jeannie was diligent in convincing her father that she had forgotten about the existence of a mother and France, although the school curriculum involved French and Jeannie was very good at French, and it tore her heart out every time she had to utter a word of it. This was the language her mother would be speaking now. Would she be fluent? Would this be a way they could communicate? Jeannie could pretend to be French. Could get a summer job at a gites. But she dropped French in Year 9 and chose instead Spanish and German.

There was something about language for Jeannie, something about the difference of babble, as if in rolling a sentence off her tongue in Spanish she was letting go of something. Easing and smoothing herself, for herself. Jeannie was diligent in smoothing and easing and not causing any fuss.

There were lots of friends. Who weren't really friends. They weren't really people that Jeannie could confess anything heartfelt to. Social butterfly that she was, by the time she was in Year 11 she was relied upon for her organisational skills at a lot of school events, school council meetings, fund raising. If it needed to be done, ask Jeannie. When people looked at Jeannie Gaffney they saw her long shiny hair and her shiny bright face, smiling as if she was Miss World. Everyone liked Jeannie.

Except, quite frankly, for Jeannie herself. She thought being Jeannie Gaffney was a bit of an effort, it took a lot of concentration. It wasn't just the hair and the make-up and stretching her face muscles into that optimum smile. No, it was heavy industry, the twenty-four-hour mental mechanics of

*keeping her thoughts and emotions in check, trying not to
ruffle people or let them know if she disagreed or was grumpy
or low or bereft. People had enough to cope with without
having to cope with Jeannie Gaffney.*

The year that Jeannie Gaffney turned seventeen was the year
she found out too much about herself. That was the year that
she worshipped Elspeth Rideout.

Elspeth Rideout. The academic supernova of the school.

*The thing about Elspeth. The aura. The sounding note.
Was that she was just Elspeth. She was not afraid to be herself.
At least, that's what Jeannie always thought back then. She'd
wear the uniform, probably the only girl in the school to wear
the absolute regulation kit, and yet she made it her own. She
made it her own because she didn't follow fashion. She didn't
follow anyone. She didn't lead either. She just was.*

*She used to travel to school on a boy's racing bike. Jeannie
would be dropped off by the bus stop at the end of the road.
She'd be milled about with the crowd of other kids who hogged
the bus and annoyed the early bird pensioners just by their
youth and smoothness. Jeannie felt constricted on that bus,
hemmed in, and not just by the girl who sat next to her, turned
her back to talk to friends in the seats behind. Jeannie felt
hemmed in by the noise, the sharp voices, the loud laughter,
the wearying quality of people who think they are rebellious
and, knowing it all, are devil-may-care. Jeannie felt hemmed
in by the smells. Chemical perfume. The sticky choke of hairspray. The bitterness of smoke.*

*Jeannie wasn't very good in the mornings; it took her a
while to find the right gear. None of her social butterflies took
this bus with her. And that's it, that's what she was really
hemmed in by. Because on that bus in the morning she was*

171

alone and she was entirely and truly Jeannie Gaffney. There was nowhere to hide.

And then there was the morning when she stepped off the kerb and her brain was on a poplar-lined road in rural France and there was a woman with her back to her in the daydream. A woman wearing slim black trousers. And Jeannie found herself almost mown down by a tall, rangy girl on a racing bike.

'*Watch it!*' Elspeth Rideout called out. The bike veered across the tarmac, cars pipped. That's how it is with people. They crash into your life and yet you are just on the kerb of theirs. Some pedestrian, glimpsed on the periphery of their vision.

I've never…Jeannie had never…been tall or rangy. Sitting here now, in this room telling this story I can see that who I really want to be is the girl on the bus. Afraid of herself, yes, but knowing exactly who she was.

Later in the empty staff corridor by the lockers Jeannie saw Elspeth Rideout walking towards her. It was one of those slow-motion moments and Jeannie endlessly replayed it in her head. The motion of Elspeth's body as she walked, the length of her stride. There seemed to be an exacting balance between all the bits and pieces of Elspeth. She appeared engineered, the long range legs, the precise torque and thrust of her hips. A carving in of waist above the band of her skirt. The easy but pendulum-precise sweep of her arms. Elspeth's hands too, their square practicality. Graceful. Sculpted.

'…right?'

Jeannie was so deep in the daydream that only the last syllable arrived on time. Jeannie Gaffney looked round. Elspeth Rideout had halted a few paces away and half turned. Jeannie looked blank.

'It was you. This morning?' Elspeth's voice. Musical of course. Jeannie Gaffney nodded.

'You're all right?'

She nodded again.

'You're a public danger.'

Another nod. But Elspeth was striding, giraffe-like, onwards.

Jeannie found herself walking home, trying out a graceful, long-legged stride. Stood in front of the mirror trying to make her school sweater sit the way that Elspeth's did. Elspeth's looked soft, it didn't pill or ride up. There was no puckered stitching at Elspeth's shoulders.

Jeannie knew she would be an utter failure as Elspeth, but she felt drawn. Each day she looked out for the figure on the bicycle, felt the anticipation. Then, the freedom, the physicality of Elspeth powering the bike. As if in turning the pedals, in the flex and contract of calf muscles, she was somehow powering Jeannie. As if all was right with the world. Elspeth Rideout became her balance, the anti-Jeannie. As long as Elspeth was there the equilibrium couldn't falter.

It was unfounded. Faintly ludicrous. But it worked.

Ted Gaffney worried more when That Bloody Ryan Boy took an interest in his Jeannie. Jeannie was in the Lower Sixth, was seventeen, was, he knew, about to step off into the world. After fifth form exam success Jeannie Gaffney was diligently plotting her course for a matching set of A-Levels. She had even picked up an extra language, she'd been taken on part-time at the local university's language school to begin Russian. She was part of a small group, gifted in languages, all being specially groomed. Part of a new enlightened local education policy to offer greater opportunities. The language hothouse, one councillor had called it.

What chiefly worried Ted Gaffney was the notion that there would soon be a parting of their ways. It wouldn't be too long before he'd be packing her worldly goods into the back of his car and driving her to university. Just a few terms. He felt excitement and doom in equal measure.

You know, he never told me about Geraldine. That here was love, but first, he had a job to do.

And then That Bloody Ryan Boy. Ted Gaffney knew That Bloody Ryan Boy's father and his three or possibly four brothers. They were all lumbering trees of men and it was hard to keep count. Plus there were one or two other lumbering-tree sons dotted about the locality, all of whom seemed to come from Ryan rootstock.

That Bloody Ryan Boy was Sean, the second eldest. Arrogant, but bright enough not to let it show. Just to know he was God was enough, bragging about it would put people off and Sean knew that with a smile he had ultimate power over most people. Generally those who weren't impressed weren't worth bothering with. And then there was Jeannie Gaffney.

Jeannie Gaffney didn't fawn or fold up. Jeannie Gaffney, when he deigned, that first time, to speak to her, simply stood her ground and spoke back. He was used to girls who melted or bleated or made a feeble attempt to be smart. He was used to power, like making small dogs do stupid tricks. He liked to make them jump through fiery hoops of desire.

I know you want me, but I don't want you. At least I won't, not after a few minutes. You'll bore me.

'Could you open the window?' He'd been sitting in the sixth form common room, in one of the low-slung junkshop armchairs, skimming a book for English. He wanted to impress the English teacher, who was singularly unimpressed with him. Chemistry and physics were at his fingertips, leaching into and out of him by osmosis or electro-magnetism depending on which lab he was in. He spoke fluent maths too, as if he just had to turn to a channel in his head. But English, what a fucking foreign language. He had failed it, and he needed it. It irked him that charm and good looks weren't enough in Miss Butterworth's class. She laughed at him.

Sean Ryan thought that he would shock her by actually reading the set book they were currently dissecting, but he hadn't got very far. Now he was skimming, hoping to cram in a few sentences that he could drop into the lesson. And it was hottish by the window.

'Could you open the window?' he said to the girl seated at the nearby table. For a second time. He looked up. The girl was unconsciously twirling her hair round her finger and he was surprised to feel his cock twitch.

'Could you open the window?' he asked again, squinting at her. She surfaced from the book. Looked at him, vague and blurry.

'Sorry?'

'The window. Could you open it?' She looked up at the window.

'No. Sorry. I'm not tall enough. Sorry.'

His cock twitched again. There was something here, and he didn't know what. He stood up, moved to the window behind him and tried to open it.

'That one's been painted over.' She stated the fact. Twitch. His cock was never wrong. It was like a divining rod. Who the hell was she? He couldn't put a name to her.

'Who the hell are you?' he asked Jeannie Gaffney at last.

When I pull out that memory from the back of the drawer I still get that crackling frizzle of electricity between my legs.

Everyone knew Sean Ryan and that he was only to be trusted to break your heart. He was so much the master of his own fan club and yet everyone wanted him. What I remember about that day is feeling good that I didn't melt or bleat or fawn. He was taller than me, he could easily reach the window; me, I mean, the Jeannie me, she'd have to stand on the chair first.

That day, Jeannie Gaffney felt defiant. Powerful. There was a long pause then. You could hear the wide open space of the kids outside on the playing field running round the athletics pitch. A motor mower was buzzing in the distance like a diesel bee.

He asked if I'd read the book he was reading. Which I had. I didn't even turn, I just kept on with my work, making notes. He was trying to persuade me to talk about it, give him some crib notes for his English lesson and I wouldn't. What I felt, I mean, Jeannie, Jeannie Gaffney felt this. It should be written across my head: 'Jeannie Gaffney felt this.'

What Jeannie felt was scorn really, that he thought it could be so cheaply won. I'll ask her and she'll give me. So she didn't. Jeannie Gaffney had nothing to lose, wasn't in Sean Ryan's League of Blondes or anything. He moved then, to sit on the table beside her, looking down at her as if he didn't realise she could work out that game plan. It was exhilarating. What she remembered best was the moment she had to leave, standing, gathering her books from the table, looking at his face, the shock and bewilderment on it. How have I not won out here? What is this thing called 'no'?

All the time Sean Ryan wasn't really thinking about the book or the English teacher. He was thinking about putting his hands into ice water and then putting them inside the cups of Jeannie Gaffney's bra, how the nipples would harden under his iced palms.

Know what? Jeannie Gaffney was thinking about that too.

Fast forward to an evening before the end of the term. Balmy, the day sweaty and tired with the heat of itself. Sean Ryan, with his trousers round his thighs, felt the buckle of his belt flash cold against the hot of his skin. It was his brother's car and the seats folded and sagged against each other, the leatherette used to the familiar drill of girl and nature reserve carpark. That Bloody Ryan Boy wasn't thinking that her head was banging against the hatchback door and that she was trying to shimmy downwards to avoid concussion. He was thinking about how he wished he had bigger hands so he could grasp more of her gorgeous overspilling arse and he was thinking about the heat of her and then he found himself panting, 'Fuck...oh fuck Jeannie...fuck...'

(But Jeannie Gaffney was three miles away sitting on a piano stool playing a Clementi sonatina as her dad fished pondweed out of their pond with an old rockpooling net. 'Frog. Jeannie...A frog...' he shouted, and Jeannie stepped out into the honeysuckle-scented air.)

Elspeth Rideout was not red-eyed and did not want sympathy. Jeannie Gaffney still saw her in the sixth form centre and in the corridors looking as elegant and rangy as a borzoi dog. Jeannie Gaffney had no idea that Elspeth even knew she existed. Jeannie Gaffney had no idea about what had happened in the nature reserve carpark. So Jeannie Gaffney was puzzled when she caught Elspeth glaring at her, watching her, and once or twice, following her home. On that racing bike, tagging behind the bus. And one afternoon when she was late out of a music class and had missed the bus, Jeannie walked home. And as she strolled through the park Sean Ryan emerged from the trees like the big, bad, wolf.

See, there are all these things going on behind your back. You just don't have all the information. How was I…I mean, how was Jeannie Gaffney to know about Elspeth and Sean Ryan? No one told her. They didn't tell anyone. They kept it quiet and Elspeth kept their break-up even quieter than that. Jeannie couldn't know their secrets. And that's always the killer blow isn't it? The secrets.

That was the summer that Jeannie spent all her time in the forest with the big bad Bloody Ryan Boy, the summer that she didn't really talk to her dad and in her not talking she said absolutely everything.

On the outside she looked like your normal everyday Jeannie Gaffney but Ted Gaffney knew. He'd seen That Bloody Ryan Boy in his car at the end of the road and he had no idea what he should do. He wanted to shout and rant and warn her but what was the use? This is it, this is the process; this is her life.

He did, one evening, let the tyres down on That Bloody Ryan Boy's car. And of course, the worst evening of all when he was out at the forest with Geraldine walking Bilberry, her stupid mutt of a dog, and he saw That Bloody Ryan Boy's car in the carpark. And then there were leaves in Jeannie's bedroom and one night, when Ted Gaffney just couldn't bloody sleep he was on the landing, heading downstairs for a cup of coffee that would keep-him-even-more-awake-but-whatthe-bloody-hell-he-didn't-bloody-care, when he caught the dry incense scent of forest floor, of compacted earth holding onto the dampness of the last rain beneath a covering of castoff needles and the rich brew of leaf mould.

After the coffee Ted Gaffney had terrible dreams of trying to catch a centaur in the forest. He couldn't manoeuvre his way through the trees, they blocked his every move, tripping him with their roots, slapping him with their branches and the finale, the bright silver of heavy hooves clomping against his skull.

I just have to be there. That is what I have to do, he thought the next morning. As he watched the steam rise from his fresh coffee and Jeannie fetched him the painkillers for the ache in his head.

It had been a lookout point for forest fires at one time, although the forest was no longer vast enough to warrant it. The furthest edge had been felled for a golf course years back and seared across by the new dual carriageway to the city. It cut right through the heart of the forest, leaving a scrap of a few hundred acres trapped on the far side of the tarmac. There was a footbridge that was hardly ever used. Most people walked their dogs to the boundary and walked back to the carpark.

It couldn't really be classed as a wilderness if there were toilets and a kiosk. But there was wilderness if you cared to find it. It was just like a fairytale, all you had to do was trip-trap over that bridge.

They, someone, had built a wooden walkway into the trees that climbed slowly but surely through the tall trunks and ended in a tiny treehouse. You had to climb inside, lifting yourself up the rungs of a makeshift ladder. Once inside there were three windows looking out onto different aspects of the forest.

Sean and Jeannie had had to cross the footbridge, the traffic scudding below. He did not hold her hand; rather he walked just a step ahead so that all the way across she had a view of his back, the armour plating of his shoulderblades under his white T-shirt. He didn't turn until he reached the other side where he waited, made certain she was with him and then carried on, down the steps and held the small wooden gate open, the gate that led through the fencing into the forest.

They walked into the crowd of trunks and the dampening effect of the forest floor, the musty, herbal crust of discarded needles and leaves. The sun striped through to the left and there was the busy sound of chainsaws as the foresters cleared an acre or two. A sappy smell filtered through, almost metallic, like blood. But Sean moved off, halting only to half turn and half smile as Jeannie Gaffney followed.

They moved uphill. Sean Ryan knew the way. Jeannie Gaffney looked back, unable now to see the primary-coloured blinks of cars in the distance. The trees closed in behind her. Just birdsong and footsteps and the rustling of leaves, the creaking of wood. She had noticed the planks of wood lifting up into the trees. They were a seasoned slope and a gnarled handrail moving from the forest floor up into a sprawling clutch of pine trees. They looked like some strange disjointed wooden snake. Sean paused, as if he hadn't noticed, was looking over the landscape of trees at a fork in the path. Coniferous or deciduous, which was the way again?

Jeannie halted, aware of the sweat trickling down her back like a finger tracing her spine. She couldn't breathe, and it was not the exertion of the forest climb but the wish that it was Sean standing behind her, his finger tracing the sweat's tributary. She put a hand onto the handrail. The wood was silky and warm to the touch. She looked upwards along the length of the snake and couldn't quite see where it led. Sean half turned again.

'Want to see where it goes?' he asked, casually, as if this was an adventure.

He didn't touch her until they had climbed up to the wide ladder that led into the hide. He had hardly spoken and hadn't looked at her. Now they halted, the ladder seeming steep, vertiginous. Sean paused, looked right at her, stepped towards her, kissed her on the mouth, slid his hand into her hair, his mouth open now and his body pressed against hers, pinning her against the wide slats of the ladder.

Leaves. Breeze. Creak. Creak. Hide.

But they were not hidden. They were watched.

The week before the A-level results. The day the thunder was building overhead and Elspeth swooped like a golden eagle and dropped Jeannie from the nest.

Did she fall? She was pushed. Elspeth waited and waited, such a very patient young woman and such a battle in a confined space. Skin and fists and the fury in Elspeth's eyes and Sean's first thought was to pull on his jeans, fending off blows with one hand. As if she was just a gnat really, as if the thing he really had to protect was not Jeannie. As if the thing that was precious to him was not Jeannie at all. It was all just a confusion in Jeannie Gaffney's concussed head.

Later, at the farthest end of that afternoon, Jeannie Gaffney was found by birdwatchers. Two gentlemen in khaki shorts, their necks laden with spotting scopes and an Ordnance Survey map in a see-through pouch. They found her like a chick on the forest floor. They covered her in a pac-a-mac and called the police and the ambulance. Then they stood by, watched anxiously as the uniformed policeman picked her up. Had to carry her, so carefully, through the roughshod forest terrain to the waiting ambulance.

And then there was Dad, summoned from home with a bag of clothes. Such a very very patient man and such a battle in the confined space of his head.

'Ready to come home?' was all he said and, as they crossed the hospital carpark and he opened the passenger door, just the lightest touch of his hand on her elbow. And in the car, travelling home, she started to cry. In the driveway, shielded by the hedging, he stopped the engine, put his arms around her and she sobbed and sobbed. And then nothing more was said.

'What do you want me to say?' he asked later when, sleepless, they sat in the kitchen. Jeannie shrugged. Ted Gaffney was desperate to think of ways to communicate. How not to say, I wish I'd told you so. I should have warned you. This is how life is. Older and wiser. Say nothing Ted, for this is punishing enough. And then it came to him.

'It has been a rite of passage.'

Bugger that, he wanted to staple gun That Bloody Ryan Boy's genitals to a park bench for the starlings to peck at. How dare you. How bloody dare you. And couldn't say it.

It was front page that week in the local paper. Some unkind person had given the paper a school photograph, Jeannie's head ringed in newsprint. The local paper, which sat around in the chip shops and Chinese takeaways until at last it lined pet cages and mopped up paint drips while the townspeople decorated. By September there were a few issues lurking in the bottom of recycling bins or saved up for art projects. The newsprint stuffed wet shoes, was made into some papier maché balloons for a Montgolfier and Flight project at a couple of primary schools.

Elspeth Rideout set out for Oxford that September. Sean Ryan might have joined the army or the foreign legion but more likely, according to local rumour, his father and his brothers knocked him unconscious, stripped him of his clothes, shaved him and shoved him, bound with duct tape, into the boot of his dad's car and drove him to Inverness.

Mr Ryan senior did not come to apologise to Jeannie for his son's cowardice in leaving her for dead in the forest, but on her return from hospital the contents of a nearby florist shop were delivered to her home. Anonymously.

Ted Gaffney worried that the flowers were from That Bloody Ryan Boy and only when he happened to pull into the petrol station by the leisure centre did he see Ryan senior at a neighbouring pump and find himself on the receiving end of an acknowledging nod. And when he entered the kiosk to pay, the girl wouldn't take Ted Gaffney's money.

'He paid,' she said, and pointed at Ryan senior, pulling out into the traffic.

The following September Jeannie Gaffney passed all her A-levels but did not take up her place at university in York. Instead she stayed at home, started work in the greenhouses for Parks and Gardens. Ted Gaffney kept talking about a gap year. Ted Gaffney kept York University in their conversation until the following August, when he shut up. Then, a visit to the library enlightened him about the glories of the local Agricultural College. He left out the leaflets on 'Horticulture: The Growth Industry!' and 'Becoming an Arborealist – Our Roots and Branches'. Accepted that she had made her choice.

Jeannie Gaffney had green fingers.

Only to be expected I suppose, after all those afternoons in the forest.

Amaranthus hybridus

green amaranth

---

healing and invisibility

When she wasn't at the college double digging beds for the stern tutor, Mr Mathieson, Jeannie Gaffney was heaving a sigh of relief in the nursery at Cromwell Park. Her first day there it felt as if she was taking a deep breath, sloughing off skin, and the feeling intensified as she walked from the park gates up the tarmac road, Park Hall in view, perched at the top of the hill.

Then the curving right onto the gravelled carpark towards the wall. The heavy brown shed, doors slung open on hooks, a verandah filled with greenhouse staging and whatever perennials, evergreens and bulbs were for sale; above them the pokerworked sign, CROMWELL PARK PLANT SALES. Beyond that the wall stretched long and high. Stone, with a wooden gate cut into it. NO ADMITTANCE, it said, but Jeannie Gaffney pushed it open anyway. She had to put her shoulder to it, the gate was old and swollen.

Inside it was another world. A long stretch of greenhouses along the top wall to the right of the gate. Below that, beds and terraces and cold frames. Now they would call it a micro-climate but then Jeannie wanted to call it home. She felt shaky suddenly, as if she'd sucked in too much air.

'You all right?' hissed a voice, through an inward breath of cigarette smoke. 'You look a bit peaky.'

Jeannie's first view of Col Bash, he was standing in the doorway to a pent-roofed potting shed, his hands claggy with soil, his fingers pinching delicately at a newly lit roll-up. He wiped at his nose with his sleeve, keeping his muddied hands out of the way. Jeannie saw him speckled all over with tiny black dots, falling inward like stars. Don't faint, she told herself, take a deep breath. So she took in a deep breath of coffee and dirt and tomato stalks.

'Yes. Thanks. I'm Jeannie Gaffney.' She could hear the uncertainty in her voice, as if she was asking him to confirm it—I am her, aren't I? He nodded his head toward the shed.

'You can help me finish up in here. I've coffee brewed.'

He offered his hand then. Muddy as it was. 'Col Bash.'

Jeannie looked into his face, saw a last tiny black star imploding by his eyes and didn't hesitate to grasp his hand. Shake firmly. And a smile stretched catlike across his dirty face.

'You'll do, Gaffney.'

Inside the long potting shed there was a two-ring stove with the pot of coffee almost always on the go. It was one of those metallic cone pots and that first day Bash showed her how to fill it with water and coffee grounds and put it to boil. He brushed the worst of the dirt off his hands before reaching down two large thick mugs. Blew dead woodlice out of one.

Jeannie Gaffney potted up cuttings as instructed. Later they dug out a couple of beds together, Bash watching her carefully, making the hairs on the back of her neck stand up. But he was watching how she worked, Jeannie could see. And she wanted to do well. No more kerfuffle for me, she thought. And if Col Bash thought she looked a bit familiar and hadn't he seen her somewhere before, he didn't say so.

Later, standing amongst rhubarb forcing pots in the back end of the largest of the cold frames, he gave her a long thoughtful stare.

'I've seen you, you know. You're not Bill Holdway's youngest are you?'

Jeannie shook her head and as she did she saw the light dawn in Col Bash's eyes. She waited for him to start on about the forest chick story that he'd probably read over and read over each time he had to wait in the Golden Monkey Chinese Takeaway. Jeannie braced herself and he saw it. But the light flashed electrically bright and burned out. Then he reached into his pocket for his cigarettes again, with his lopsided smile.

'Nah. Forget it. My mistake.'

They got on well. Bash seemed to forget she was female. There was nothing he didn't deem her capable of or trust her with. They put up sheds, they dug out beds, they hacked and sawed and trimmed and mowed. Jeannie loved to ride the motor mower, starting her stretch down by the boat hire sheds at the lake and mowing her way across the wide open sward of parkland heading back up towards Park Hall, buzzing and clipping as she went.

With her protective earmuffs on, all sound was dulled and Jeannie Gaffney vanished into her own world. She could hear music some days. It would be some Schubert impromptu that she loved, or the Elgar they'd all been playing the night before. Her father and his small ensemble, together in the college rehearsal rooms, fellow lecturer Geraldine on the cello, Jeannie at the piano, their students on violins and violas, a clarinet, a flute. The evening bending and stretching around them; Jeannie transported. The smells of the college seeped into her skin. The wood polish. A leatherish smell she could never quite place. The rotted smell of old flowers in a vase on a far table at the back. The dust of the tall brick red curtains. Rosin. The soured oniony scent of that blonde girl's armpits as her elbow sawed up and down, back and forth. All of this weaving through the music. The wrong notes, the repetition, the going back, the skipping forward.

Nothing like the stone cold of the agricultural college, where Mr Mathieson disliked her and Jeannie ignored it as far as she dared. The stone cold lecture rooms where she breathed in must and mould, where she found she was photo-synthesising the knowledge in spite of him. The bright cold spring in the nursery fields behind the College, where she worked in the soil and longed for the moment she'd be released back into the wild, to go home. To the walled garden.

In the walled garden everything they had sown was begin-ning to grow. They were asked to help with a vegetable growing project for local schoolchildren.

'Bloody hate kids. You do it, Gaffney,' Bash said one morning, snapping the last biscuit in half for them to share. 'You're a woman. That's your territory.' And Jeannie helped them plant courgettes and tiny carrots while Bash disappeared out through the back gate, wandered off down the overgrown path with a wheelbarrow and a rake. As the school parties arrived in their neat uniforms and began watering and pinching out and sitting cross-legged to draw the new shoots and label all the parts of the plants, Jeannie found herself looking towards that back gate and wondering where it led. It was overgrown and the padlock was rusted. She knew because yesterday, when Bash had been out on the motor mower she'd checked it out. The gate peeled its paint. She could peer through a tiny slit where the planks of the door had started to warp away from each other. There was a dirt path. Just. It looked like a badger run.

But she did not ask. She did not say. Bash was older, nearly forty, and he was keeping her secret. She would let him have his.

But his vanishing act started to throw her. She'd have been busy all morning in the rose garden and she'd come back to the walled garden and the shed and find no coffee brewed and no sign of Bash. There'd just be a spade upright in the earth. And her eye was always drawn to the back gate. She thought she could smell the damp earth under the brambles and hawthorn, could smell the green edge to the leaves that sheltered the way. Could smell the coffee and soap scent of Bash on the breeze.

If she worked in the beds or frames at these times she made certain she had her back to the gate. She didn't want to see him arrive back. He would suddenly appear behind her with a mug of coffee and a set of instructions about tying up the pear trees on the south-facing wall, or what they might do about the bindweed that was strangling everything in the borders by the boating lake. Jeannie looked into his face and could only think of the word 'secrets'. As though it was written on his face.

It was nearly Easter and she was potting up daffodils and narcissi for sale at the EasterFest in the Park. They'd got hundreds of them to prettify in terracotta pots with yellow ribbon. The man blocked out the light in the doorway. His shoulders made a sagging square in the soft leather of his well-worn, well-kept jacket. He had clipped hair, a beard and moustache so expertly groomed they might have been barbered with a set square. These were the bare outlines she could see from his silhouette, the details of his face were obscured by the sunlight behind him.

'Bash around?' was all he said, and she directed him out to the bottom rank of cold frames. He didn't stay long. Five or ten minutes later she looked up as he walked past the door again on his way to the gates. She heard an engine gun and tyres screeling on gravel.

Later when a muscular roll of ten pound notes fell out of Bash's pocket and landed at her feet she picked it up, handed it back. There was just a moment as she looked into his face. It was important for both of them. Jeannie felt the secret unearth itself. I know. You know. Nothing more needed to be said. Jeannie turned back to tying the ribbons.

She was deep in the maze walk, busy putting up the last of the new bird boxes. Jeannie was thinking about the blue tits and finches that visited, hoping that they'd be back this year, that they'd enjoy their new homes. Bash seemed to pop up out of the earth.

'You're saying nothing then?' he was edgy. She had never seen him edgy before. It was as if he'd found something he might deem her not capable of at last; something he might not be able to trust her with. Jeannie looked at him for a moment, his hair slicked back as usual, striped through on just one side with grey.

'About what?'

He hesitated. His eyes didn't dart around, they held hers, intent. Jeannie turned away first, reached for the last of the nest boxes from the back of the trailer. Bash held the ladder, handed her the hammer. 'If I tell you, you can get me into trouble.'

Jeannie felt challenged. This was not what she wanted to happen. She wanted the balance, the equilibrium. And it came to her. 'If you tell me, you could get *me* into trouble.'

She looked at him as she took the hammer, squinted in the pockled sunlight through the trees. Bash grinned, broad and clever. He ruffled her hair, as if she was an apprenticed lad. 'Fuckin' hell, someone screwed your head on right. You'll do Gaffney.'

Jeannie thought she would do. She would do very nicely thank you. Things were straight now. There was not knowledge but there was awareness. All she knew was that since starting work at the walled garden she slept deeply and well. In the mornings, winter or summer she was itching to pull on her shoes and her jacket and head out. Whatever Bash got up to was outside the wall. Let him get on with it. She did not want to tip the balance.

Jeannie thought Mr Mathieson was standing just a centimetre too close. He was almost having to squint down his nose to focus on her. He was wearing his clean wellies, the wellies he hosed off at the standpipe near the old stable. He was wearing his checked shirt and his jumper and over that his waxed waistcoat pitted with pockets, some that poppered and some that zipped. But Jeannie always seemed to see him with a riding crop. A crop that he snapped at her. A crop that didn't exist but seemed to catch her on the side of the face whenever he spoke with her.

Jeannie was afraid of him. Mr Mathieson didn't think there was a place for women in horticulture. Floristry, yes. He seemed to vent this prejudice only on Jeannie Gaffney. There were two other women on the course, Abbie and Tanya, but Mr Mathieson couldn't reach them. They were very far away in a little pink universe of their own, as Mr Mathieson put it. Not that Tanya and Abbie cared about the abuse or the scorn. They were oblivious. But Jeannie did care. So he punished her.

She was doing very well in spite of him. Other tutors were supportive and helpful, coaching her further, recognising that she had a talent, that it came naturally. Not Mr Mathieson. He marked her as harshly as he dared.

Then he missed a session because he was in a meeting with the course manager, Alan. After that he marked her less harshly but more grudgingly. Generally he marked in green ballpoint. He wrote her grades and markings in red. *They have made me do this. You are still worthless*, the red ink seemed to say.

Alan called at the house one evening. Ted let him in, showed him into the garden where Jeannie was filling beer traps in Geraldine's new herb garden.

'I wanted to offer you a sideways move,' Alan began. Jeannie could barely hear him above her heartbeat, her blood turned to Niagara Falls. She felt thick and light in the same instant.

'Oh?' Her voice came out very quiet, very small.

'Thought you might be interested in joining Amy Fitz's tutor group. For your final term. What do you think?'

Jeannie felt sick. Panicked. What had she done? This was to do with Mr Mathieson.

'Have I…is something wrong?' She was tentative, imagining she was maybe moments from being asked to leave college. Asked to leave her placement at Parks and Gardens.

'No. No, god's sake no Jeannie…Look, I can be honest with you. It's felt, that is all the course staff, we feel that it would be better if you left Mr Mathieson's tutor group.'

She couldn't control her face as the blood drained out of it. The vomit of panic lurched up into her throat like a dog at a gate.

Alan said quickly, 'For your benefit. Don't misunderstand...You are not the problem. I can only apologise Jeannie, for not having dealt with this sooner.'

'No. That's fine.' Jeannie heard the words coming out of her mouth.

'Seriously Jeannie. Amy would love to have you. She's been impressed with your work on the foundation module on garden design you've been doing. This isn't a problem. This is a solution.'

Jeannie couldn't do it. She knew. It would be running away. He would have won.

'No. That's all right. Thanks. But it's just a couple of months. I'll...' She hesitated; what would she do? 'I'll stay where I am.'

Alan looked fazed. Jeannie could feel her smile wobbling. She was willing him to go. Go away. Leave me to it. She had had no wish to get Mr Mathieson into trouble. It was her problem. She could cope with it.

When August came, she passed her examinations in spite of Mr Mathieson. The day she came into college for the results she left it until the last minute. Finished her day at Cromwell Park first and walked up instead of catching the shuttle bus, but Mr Mathieson had waited her out. Standing sentinel in the common room, her envelope in his hand instead of placed alphabetically on the desk. She would have to take it from him. She had done exceptionally well and she saw that it galled him.

What she didn't see was that he felt beaten; he had not driven her away or made her give up. That last day, he should have been out at the golf course with an old school friend and instead he belittled himself waiting and waiting for her and in the end he did not get a reaction. She did not smirk or rant or rail or have any parting shot at all. She didn't know she had won.

A celebration for the outcome. Champagne. Dad laughing in the garden with Geraldine. His face scrumpled up. The laugh loud and uproarious, the soft fall of his fringe as his head threw back, the slap of his hand on the garden chair. The wheezing amusement and Geraldine, still in the middle of her story, reaching across her hand, touching his arm, her eyes looking at him with love and brightness.

'Hang on Ted, that's not it…that's not it…wait…listen…' and her own mirth, hardly able to speak. And Jeannie drying the pots in the kitchen, hearing the sounds reflected off the open kitchen window and thinking that she couldn't remember the last time that Dad had laughed that hard. Couldn't get out of her head the picture of Geraldine's neat and freckled hand, the garnet dress ring on the fourth finger, like a ripe blackberry. The tenderness of that gesture. The way they fitted. The way the lights had come on inside her dad.

That was when Jeannie walked past the garden flat in the row of redbrick Victorian villas on the road running alongside the park boundary. To Let. And Jeannie found herself in the estate agent's asking about looking around. Saw the view through the bedroom window to the garden. Saw the view through the French doors in the tiny living room, out to the garden. Beyond, the green of the park. Liked the way the light fell through the skylight in the kitchen extension. Found herself thinking about sitting in that garden to have breakfast.

For those were the days when Geraldine came round in the evenings and Jeannie felt squeezed out of the old kitchen at home. Felt squeezed out of the house because it wasn't hers. Felt she'd squeezed her dad into a different life. Maybe it was time for them both to spread wings.

So she put down the deposit and the first month's rent and Geraldine bought her a box of kitchen utensils. They shared a look over the serving spoons and spatulas, Jeannie aware of the significance of the present. Geraldine didn't fudge it, she laughed. As she did the light caught in the flecks of grey amongst the deep auburn of her hair. The grey strands flashed like spun steel. Jeannie knew then that someone else was thinking about what was good for Dad.

Dad was sleepless. Jeannie came down to the kitchen because she could smell the coffee and was thinking about Bash, dreaming of him unlocking the back gate, of him turning and looking at her. In the kitchen she made toast and said simply to Dad, 'It's a rite of passage.' And was completely understood.

Then it all got turned on its head when some idiot at the council sent the lad for work experience.

Lazy. Moaning. Losing every bit of kit that wasn't nailed down or pegged up. Troy was his name, and he was the bane of their life. No more coffee because it pained them both to have to sit in the shed with the whining, sour youth. He couldn't do anything unsupervised and so their lives became a rota of babysitting. Every task he was set seemed to take four hours longer than it should, because it had to be done and redone and done over.

Jeannie found herself one bright May day wanting to take the spade he was bitching over and whack him around the head with it. They could dig a trench and bury him and see what hideous weeds grew out of him. It would be something rampant and full of thorns with sap that would raise welts on your skin. Troybane, Jeannie called it in her head.

Bash and Jeannie relished the time when he began turning up an hour late, using the extra sixty minutes to have a cup of coffee together and breathe easily. Of course, his mother spoilt that with her dastardly plan to drop him off each day. She had the measure of her son, that was clear, and she seemed determined to do something about him. If he was going to be late then he was going to have to be dropped off, like a baby. Jeannie heard them from inside the shed. Her voice was a low bark, angry and stiff as she escorted him, police fashion, onto the premises.

'Like a *baby*,' she spat at him again. Jeannie could see him squirming. His face red. 'Get on with it. Get me? Or it's end of story.' Her hand made a definitive slicing gesture. He made no response. She gave a frustrated grunt and with a chinkle of car keys was gone. He caught Jeannie looking through the crack in the shed door. He wouldn't forgive that.

Jeannie was in charge that morning, Bash had been summoned to County Hall to talk to Morag, who supervised and managed the Parks and Gardens. Troy was supposed to be laying in newspapers and organic matter in the sweetpea trench.

'Shit shovelling,' he complained.

'Ready for planting out.' Jeannie kept her calm and once he'd gone off with the spade and wheelbarrow she manned the till at the plant sales. She thought she'd be five minutes, tops, but the sun was out and had brought people into the park with thoughts of the bald spots and bare patches in their own gardens. Jeannie found it was nearly lunchtime and she was half-starved with the thought of her lunchbox and the piece of Geraldine's chocolate cake.

As Jeannie came through the gates of the walled garden she saw the spade abandoned in the trench, slumped over on the banked up earth. Troy was at the padlocked gate trying to pick it open with bent out wire. It was clear to Jeannie that Troy had seen Bash's vanishing act. *Danger. Danger.*

'Finished the sweetpeas then?' Jeannie called to him, her voice firm and hard. He jittered away from the gate, dropping the wire. Then, seeing it was Jeannie, his edges smoothed.

'No. But what you going to do about it?' he challenged, swaggering towards her.

'Tell your mum,' Jeannie bit.

'Bitch.' He spat as he said it, the gob missing its mark. He couldn't get anything right.

'Me or her?' Jeannie didn't look back as she moved towards the potting shed. She didn't feel hungry then. Didn't eat the cake until nearly six when Bash got back and she cut it in half so they could share. Three quarters of an hour after Troy's mum had come to drag him home.

Troy had said at the start, in a very tiresome way, 'I knows you,' although he didn't have any theories about how. 'I knows you, I seen you,' and Jeannie ignored him. But at last he realised where he'd seen her. That first morning, when the knowledge came to him, he was triumphant. On one level Jeannie Gaffney was relieved that he had, after all these weeks, found something to bloody smile about. Not that his smile was any real improvement on his scowl: the taint of nastiness made it look more as though someone had slashed his face open. He had a habit of licking his thin red lips exactly like an animal licking wounds.

'Got your knickers on today then?' was his opening gambit when she emerged from the potting shed. Jeannie didn't twig his meaning, was only half listening. The general tone of everything he said was abusive so it didn't seem anything had shifted. But Troy worried at it. Worried at her. On and on.

'If you go down in the woods today,' his cracked voice carried across the cold frames. Something about the childishness of the song struck her. Was Troy really singing 'Teddy Bears Picnic' as he worked? What was he, one of the seven dwarves? He whistled on. Jeannie felt a thin sliver of unease slice into her. She ignored it. But then he was up close, standing too close over her, legs astride, as she knelt in the border planting out the herbs.

'You go down in the woods then?'

Jeannie caught the meaning like a slap in the face.

'Bare-arse bitch,' he spat again and sloped off. Later, heading out on the trailer with Bash, he barged her as he picked up his jacket. 'Badgerfucker.'

And Jeannie could see her own face, ringed in the paper that week, that month, that year. Could feel the whited-out newsprint noose hanging about her now.

He found new digs and jibes until, by the Thursday, he hit upon his masterpiece. 'Want me to stick a cuckoo in that bushy nest of yours, Badgerbitch?'

Jeannie was filled with poison. No more. She stepped forward, too close to him then.

'You?' she asked, harsh. He lifted his head back, as if looking down at an angered dog. Found he couldn't step back because of the boxes of spring bulbs that had been delivered that morning.

'You?' she nudged closer, her breath pushed back at her from his face. She picked the secateurs from their loop on her belt. Made them glint on his face. White. Flash. Stab. Stab.

'Let's see it then.' Glint. Glint. Flash. Stab. Troy's edges wavered now, his face struggling to hold onto his cocky slashed-skin smile.

'You're fuckoo cuckoo you are,' he blarted at her. Jeannie didn't move. Then all it took was a subtle feint at him, her eyes unblinking. He flinched and inside Jeannie felt trumpets sound. He had flinched. She felt cruel. Wanted to make him do it again.

'Fuckoo,' he said, spooked, and pushed her out of his way. Jeannie's balance never faltered. Troy's foot caught on the edge of the lowest box of bulbs and he stumbled out of the potting shed.

'Fuckoo.' He thought he'd hit the mother lode with that one.

So what, she thought. But, dammit, it ravelled into her nights. She dreamed she was running naked through the walled garden under the midnight sky. She was always running towards the locked gate. She shouldered it open and the forest opened deep below her. She always woke as she fell. Well, after all, that's what everyone does in their dreams.

Jeannie's petty revenge was to make Troy do the most boring tasks and to smile with scorn when he showed he couldn't do them. But her worst revenge, unintentional, was when she asked him to do the labels for the hardwood cuttings they'd just taken in the Italian garden. She thrust the marker pen at him. He did not take it; looked at her, his eyes flaring. With shame? Hatred? And she knew. He couldn't write.

Jeannie's breath was taken away for a moment. She felt the blush burn through her as if she was paper igniting, she hadn't meant to do this, it was an accident.

'Fuckoo,' he muttered, throwing down a trowel and

clomping out of the shed to have a not-very-sneaky ciggie round the back. Bash had already found him there once or twice before and took a satisfying revenge by switching on the power hose and shouting 'FIRE!'

Troy never dared say his pet phrase when Bash was around.

If Jeannie thought they had reached the lowest point she was sadly mistaken. She came back in the trailer with the prunings from the rose garden to find him, ciggie in mouth, riding around the walled garden on the motor mower. It was clear from the agonised screels that the blades were down, chewing up gravel, and somewhere a cog was trapped; some piston bent and contorted because the machine was screaming with a cold steely fury. The exhaust was billowing black smoke and when he saw her running towards him he cut across the dahlia bed. Jeannie's pride. Her joy. He hit the scalloped edging at a bad angle and the mower tipped him, motor choking, wheels spinning as if it was scrabbling at the sky, trying to right itself.

Jeannie was on him, anxious to see he wasn't damaged. She didn't want his mother's face to become any more pinched and taut than Troy had already made it. As she grabbed him by the scruff of the neck, aware that the left side of his face had grazed across at least three feet of gravelled path, that he was dripping blood, she felt him rise beneath her. She didn't have to lift him, he seemed to launch himself vertically, his face puce with anger.

'FUCK YOU!' he bellowed, one hand lashing out to grab her by the throat and dangle her in front of him like a rag doll as the other hand freed itself from a tangle of massacred dahlias to land a punch. Jeannie felt her teeth give in her jaw, saw the black stars supernova. She was moving without walking as

Troy hurled her backwards. His foot flew up at her. She turned herself away and still felt the imprint of the sole of his boot as it grazed up her back.

'*Fuck you,*' he spat and something fired in Jeannie. Her dangling legs swung upwards to kick against his waist. He was toppling and growling. His hand let go of her neck as his other arm flew up again, carrying another punch. Jeannie's arm shot up unbidden and their bones cracked together like clubs. She was fighting back, pushing all her weight against the strength of him. Rage boiled and bubbled in both of them but she was losing. She could feel it. He was too big for her, too strong but SO WHAT, FUCK YOU TOO.

The scalloped edging saved her from the killer punch, and sent her sprawling backwards into a fountained batch of cardoon. By which time Bash was there, his hand clutching the scruff of Troy's neck, wrestling him off her, manhandling Troy along the side path into a small redundant outhouse and locking the door. Troy spat and battered like a trapped cat as Bash picked Jeannie out of the undergrowth.

Patched her up. The leather of his hands. The bitter aroma of the antiseptic from the first aid box, bandages gone mouldy from too long in a damp, weatherbeaten shed. Not a word. Even when, as he leaned in to pick some bark from her eye their faces almost touched. As he leaned forward to reach back into the tin for the tin of plasters his body close against hers. Just the smell of him, the sweat and soap smell of him, made her feel better.

Troy's mother took him away in the back of her big car. Put him into the hatchback boot separated from the rest of the car by a dog fence. He almost protested. Hot faced, tantrummed out from his stop in the outhouse. But she pushed at his middle and he folded like paper, folded onto the hair-strewn dog blanket. Jeannie noticed that there were so many hairs it seemed as if the dog had been there only moments before and had suddenly vanished. Popped, perhaps.

They drove off. Jeannie and Bash aware of Troy's mother's stinging tears. She had been trying so hard to hold on to her dignity. Had managed a severe nod before moving to the driver's side, fumbling her keys from her pocket.

Bash stood looking over the trail of destruction, the chewed-up beds, the broken cold frames. He lit up a cigarette. After a couple of drags he pulled a face as if it tasted bitter and dimped it out with his fingers before putting it back in his pocket.

'Bugger this. We're off down the boating lake,' he said.

They were heading to the island in the middle of the boating lake to root out some ground elder that was taking hold. For this they were supposed to be able to use the little motor boat that the boat-hire supervisor, Micky, used to fetch in errant boats, but there was an engine problem. Micky had been 'keeping up the maintenance' and had stripped it down. There had been 'a problem'.

'Problem is you haven't got the map of putting it back, have you?' Bash laughed. Micky drank deeply from a mug of tea, standing amongst the three-dimensional jigsaw puzzle of engine parts and oily mysteries.

'Row out,' Micky suggested with a knowing smile. 'Lazy arse.'

Bash gave a scornful laugh and then looked at the bright weather. The blue sky. The sun-sparkle on the water.

As he loaded the kit he handed her an oar.

'I'll steer. You row.'

Jeannie looked at him, uncertain. Confessed she'd never been in a rowing boat.

'That's buggered your plans.' Micky held the boat against the dock.

'Never?' Bash said, looking as if this was a serious gap in her education. As if rowing a boat was something that should be on the curriculum, like past participles or quadratic equations.

'Never. Don't know how.'

Bash was open mouthed. Then decisive. 'Time you learned then eh?'

'Ingenious.' Micky laughed, shaking his head as Bash moved into the stern of the boat. He settled her on the bench, showed her how it was done and then they pushed off. He was the harshest of taskmasters.

'For fuck's sake Gaffney. Don't be such a bloody girl about it.' He leaned forward from his seat and took the oars, put his current cigarette into the corner of his mouth as he rowed and instructed. They moved the opposite way now. She watched his arms working, saw the indian-ink blue of his tattoo, the words old and blurred. Watched the flex and twang of sinews, of strength, of effort.

'You've got to put your back into it. Forward and *pull*, forward and *pull*.' He handed the oars back, gestured at her to get on with it. Busy untangling himself from the rudder strings, he had one intent eye on her technique. 'Lean into it and pull back. That's it. That's the way, girlie. Use your strength.'

And then he was surprised by her strength, rolled a fresh cigarette and gave her a round of applause. 'You'll do Gaffney. Knew you could.'

Steering them round the lake, Jeannie losing herself in the physical effort, the sound and smell and cool of the water. Bash humming a tune that had been on the radio that morning.

'This is the life eh? Getting in your stride now. Rowlocks to it, take us round again,' and she rowed around and around the boating lake as the day grew humid and cloudy. They landed on the weed-choked island at last, Jeannie's arms buzzing with the effort. There were more muscles to pull wrestling the ground elder, digging and stabbing and hacking and chopping. And then, of course, as the sky started to pink, she was rowing them back. They locked up the tools, set the prunings and rubbish ready for burning. Bash took the matches from the potting shed. Jeannie brewed coffee while they watched it burn into the evening.

'Is there nothing you can't do then Missus?' he puffed cigarette smoke into the air between them. Winked.

Bash had been edgy the following week. He'd sneaked more cigarettes than usual, disgusted with himself each time, pinching out the cigarette after a few desperate puffs. Jeannie had a feeling it was the same cigarette, it just got shorter by tiny degrees.

One afternoon she walked back from the tea rooms by the boating lake where she had taken her lunch. She was moving towards the greenhouses, ready to start pricking out the sunflower seedlings. There were big plans for an Arts Week event later in the summer, tying in with the art gallery and the museum. All the parks were going to participate. They'd drawn a Van Gogh theme. But as she turned she heard the gates creak, saw that Bash was locking them up.

'You. Now,' he said, moving past her. Businesslike. He was reaching deep into the sagging pocket of his jeans, pulling out a small key.

The path had an earthen smell baked by the speckling of sunlight that tried to poke its way through the thick canopy of elderflower and hawthorn. There was a soft heat in the air as she followed Bash down the incline. It turned slightly and for a moment he was lost to her sight. By the time she rounded the curve she could see he was at the door to another shed, turning another key in another padlock. But he waited for her by the door, didn't open it.

'Going to show you something. Something important.' His eyebrows raised up, earnest. He looked right into her face; then a brief glance over her shoulder as if he was anxious they might have been followed.

The heat inside the shed was sultry. The light was Mediterranean sunlight hot. Made you want to stretch naked. He'd got the lamps rigged up and wired into the connector that they used for the Christmas lights in the stone grotto behind the shed. The hothouse heaters kept the forest of marijuana in a state of lush greenness. Bash showed her what he was doing, how to tend the plants.

'Why are you showing me this, Bash?' Jeannie was uneasy. She didn't want to be part of a secret.

''Cause I reckon they're onto me on account of that gobby little shite.'

Jeannie felt a pang of guilt. It was her fault. For getting under Troy's skin. This was Troy's revenge. She'd tipped the balance again. Clumsy. Stupid.

'And 'cause I trust you. Which, believe me, is saying something,' he added. Jeannie said nothing, felt the spit dry in the back of her throat and knew it was nothing to do with the heat and the lamps and the claggy smell of the shed. I don't trust me, she thought.

Later Bash took a small paper bag from his inside pocket, rolled and lit a spliff and offered it to her. Jeannie didn't smoke, never had. It didn't smell appealing. It smelled fuggy and acrid. In the confines of the shed it began to make her head ache. The only effect it seemed to have on Bash was to make him smile like a dog dreaming. She felt so muzzy-headed later that Jeannie Gaffney hardly knew how she got home to the flat, only woke up, late in the night, as if she'd been asleep since she was seventeen and the forest and That Bloody Ryan Boy and Bash in the walled garden and the Secret Spliff Shed had all been a dream.

A month later. Jeannie was in the greenhouse deciding that she hadn't the heart to abandon the weaker sunflower seedlings. Bash had said she was to pick out the feeble and spindly ones and toss them onto the compost heap, but she just couldn't. All the seedlings had made the effort even if some were more energetic than others. She couldn't do it to them, not after all that hard work pushing up through the earth. Jeannie was going to plant the lot in the prepared bed they'd cut into the boring lawn that sprawled before Park Hall. She was loading the first few trays into the back of the trailer. She went back into the greenhouse for the next batch.

When she turned there was a man standing in the doorway. Not the neat-haired marijuana man of old. No. This man wore a suit under a sludgy green raincoat. A white shirt. This man had expertly shaved hair to disguise approaching baldness.

'Morning,' he said, authoritative. 'I'm looking for Colin Bash.' His voice rumbling, crisp and enunciated.

Like a Roman senator, perhaps. Or God.

Rosmarinus officinalis

rosemary

---

for remembrance

Nathan Flynn didn't announce straight out that he was a detective. However, there was something different about his demeanour that told her he wasn't here to pay Bash for his latest crop of marijuana.

'Do you know where he might be?' Again that voice. He was a block and tackle of a man, physically confident under his crisp white shirt and his clipped hair. Jeannie didn't bristle. She didn't quake. She continued potting on, just glancing at him, casual.

'He's not here at the minute. Want to...'

'Where is he if he isn't here?' His voice was interrogative but polite, as if he knew all the facts already and was just testing her.

'Somewhere else?' Jeannie volunteered. He took one step nearer, dug his hands deep into the pockets of his raincoat. Jeannie felt suddenly as if she had disappointed him somehow. She didn't like the feeling. She abandoned what she was doing and brushed off her hands against her trousers.

'Any more specific ideas?' he asked. She noticed that he

had a very direct and inescapable look. Jeannie found herself suddenly having to squint at him, the cloud cleared behind his head and the sunlight was suddenly glaring, like an anglepoise lamp pointed directly into her face.

'It's a big park. I think he was cutting back the rhododendrons in the maze walk. Want me to show you?'

For answer he stepped back, against the open potting shed door and swept his arm across himself like an usher, showing her the way.

So they walked towards the maze walk on the far side of Park House. Not that Bash was there. Jeannie knew for a fact that he'd vanished only half an hour or so before this detective had arrived and that he was probably, right at this moment, busy tending his crop. Hopefully, this little stroll to the maze would give Bash time to get back to the walled garden. She hoped he wasn't rolling himself a spliff and not thinking straight. If and when he got back he could brew coffee and when she returned with the detective he'd be on his own. There was no reason to give him away, to show the detective, 'Yes, certainly sir, he's in his marijuana shed at this very moment.'

But as she and the detective walked he seemed less interested in hearing about Col Bash and more interested in hearing about her. Questions. Questions. Of course, that was probably his investigative technique, find out what he needed to know, how dishonest she was, from what she might say about herself. In spite of herself Jeannie found herself talking easily to him.

'You ask a lot of questions,' she mentioned.

'Do I?' he asked.

It was the park, the outdoors smell, the creak of the swings. Or maybe it was the deep slate black and green of his eyes, their watchfulness, their carefulness. There was just something. Indefinable. Dangerous probably.

'Detective Constable Flynn by the way.' He introduced himself as they pulled down the hill towards the boating lake. He offered a hand, dredging it from the deep raincoat pockets. He had strong hands—gripped her as if he was saving her from drowning. Jeannie found it disconcerting that whenever she looked up he was looking right back at her. Didn't he blink? She stared at his eyes for a few moments as she waffled on about the fact that the rhododendrons were taking over. He didn't blink. It was like a competition.

And then they passed into the maze walk, finding green shade in the tunnel of arches, grown over with a hard-to-distinguish collection of climbers and climbing weeds. The maze walk branched off in different directions leading into a central woodland area. There was evidence that Bash had been there earlier—the tractor abandoned, an unattached trailer loaded ready with rhododendron clippings. The debris and detritus. Now she turned and stared once again into Detective Constable Flynn's eyes as he spoke. It was incredible, this unblinking.

'What's your name?'

Jeannie continued to stare at his eyes. Now, there was more, a twinkled look. Now, raised eyebrows as he waited for the answer.

'Rumpelstiltskin.' She couldn't believe the name came out of her mouth. Cheeky. Flip. She was doing her level best not to blink back now. And then he did it, a fleeting moment in which he crossed his eyes, jokey, just for a second. Jeannie gasped. The timbre of his voice did not alter as he said, straightforward, 'Got you, Jeannie Gaffney.'

Jeannie's eyes locked his, again the twinkled look, and

she saw his lips struggle against the forces of smiling. Those articulate eyebrows expressive and questioning. Furred brown caterpillars above his eyes.

'If you knew, why ask? Did you think I would lie?' she asked.

'Did you think you would?'

Jeannie thought she had learned her lesson with That Bloody Ryan Boy. She should stay out of the forest, shouldn't she? Keep to the walled garden. Because here she was again, in the green, feeling tempted.

Jeannie moved towards the tractor and started hitching up the trailer of cuttings. The keys were in, they could take it back.

'Want a lift?' she asked and Detective Constable Flynn nodded, climbed up beside her.

What if he hadn't? What if she had just shopped Bash that day? Where would Jeannie Gaffney be now? Happily married and running a garden centre, with a litter of children and a nice four-bed detached. Would Geraldine have played grandma on some well-kept back lawn? If stupid, thoughtless Jeannie Gaffney had got on that tractor and taken only the trailer of scraps back to the walled garden. If she'd never laid eyes on Detective Constable Flynn, what might have happened? But she didn't. And whatever might have been wasn't. And now it never can be.

She warned Bash.

'There was a detective looking for you. I don't think he was a customer but you'd know better,' she said. And she was surprised how much Bash paled at the news. Jeannie had assumed that if he was willing to run the risk of growing the stuff then surely he couldn't really have any qualms about it. Couldn't really be surprised that a detective might come sniffing around. She berated him later, slotted in behind the potting shed, in Troy's old spot, for chucking away the dog end of a cigarette into the leaf mould.

'I'm off,' she said, pulling on her jacket, her bag dangling off her shoulder. 'See you tomorrow?' and she couched it as a question on purpose. Bash only shrugged. Jeannie turned to go.

'Gaffney?' he took a long and desperate suck on a new cigarette as Jeannie looked back. 'Thanks.'

Detective Constable Flynn was waiting for Jeannie as she left the gates. His car was the only one parked on the small gravel stretch. He was leaning against it and waited for her to draw level with him before speaking.

'Can I repay the favour of the lift?' he asked. Jeannie shook her head.

'That's all right. No big favour. I happened to be going your way.' Jeannie kept walking towards Park Hall, passing the orangery now where the tea shop was, rounding the side of the house where the vista opened up, showing the city sprawled outside the hemmed-in greenery. The road, the bus stop just visible. Detective Constable Flynn locked his car up and followed.

'Police escort?' Jeannie asked keeping her voice calm and steady. He shrugged. His eyes unblinking again, asking to be looked into, demanding that she look right at him, as if there was something he wished her to see.

'I'm going your way.'

Jeannie felt again that she was disappointing him somehow. She shoved the thought aside. It was just a guilty conscience; she should say something about the marijuana crop, about the shed and the padlock. But actually, he hadn't asked.

'You know he's been in prison?' Detective Constable Flynn offered, kicking at an errant football as they skirted the top edge of the playing field. Jeannie did not avoid his gaze. Once again they were locked in a staring competition and she knew exactly what he was reading from her eyes even as she couldn't make anything out in his.

'I do now.'

In that moment he had changed her perception of Col Bash. In prison. For what? What crimes had he committed? She didn't think she wanted to know. Now who was disappointed? With herself mostly. Disappointed that she could let something like this spoil the way she thought about Bash. He was just Bash. Laidback. Kind. No questions asked. Did it matter?

'Theft. Burglary. Bit of credit card fraud.'

'Not a lot of opportunity for that in Parks and Gardens,' Jeannie replied. Detective Constable Flynn nodded agreement and checked his watch.

'I'm off duty as of ten seconds ago. Would you like to come out for a drink?' He didn't miss a step. Jeannie looked at him, then at the bus as it pulled up.

'My bus is here,' she said simply.

'Miss it,' he challenged her.

When the bus pulled away she looked back, saw he was still standing by the stone gateposts, still watching. He didn't wave. Then he turned and walked back up the hill towards his car.

The next morning Bash did not show up for work. The first thing Jeannie did, apart from start the coffee pot brewing as if nothing was amiss, was walk over to the padlocked gate and dirty up the padlock. By the time she'd finished, it looked as if it hadn't been used in years. There were a couple of the planks that they used for walking across the beds stretched across the path and Jeannie angled a couple in the doorway.

If you had stood in the potting shed that day, sipping hot coffee and asking Jeannie why she'd done this she would have said straight away, 'Elspeth Rideout'. She felt she had already unwittingly betrayed one person and she was not going to betray another. This time, she knew the secrets. It was not as if Bash had asked her help in burying a body under the asparagus beds. It was just some plants. It was none of her business. But Jeannie felt it had been made into her business on the day that she had walked into the walled garden and he had said simply, 'You all right?'

This is who Jeannie was. She couldn't cast things off.

Who am I kidding? This is who she was? This is who I am? I've tried casting it all off, I've tried and I feel like Atlas holding up the world. I can't take a step forward or I'll topple. She'll topple. My twin existence. If she goes, I know I go.

Nathan Flynn appeared daily for the rest of the month. Jeannie assumed he was dogged in his pursuit of Bash. He seemed to appear out of the air and there was always a slight twinkle in his eyes when she startled. Jeannie lost herself in her work. They were moving into peak season and the walled garden was beginning to burst with flowers and produce and Jeannie, true to her form, was tackling it all virtually single-handed. She instructed the college lads and sent them on their ways around the park. She was in every morning by six and never home before eight. Her own small plot at the back of her flat was overgrown and wild.

'It's like the Garden of Dorian Gray,' Ted Gaffney joked when he popped round one evening and, as they opened the French doors to sit with a cup of tea and let the summer air in, the tangled entwinement of ivy and honeysuckle and bindweed burst into the living room. Ted Gaffney propped it up on the top of Jeannie's stepladder. Later that evening as Geraldine arrived with lemon chicken and rocket salad and wine, they all took scissors and secateurs and cut back and pinned up and revealed a canopy of stars in the ink blue above. The fresh cut scents of earth and grass and sap perfumed the evening. Geraldine and Ted headed home very late.

Bash had not officially been seen around and Jeannie had heard the agricultural college lads chewing over the rumour that he'd skipped out of town altogether. Jeannie thought about his last crop damping off in the shed. She had the key. It had appeared one afternoon looped over a hook on the back of the door and Jeannie knew only Bash could have put it there. She put it into her pocket attached to her keychain. Was that what he wanted? Safekeeping? What might it mean if a criminal trusted you?

Jeannie found herself worrying that Bash might need the money from the last crop. What did criminals on the run do? How did they live? Perhaps even now he was brewing coffee in another potting shed in another town park.

At first, Nathan's time in the walled garden seemed to be taken with standing, hands in pockets, asking about her college days. Asking about her home life. Asking.

Jeannie felt hedged in at first, suspected his motives. He was a policeman. He wanted to get his man. But then he also appeared to want to get his hands dirty, squatting on his haunches to hand her bedding plants or bulbs. Holding the apex of a pyramid of bamboo canes, taking over the tying off if her fingers fumbled or cracked with mud.

She looked at his face in those moments, at the lines and curves. Tried to see what he might be. Looking away from the fact that what he wanted was her, that no petty criminal marijuana farmer was worth all these hours of investigation. It worried her, that she grew to miss him, to anticipate him, to want to see his eyes looking back at hers with their intelligence. She worried that she was seeing things from the wrong angle. That after all, he was a police officer. He thought that she was in league with Bash, that she might, at any moment have a slip of the trowel and tell him all.

There was nothing to tell. Except of course, the spliff shed was still there.

Jeannie had been down the path once to check on the crop. She realised that Bash had known exactly what he was doing in giving her custody of the key. He had known she couldn't stand by and let the plants die. This was a woman who couldn't prick out any seedling that had bothered to germinate. She watered and she tended and thought about Nathan Flynn, hands in pockets, half expecting him to materialise behind her, cuffs in hand.

After two months it was official that Col Bash was not coming back. Morag from the small cramped office at County Hall arrived. Her runabout car churned over the gravel and she reached her clunky briefcase, like a heavy leather brick, out of the hatchback boot. Jeannie saw her take out her purple flowered wellies. The boot of Morag's car was obsessively neat. A colour coded range of plastic crates organised everything.

Morag had come to ask Jeannie to take on Bash's responsibilities. She was displeased that Jeannie had used her initiative and gone ahead with all the tasks anyway. Morag had lots to say about her own failure to 'rehabilitate' someone like Bash. She was keen to point out that she hadn't been keen to take on an 'effing jailbird' in the first place. It was that woolly-headed twat in HR that liaised all the time with the halfway house people and the probation service.

'They couldn't wait to take him on. All because he got a silver gilt at Chelsea with some effing prison garden. Effing Chelsea my left eyeball.'

Jeannie didn't like Morag.

'I can't pay you for what you've been doing, you know that? There won't be back pay. I haven't the budgetary capacity.' Morag looked harassed. Jeannie didn't care about back pay. She cared that the park looked lush and jungly, that people were assailed on all sides by scent and flower. She cared that she'd put out bird feeders and people had sighted bullfinches and jays. She cared that she had coloured the park in. It was hers.

After Morag left Jeannie took a walk around her territory. She paced every section from the steeply hummocked rise housing the radio aerial tower in the north, winding down to the Farm Zoo and the cleared space where the ornamental birds had been and the new wildlife ponds were being dug out. Along Copper Beech Drive to the boating lake, around in a sweep through the dense trees towards the Folly, a huge archway in stone buttressed by carved satyrs. She had let it become just a little overgrown here and got some of the work experience lads to move the stone benches from in front of Park Hall. Then, back, up, up, up the long pull towards the walled garden in the East. To the potting shed. To the smell of fresh coffee, although that she hadn't left any boiling, and some of the strawberries.

To Col Bash, waiting with two mugs. He was looking thinner than usual and had the beginnings of a beard to balance out his newly shorn hair. He had waited to make certain she was alone before appearing. Who knows how long he had been hiding out in the outbuilding, biding time. Not a word. Just put the mug of coffee down on the countertop and picked up her keys.

Jeannie moved down to the spliff shed with him. The crop was wild, but still harvestable. Bash looked at her, his eyes almost teary with thanks. A nod.

'You. On your way.' He winked. Jeannie turned. She had some planting to do in the new wildlife ponds. She walked. Did not look back.

When she returned much later and much wetter, the padlocked gate stood wide open. The shed too was unlocked, all evidence of the plants removed and in its place a collection of broken wheelbarrows and old pots.

In the potting shed a week later she found the parcel of money in the pocket of her battered leather jerkin. She had felt in there for the KitKat she'd stowed there yesterday and instead her fingers touched the ribbon. A yellow ribbon, it turned out, from the Easter pots they'd done. She lifted the roll of money. There was a smudge of a thumbprint. The smudge of a memory. Bash that first day, muddied hands. *You'll do.*

It didn't seem to matter how late she was, Nathan Flynn managed to wait for her. His working hours were as erratic as her own but he tried to walk her to the bus stop each night. Once as the 8.35 evening bus pulled away she caught sight of him in his car drawing up at the park gates. Another evening he was asleep in his car and she waited for him to wake, finishing the last of the small tidy-up jobs, until she dropped the secateurs and he was there to pick them up. Another occasion she saw him again from the bus. Running, too late, down the hill towards the stop.

One morning she arrived at six a.m. She had walked from town in the clean early sunshine with a bag of almond croissants from the French patisserie. She had been thinking about Nathan, about a dream she'd had. She'd been, as ever, naked in the walled garden. She pushed open the gate but this time when she fell Nathan Flynn caught her. He caught her and she woke as she landed in his arms.

She was startled now to see his car parked by the gates. He was inside it, sleeping again. The driver's seat tipped backwards, his raincoat pulled around him. Jeannie opened the gates, brewed coffee in Col Bash's old pot. Put the croissants in the heated propagator. Later they ate together, saying nothing.

Those were the days when the local news rechristened the town Dodge City, when two rival gangs of drug dealers started killing each other in the shopping precinct and at the supermarket and at the nightclub in the High Street. You could find yourself walking along the pavement thinking about a loaf of bread or whether you needed milk, and you might not even notice the heavy brown bloodstain on the paving stone.

It was as if Nathan existed in a parallel universe of guts and bullets. Once night fell all the monsters came out and Nathan and his colleagues had to wrangle them. In a world lit by electric bulbs he stepped over gunshot corpses, and questioned men perfumed with drugs and lapdancers and vomit.

Nathan was first on the scene for two of the three major murders. A head spiked onto the railings outside a councillor's expensive home. The councillor implicated in the drug running. Everything Nathan saw was on a spiral downwards and he could trust nothing. Except, apparently, some quiet gardening woman with a dirt-besmirched face who waited for him in the walled garden at Cromwell Park.

You can think back and see that the shadow was the reality. You can think back because now you are skewed too and see the differing angle. But then, then he seemed like a knight, armoured and brave and worth something. But Knights crave battle. Armour shiny. Sword sharp.

It was not so much a courtship, more a wearing down. Nathan was always going to have her. He had decided that long ago. There were secrets he kept from her even as she felt he was revealing everything. She thought she was his refuge. She was aware that when the day had been harsh he could come through the gates to the walled garden and he could breathe again.

She thought she could ask at first, thought that he might need to talk. He shook his head. He needed, he said, to slough off the dirtied skin. So she handed him the small piece of pumice she kept by the sink.

'Who do you think I am?' he said, reaching for the soap, slicking his hands around and around so that he looked as if he was wearing white lace gloves. Jeannie watched him for a moment. Wondered what answer he was looking for.

'Good guy? Bad guy?' He held her gaze. Jeannie did not look away. Did not want to look away from that face ever.

'I think you're Nathan Flynn.' And threw him the towel.

Then work would mean he had to stay away for a couple of days. On his return he would seem more battered than before. If this was a fairytale, and at the time it seemed that way to Jeannie, then he was off battling dragons daily, and he came back to her scorched.

She remembered the first day that she missed him and the jolt of surprise, of desire two days later when he arrived at the walled garden mid-morning. She knocked into the potting table and sent a leaning tower of terracotta plant pots shattering across the paved patio. She saw his face react.

Jeannie made coffee and he stood in the doorway. Asking questions. This is your territory isn't it? You enjoy what you do? Jeannie had come to realise that he took in details, even the smallest small talk was logged into his memory. He took notice. He gave her security advice for the tool shed and the equipment. Talked about the bouts of car thefts the park suffered from. Just recently the carpark nearest the golf driving range had been targeted. Nathan had used it as an excuse, as if he was only here for the car thieves. Windows were smashed, petty items taken. Gloves. CDs. A muddy pair of hiking boots. An umbrella. But they reckoned without Nathan and his detailed mind.

The day he apprehended the teenage car thieves and handcuffed them to the castle in the adventure play area Jeannie felt flustered and wild. What she wouldn't give for this man to handcuff her to the castle. He would have to keep his raincoat on. His shirt buttoned up. His white, white, white shirt.

He made her feel that she was what he needed from the world. Each day he would move away from the dark world of work towards the place where Jeannie was. The place of sunshine and plants. Things living and being nurtured. Jeannie found her days being regulated by whether or not she saw him, by whether or not she was thinking about him. It was like hypnosis. He insinuated himself into her landscape so that after a while she forgot the time before Nathan. If his car wasn't parked outside the wall on the gravel it felt as jarring to Jeannie as if someone had cut a tree down.

They had been talking about the boats on the lake. She was moving out of the confines of the shed towards the pear trees. She'd picked up her string and her secateurs, took the three steps to the doorway. He blocked the doorway. A brief standoff moment in which he could probably echolocate her heartbeat, feel the sound of it vibrating through the air. She didn't back off. Jeannie stood as close as she dared, the blade of her secateurs glinted in the afternoon light, tilted and glittered across his face, like a shooting star. It seemed like a test. She tilted her head upwards. His hand reached for her, his thumbs tilting her chin. His eyes, taking in every detail of her face, then, his mouth on hers. Time stopped for a moment. All the birds silent, beaks open in the tops of trees.

At the bottom of the hill he stood closer than before. Her arm brushed against that white shirt as she moved past him, as he opened the gate for her, ushered her through, the bus chugging towards them, brakes hissing.

'This is my bus,' Jeannie said, as she had said many nights before. Only this Wednesday was different. It was past nine-thirty in the evening. The light around them was purplish and warm as the sun set. The sky seemed inflated with the heat as if it was stretching lazily outwards after a hard day. Summery clothes and white cars seemed to shimmer around them. Nathan was wearing a crisp white shirt and it was cooling to look at it. Jeannie felt the day's grime and sweat at the roots of her hair, felt the skin of her hands, dry and papery. Wanted to lean against that shirt's smoothness. Lean against him.

'This is my bus,' she said. Now she thought that he might not say it. He might not cast the spell this time, because she had cast it off so many times before. The bus doors hissed open. Hot and bothered.

'Miss it.'

Canada geese flew above them, an arrowhead, she remembered. Jeannie and Nathan walking, his hand, resting in the small of her back. Up the hill. Together.

Lunaria annua

honesty

---

repelling monsters

It was a slow-burning fuse that he lit. Nathan let you know what was on his mind. He didn't care if he shocked you or upset you, there were things you needed to know, things he needed to know.

'Your mum ran off. What was that about?'

Or when she asked about him, 'You don't want to know, not the details. My dad's a turd. Curled and brown. Waste of space.'

Or: 'You ever think the lowlifes and the shitfaces are winning?'

He said this one afternoon, as matter of fact as if he'd asked what she thought the weather was turning to. And later, helping himself to more coffee, rooting out the tin he knew contained biscuits, 'Look at this fucking place Jeannie. Fucking wasteland before you got here. Fucking Bash growing his hash and what the hell. Those fucking bizzie-lizzies in all the colours of some Seventies fucking rainbow. Look at it Jeannie. Fucking look around. You've made this place. You.'

Kissing her. Knotting his hands into her hair as if she was

a lifeline. Hugging her to him until she thought a vertebra would snap. He always swore more when the day was hard. She could only guess at what he was involved with. Only the previous week someone had shot a traffic officer who'd pulled them over for a faulty brake light. The morning's paper had been full of a local stabbing, the victim bleeding all over the front pages even before they had been wheeled from the scene on the ambulance gurney.

The air ambulance helicopter hovering over town. Jeannie had been in the garden with Geraldine watching it yaw and tack over the back gardens before landing on the other side of the dual carriageway, fusing the traffic into a metallic spine through town. Dad calling on his mobile from the middle of it. Drivers getting out and the rumours seeping quickly. The air ambulance was down but not going back up, therefore whoever it had been summoned to help was beyond it. At first the rumour was that it was an accident, some hideous nudge-and-shunt catastrophe but by seven o'clock everyone knew. Someone was out there. A murderer. Someone being pursued.

That evening Nathan waited for her. But instead of walking to the bus Jeannie moved to the car, put her hand on the passenger door handle. It was locked. There was a moment of eye contact and then Nathan chachunked the door. The car unlocked, Nathan moving towards her, opening the door.

They didn't get home. Instead he drove them to the farthest, wildest part of the nature reserve. To the Watch-tower bird hide. In the reeds. By the lake. With only the distant trundle of traffic to remind them of reality.

Clues. He gave you the clues Jeannie. You just didn't know there was a crime.

He hid the dark-circled side of himself from others. In

company he was always hail-fellow-well-met. Everyone knew you could ask Nathan. Nathan'll do it. Be up for it. Help out with it.

It reminded Jeannie of her old, school self. Nathan's strong smile would stretch across his face, his hand out ready to grasp yours. Smiling as if this time he was Miss World. He remembered names. He recalled the details. He surprised and impressed. Jeannie loved him. Wanted to be with him for all the days that God sent. To be the beacon calling him home at the end of a hard day with the lowlifes.

Geraldine approved of him from the first moment she opened the front door to him.

If only. If Jeannie could ravel time she'd barricade the door. Nail boards across it. Duct-tape Geraldine to a chair. Give Nathan the wrong address so that he would never arrive. But he was handsome and kind and beloved and so they let him in. You assume that a bell tolling doom will have a sonorous quality, it will be vast and cast in bronze by the bastards of the gods at least. It will be patinaed and cold. You don't think it plays Westminster Chimes or Friesland.

Most people knew Nathan. He'd done the road safety talks at the schools before he became a detective. He was a local man. A community man. He was on the Buzzards rugby team.

They were known as the Bastards, unofficially. Big. Tall. Bruised. Battered. Boozy. Jeannie didn't feel at home at the club but then, she reasoned, she wasn't supposed to. They ran gentlemen's smoking evenings, not needlework nights. Nathan's job was stressful and he needed to let off steam.

Jeannie showed her face when she had to. She noticed that the marriages fell like dominoes and girlfriends were interchangeable. It was smoky and rank. Not even a few hundred thousand pounds of refurbishment the previous summer could rid the clubhouse complex of the underlying aroma of sweating testicles and picked-at athletes' feet.

It was their anniversary. A year since the day they had met. Nathan remembered. It coincided with the Bastards club dinner. Nathan had said they would show their faces and then leave. But that wasn't possible where the Bastards were concerned. One drink led to another and then Nathan was presented with The Players' Player award and they just had to stay. Jeannie watched them worship him. Loud singing, beer after beer after beer. Jeannie considered that he was, as they put it, The Bastard in Chief. They didn't see him, she thought. Only she had that privilege.

'Five minutes more,' he said, kissing her. 'Five more. I just have to catch Jez and we're free.'

More kisses and then she was abandoned. After a wave of jealous women and their fake congratulations that she, of all of them, was with the Chief Bastard, the Grand High Bastard of Bastards, after their fake smiles, their air hugs and air kisses, faint and insubstantial as the cigarette smoke that smarted in her eyes—after them, the land mass that was Liam.

Liam. A dark-haired man, six feet five tall and almost as square, he positioned himself like a brick wall in front of her. He had a way of leaning down to try and hear what she was saying over the loud music and in the leaning down he kept trying to snatch a kiss. His breath hot and herbal from the bitter he was drinking and Jeannie found herself squirming away, trapped. Jeannie couldn't see Nathan in the crowd at the bar, in fact she couldn't see daylight beyond the looming figure of Liam. He brushed a meaty hand across his shaved scalp. There was a pale moon of a scar that she noticed above his forehead. A patch of sweat on the armpit of his shirt wafted out a harsh soapy masculine smell. The moment when, in pressing forwards to let someone squeeze past them his hand reached up, taking his chance in the confusion to squeeze at her breast. Jeannie pulling herself away, Liam not budging. Laughing into his beer. Jeannie excused herself. Endured a brief dance of thisway-thatway as Liam blocked her this step, that step. In the end he was jogged from behind and his beer sprawled all over her. Soaked, she took her chance with the gap created as Liam turned on his beer wrecker. Jeannie took refuge in the toilets.

She splashed her face with water, dotted at the dampness with a paper towel. As she opened her eyes Liam closed in behind her. Hands clamped around her hips, pushing and lifting her skirt as he manhandled her towards a cubicle. Jeannie fought back, grazing herself against the surface of him and then Liam seemed to lift into the air, blood fountained from his lips. His teeth fell like stones and a deep animal groan, like a stag rutting, blew out of him. The metallic partition walls around her trembled and blattered. A cistern smashed. Water flooded out. Cold. Soaking into her clothes. Nathan sodden and angry stepping over Liam as he stooped to her, peeling off his jacket and wrapping her inside it. The soap and grass smell of him seemed to cover her, seal her into safety again. His face close to hers as he knelt to pick her up.

They left like thieves. One of the girlfriends, someone redhaired who'd come in with Liam was hanging around in the corridor. Nathan swept by her, putting himself between her eyes and Jeannie's prone form.

'Fuck off,' he snarled at the woman and Jeannie saw her smile.

Nathan putting Jeannie gently into his car, chunking her seatbelt. His face set hard as he sat in the driving seat, turned the key.

In the darkness they drove. Later, in her kitchen her hands shook as she reached for the tea caddy. He touched her hands with his hands. Then with his kisses. Jeannie Gaffney thought she knew what love was.

She did. Don't short-change Jeannie on this one. She loved him. It's such a short word and so overused it has become like 'nice' and 'fine'. There needs to be a new word, something Jeannie could use to describe what she felt for Nathan Flynn. Because what she felt was unique to her, for him. Don't deny her that.

Nathan had come to help collect the fruit trees from the Hanging Gardens of Barbara. It was the independent garden centre that clung to the side of a steep hill on the edge of town and Barbara had spent years terracing it. Years when she was an apprentice to Mr Rigger and years after he sold her the business. As a teenager Jeannie had had a Saturday job there for a while until exams and Sean Ryan distracted her.

When she was a child Jeannie and her dad had come here often, for plants, for the company. Sometimes for a sandwich in the small coffee shop, run by the sour Irene. The coffee shop sat in a shed at the bottom-most terrace. There was a steep drop towards the gardens of the bungalows littered below. Barbara had screened it off with berberis and white-wash bramble. You could sit for hours on a bench and look the length and breadth of the valley, see the whole town spread out before you. Jeannie had liked to watch thunderstorms from there as Irene crouched in the coffee shop shed sucking on one of her eternal cigarettes warning, 'You'll get struck sat out there.'

Barbara greeted Nathan with a kiss. In his earlier days as a uniformed officer, he'd dealt with a spate of robberies at the nursery and at her home. Petty theft and some vandalism. Barbara had come to rely on the quiet, serious young officer. That was when Barbara's hair turned white. She'd been bothered by it at first, she was only in her forties, but somehow the white looked better than the vanished sleekness of black. The whiteness of her hair made her face stand out.

Jeannie loved that face. Barbara was what is called a handsome woman. Strong featured, she had what Jeannie's mum had called 'bone structure'.

Now Barbara mentioned that she'd been to Cromwell Park and seen Jeannie's work. In Barbara's opinion the place had never looked so well tended. Jeannie was pleased and Nathan gave a wry smile.

'Couldn't send Morag a written testimonial could you?' he asked. Lovely Morag with her wellies and organisation, unwilling to promote Jeannie.

'I'd have thought you'd want to be your own boss Jeannie?' Barbara remarked and then they were distracted trying to fit the fruit trees through Nathan's sun roof. Later, over a pot of tea, Barbara said she'd thought of retiring, but wanted to pass the nursery on to someone who would really care.

'Not that bastard from the estate agents' who keeps bargaining for the developer and showing me artists' impressions of the block of bloody flats they'd like to build.' As Barbara spoke, Jeannie caught Nathan's meaning look but said nothing.

'Hint, hint,' he joked on the way home, and Jeannie laughed. Barbara had just been talking, mulling things over.

'Besides. I've got a job.'

Morag looked flustered the next time Jeannie met with her and she couldn't seem to meet her eye. Then, as they checked out the new arched bridge that crossed over the wildlife pond she blurted it out.

'I might be in a position to officially offer you the job proper. I might be. In about a month. They want to get Britain in Bloom out of the way.' Morag spoke quickly, embarrassed.

'The job proper?' Jeannie asked. 'Which job?'

Morag looked harsh.

'You know which job. Bash's job. In fact, above Bash's job. They need someone to take on Watersfoot Gardens and the Scented Arbor Gardens too. There've been meetings. Your name cropped up.'

'Oh.'

Morag looked infuriated.

'You know, it hasn't been anything personal. I wasn't denying you anything. But I have budgets. I have to manage things. Everything.'

A month later Jeannie found that Morag had chiefly been managing her younger brother's graduation from the Horticultural College. He was being groomed for greatness by Morag and Mr Mathieson. They were going to place him at the centre of Parks and Gardens and Jeannie had just been a stopgap.

Jeannie arrived for work one morning to find Morag and Menzies already in the potting shed. He was a smiling young man, full of confidence and bonhomie. Morag introduced him as Bash's replacement, Jeannie's new boss and Jeannie knew, as she shook his hand, that this was goodbye. Goodbye, despite a beautifully rehearsed 'thank you for all you have done here' speech from Morag and the hastily wrapped presentation of a top quality gardener's trowel and leather gauntlets.

*

'You did what?' Jeannie stopped peeling carrots. Nathan was leaning against the worktop opening the wine.

'Got a couple of mates in traffic to stop her car.' He kissed Jeannie as he leaned to fill their glasses.

Morag whipped by an autumn wind on the side of the dual carriageway as Nathan's colleagues had checked out her tyres, her brake lights, oil pressure, tyre pressure, windscreen wipers, paint job, anything and everything they could think of and requested her documents be presented at the police station within seven days.

'Just ruffled her feathers.'

'Ruffled her…? Why would you do that?'

'Do what? A couple of safety checks. Nothing serious. Barry was all for frisking her. Few of them were on for a full body search. I nearly had to draw straws.'

Jeannie looked at his face, at his eyes, the left one winked at her.

'Didn't you want revenge?'

Jeannie admitted she hadn't thought about it. Nathan leaned in, kissed her.

'I did.'

He chinked her glass.

'Anyway. Fuck Morag. You should buy the Hanging Gardens. Barbara dropped enough hints.'

Jeannie felt her face crease into a wry smile. She had caught the hints. They had fired up her imagination. She'd been back over at the Hanging Gardens yesterday, walked that way home instead of catching the bus. Had needed time to think. Away from Morag and the shed and the walled garden. He was right. Barbara had talked about succession and passion then too. Had in fact sought her out as she sat at a coffee shed table looking out across town. Jeannie deep in thought, thinking that the area covered by Cromwell Park seemed greener than anywhere, that birds seemed to flock and fly and hover towards that green patch in the near distance.

'There are two things you should do, Jeannie.' Nathan poured wine. Did his hand shake? Jeannie thought she saw his hand tremble, clinking the bottle against the glass. 'One. Buy the Hanging Gardens. Agreed?'

He handed her the wine glass, his eyebrows raised, waiting for her agreement. She nodded. Chinked her glass against his.

'Two.' Nathan leaned in close, not touching her, just whispered the words. 'Marry me.'

He looked at her. Jeannie felt all her breath stop.

'Agreed?'

There was just a waver in his confidence. She saw it cross the green of his eyes, like the shadow of a bird on grass.

Cirsium vulgare

spear thistle

---

the swords of sharpened leaves offer both protection and evil

Mr Ted Gaffney was businesslike in his offer of a 0% loan to assist his daughter, Miss Jeannie Gaffney, to purchase the Hanging Gardens nursery and garden centre. Jeannie felt reluctant, greedy even, until Geraldine took her aside.

'It's the money he meant for when you headed off to uni. Take it. He can be a sleeping partner. Take it, Jeannie. It's given.'

As Jeannie worked alongside Barbara settling into her new business, several afternoons found Jeannie and Geraldine venturing out in search of the perfect dress. Jeannie was delighted to get to know Geraldine, to find out how much they had in common, their taste, their sense of humour about the pom-pom and frou-frou bridal creations. She was glad to see Geraldine's face as she turned in at the path.

Finally the veils billowed like overblown candy floss, tiaras glittered too brightly in twinkling cabinets in wedding-shop windows. Cinderella seemed to have left all of her pairs of glass slippers and the twelve dancing princesses could have stocked up for life on the silk-bowed footwear. Boots laced with ribbons. Pinpoint glass-effect heels.

Jeannie zipped and slid and sucked herself into everything the flurry of saleswomen could muster. Then she pulled herself into her sagging jacket and sat in a coffee shop with Geraldine. Nothing felt right. She did not want to get married looking like a meringue or a waterlily. She was beginning to feel uneasy. She was beginning to think too much.

'None of them spoke to you. Well, unless you count "yuk".' Geraldine munched on a chocolate chunk shortbread, her glasses hanging on a leather thong around her neck. 'Where's your fairy godmother when you need her?'

Jeannie smiled, thinking that Geraldine was a fairy godmother. Thinking, *why didn't she get here sooner, when he was younger?* as Geraldine blew at the froth on her latte and drank deeply. Then half spluttered, 'I know where she is. Christ, of COURSE I do…'

And Jeannie found herself in Arbuckle's Vintage Vault wearing a gown of bronze velvet Fortuny pleats and kid button boots in a rich chocolatey leather. Geraldine and the proprietress sorted through boxes of hats to find The One, and find it they did, complete with gossamer cobweb veil. Jeannie looked at her reflection and wondered why she didn't always dress like this.

It was Geraldine's Pilates night and Nathan was on a late turn. Since things were so busy at the Hanging Gardens, Ted Gaffney and his daughter had arranged a spaghetti bolognese evening. Dad left the ragu simmering and picked her up from the nursery, helped her with the tidying and tilling up, mentioned a few other jobs he could turn his hand to as only dads can. In the end he gerrymandered a few fence panels that screened the composting area from the perennials terrace and discovered a puncture in a wheelbarrow tyre.

It was a mild evening, the light hanging around in the sky reluctant to leave. They ate sitting outside at the wooden table that Geraldine had persuaded him to buy. Jeannie thought suddenly how she had missed her dad's cooking. There was some special ingredient that she never could quite place. Dad said it was nutmeg and bay, and pork as well as beef. But whenever Jeannie made the dish it never seemed to quite follow his recipe. That night she realised the essential ingredient had been dadness, his hand on the wooden spoon, stirring.

Later, they played the piano, Dad pulling up the dining chair. They had spent many years since Jeannie had learned to sight-read trying to perfect 'The Arrival of the Queen of Sheba' and it had always proved fiendishly difficult. This, Jeannie knew, was partly due to her habit of giggling and laughing when her hands couldn't keep up with what her fingers were doing. They tangled and knotted before her and still the music came until, at last the connection was broken and the fingers untangled and slid off the keys and she was lost in laughter. Dad, raising a comic eyebrow, more laughter.

That night, a week before the wedding, there was no laughter, no eyebrow, no tangled fingers. The Queen of Sheba finally arrived. Note perfect. When they had finished they both sat in silence, could only look at the stilled black insects of the sheet music.

Ted Gaffney reached forward then and closed the book and said, with a wry smile, 'It is a rite of passage.'

Jeannie had met Nathan's father, Ray, on a few occasions. Nathan found Ray hard work and Ray found Nathan a challenge, so it was not expected that they'd spend much time visiting. Nathan's father looked to Jeannie as if he was made of plastic, his face stretched and shiny and highly coloured. His hair was so darkly black it looked painted. He smoked rank, stunted cigars and lived with a woman much younger than himself.

On the first occasion that they met at his home, the woman was Linda, a heavy-busted blonde lady of about forty who was a manageress in a local discount store. But a few weeks later when Jeannie and Nathan met up with Nathan's father at a rugby club party, the woman on his arm was a tiny thirty-year-old red-head called Shannon who owned a nail bar in the centre of town.

When Ray showed up at the Hanging Gardens asking for a family discount he was with Linda and gave Jeannie a heavy wink. Later, as Linda ordered coffees on the terrace, Ray admitted he had both women 'on the go' and mentioned a gentleman's agreement. 'A man must have his pleasures, Jeannie.' Jeannie did not want to think about what Ray's pleasures might be. And then as Ray talked to her, she became unsure what he wanted. Her silence or her participation? He was what Geraldine would call touchy-feely, his hand often glancing across her bottom as they walked back to the checkout.

She didn't like Ray much. When he asked if she could help him out with a bit of landscaping Jeannie wanted to say no. Nathan said it for her, later that evening, shouting down the phone, very loud, very clear, when he found out about his father's request.

No. And she doesn't want to see your bastard etchings either.

Just before the wedding Nathan's colleagues in uniform were called out to a fight in a pub which turned out to be Linda and Shannon battling it out for Ray's favours. It was like a scene from a porno western, one colleague had joked, with half-naked saloon girls, tits out, scrapping on the beer-soaked carpet for the cigar-smoking sheriff.

It hurt and embarrassed Nathan, made him surly and grumpy. Jeannie couldn't put it right. She tried talking and she tried bed but nothing worked for a few days. A couple of mornings he left for work without even looking at her. They had had tiffs and rumbles before but this was the biggest, the gloomiest. Jeannie felt closer to him in a way, almost pleased that he could reveal himself. He didn't have to hide now, they were together. But she did notice he tired very quickly if she felt out of sorts or crossed him in any way.

She was at the Hanging Gardens and it had been a busy day. Now the rush was off and she was going over a new land-scape display. She had been digging the bed over and leaned, sweating, on her spade. Suddenly Nathan was there behind her. She turned to him, his face blocked out by the sun behind his head. He didn't say a word. He picked her up, put her over his shoulder and strode down to the new display of summerhouses, a new line they were going to sell with lead-lined minaret style roofs. He chose the farthest one. Shut the door. He looked at her, intense. Jeannie didn't even blink. She reached around him and turned the ornate key.

Pulled the blinds. No words. Just a taking off of clothes. And as Jeannie straddled him it felt as if her body opened up and she moved into another place, as if the sky peeled back to reveal the blue of midnight and thousands upon thousands of stars burning pinpoints in the universe

And then Debbie, outside, tapping on the door. 'Everything all right in there?' in a quiet voice and further away the two lads from the college laughing and saying, 'Leave it Debs. For Christ's sake…Leave it…At it…'

They lay together then on the cushions from the wicker chairs. Jeannie inhaled the scent of linseed and newly sawed wood and Nathan's sweat and thought there was nothing in the world except being with him.

At the wedding, after a beautiful ceremony and Geraldine laughing because she looked like a panda with her mascara all over her face, Ray approached Jeannie. He had bided his time, waiting until Nathan was busy with the best man, sorting out some telegrams and bouquets.

'You made it then.' Ray took the cigar out of his mouth for just a moment. Flicked ash into a half-drunk cup of coffee on the nearby table. Jeannie looked directly at him, into his eyes, a hard wooden brown. She saw an evil glint. It was forthright—it almost had a little sign attached: *evil glint*. She had never seen evil before. Never thought to make a note of it since she didn't plan on seeing it again.

'Last one didn't.' He puffed at the cigar again, inhaled, let the smoke channel out through his nose so that now he looked like a fire-breathing demon in a hired morning suit. Jeannie felt herself flush and Ray made an annoying sigh of sympathy.

'Didn't let you know about her then, did he not?' A tutting sound. A conspiratorial wink.

'Have you had enough to drink?' Jeannie asked, wanting to be mean back and yet also wanting to be polite. 'I'm sure we can find you some lighter fuel or some meths.'

Ray's evil eyes flamed with delight. 'Get to know me Jeannie. You'd like me.' He took her hand, held it vice-like. Jeannie felt herself resist. He kissed her hand. 'Me and Nathan, stallions from the same stable.'

Jeannie stopped resisting. Just get this done with. She didn't smile and she didn't lower her gaze. Ray pulled her towards him. Moved in for a cigar-scented kiss, the shiny plastic of his face brushing against hers. He whispered.

'Best of luck girlie.'

And Jeannie was about to smile and be gracious but he halted her as he squeezed her left buttock and said, 'You'll fucking need it.'

Time spins now. Like one of those gyroscopes. At first it flows smoothly around and around itself and then, you can't see the exact second that it changes, but it begins to slow, it begins to lose momentum. It tips. It falters.

'Christ in pinstripe pyjamas why is there never any fucking JUICE.' He was rootling around in the fridge, standing with the door wide open. Jeannie was trying to move around him, her arm sliding around his waist.

She leaned up to him to plant a kiss. 'There's orange juice. They didn't have any fucking juice.' She kept her voice light, jokey. There was orange juice, in a carton on the top shelf. She could see it, until he wheeled around, grasped her wrists, yanked her towards him, slamming her into his body.

'I'm sorry?' he demanded, 'I'm SORRY?'

Jeannie's mouth babbled and he whiplashed her away from him, she knocked her hip against the opposite worktop, stumbled, caught her cheekbone on the open fridge door.

'Watch the fucking fridge door,' he snarled, his hand shooting out, the palm smacking her square in the face. The other hand slamming the fridge door so that all the magnets and messages fell.

She thought it was because he had worked very hard and not been promoted to detective sergeant. She thought it was because they had chosen to promote Barry above him. She thought it was better not to think about why. She thought it was better to be quiet and wait this one out.

'I'm making coffee. Want one?' he was saying, as if nothing had happened. The magnets and messages back in their places. After a few hours, she knew, it would seem that she had dreamed it.

A year and a half they had been married and somehow it seemed. Well. Longer. The business was doing well. They seemed to be doing well. He phoned her all the time and at first it seemed romantic. It seemed he reached out that way. His voice small and sorry. But after a while Jeannie knew. It just wasn't. He was keeping watch.

No was his answer for everything. If she mentioned a birthday evening out with the horticulture students, a leaving do, an engagement party it was No. Or a more subtle version.

'You? And a bunch of teenage students? You'll look like their mum.'

She drifted into a state where if she had the day off she didn't know what to do with it. He wouldn't approve. He wouldn't let her.

Whenever his work allowed he could be found at the Hanging Gardens. *No. Don't.* Watching her. *No. I wouldn't.* Waiting for her. *No. You don't really want to do that?* Taking her home. *No. Not really you is it?* He was charm. *No.* He was love. *No.* They all thought how lucky she was. *No.* He was so gorgeous. *No.* So attentive. *No.* Jeannie thought she was dreaming. *No.* She was mad. *No.* She was unfair. *No.*

It was an illusion and she couldn't see the mechanics. How had it begun? Just a few well-chosen words? Stupid. Bitch. Neurotic. Stupid. Neurotic. Bitch. Like a mantra. Had it begun with him taking the car keys from her? 'I'll drive,' and 'Give me the keys then.' The big hand, the beckoning gesture. It was hypnotism.

Stupid.Give.Bitch.Keys.Stupid.Give.Bitch. Stupid. Give. Stupid. Neurotic. *You stupid fucking neurotic bitch, give me the keys now.*

She couldn't seem to change a lightbulb. Stupid. She began to lose confidence in everyday abilities. Bitch. She began to draw boundaries around herself, wary of the things that might set him off, upset his mood. Stupid fucking neurotic bitch.

He spat the food at her. Surely he did, she had felt it spatter into her face, could even see the mark on her top where the sauce had stained. And yet, had he? Suddenly the kitchen was cleared. No plates. No sauce. And weren't they on the sofa now, his hand down her jumper tuning her nipples to Radio Sex? His hand unzipping his fly, putting her hand inside his jeans.

Jeannie was accommodating, polite at best and cowardly at worst. She couldn't look back from where she was at any given time—opening the gates at the delivery bay for a huge bulb lorry from Belgium—and see exactly what had happened. It just seemed that now she had to ask for permission. Even buying fish in the supermarket was starting to take on hidden danger.

'I'm not eating this.' Like a hairy, petulant child. A look of revulsion. Of a man being fed poison. 'Full of fucking bones.'

The plate shoved away as if it contained toxic waste. It seemed that Jeannie's cooking skills had been a delusion. Since her marriage she'd served Nathan a diet of 'shit' and 'slop', from fricasee to what-the-fuck-is-that. It became a strain to glide her trolley through the supermarket doors. The bright commercial lights glared at her and she seemed to spend hours indecisive over pork steaks or chicken fillets.

The honeymoon was over. Well, of course it was, Jeannie

thought to herself. Life is not a honeymoon. No. But what was this?

Work. That was her theory. His job was hard and stressful and he didn't talk about it. When she had tried early on in their relationship he had said he didn't want to.

'Just what I want when I get home. To relive the fucking episode.' His voice low, snarling at the edges. What he wanted when he got home was exactly that, to be home. Safe. Sound. Shut up.

Later. After not speaking. He stood in the kitchen doorway. Tell me about your day, Jeannie. Here, let me help you with the washing, as he took off her clothes.

What she wanted at first was to try to joke about it. But it wasn't a joke, jokes made it worse. Made the first plate smash. That white plate spinning in orbit through the room, towards the back door. There was a serene magic about it, somehow, as she felt it slice past her head, barely brushing her hair, spinning and spinning, the chicken forestiere and potatoes anna, the carrots vichy, all travelling through space and time. She had to wash out the doormat. Even now on damp days it smelled of mushrooms and red wine.

What did I do? When did I do it? If I could just find out. It was as if someone had been there ahead of her and turned all the road signs around. Jeannie quizzed herself instead of sleeping. Each night that week there were more plates until there were no more plates—'And whose fault is that? I'm sorry?'

On her knees. Down. On her knees.

When he was pleased or sated her head was flummoxed with a terrible euphoria. Then a screeching panic that she couldn't remember *exactly* how she had cooked the steak or what particular variety of potatoes she had cut into chips.

But she could remember the bedroom. The territory where she tried to make it all up to him. In the bedroom. Or on the table. Or in the shed at the bottom of the garden. They could be together. She could reach him there. She was greedy for him. Jeannie wanted to be naked with Nathan, to be astride him or feel his tongue trail over her nipples. She wanted to be queen of all the women whose buttocks his hands had squeezed at. She loved him. She took him inside her, inside her mouth. Tried to claim him. Do anything, that was what she wanted. To him. With him. For him.

If he was moody that had to be worked with. This was what being married was about. It wasn't about hearts and flowers, it was working together. She was his partner. He had a need for her to be there. She thought of what he saw at work, the mess and disaster he was trailing after, picking up everyone's pieces. He needed her. If he didn't speak to her for three days he had a reason. He was burning it all up inside and when he was ready he would be back. And she would be waiting. With opened legs.

Until.

She was with Debs, tilling up for the day. Nathan arrived unannounced.

'Let Debs do that.' A handsome, strong wink at Debs. Jeannie nodded and tried to finish counting. He simply lifted her onto his shoulder.

'Me Tarzan, you Jeannie.' And he slapped her arse, his face mocking lust. Even Irene from the coffee shop stopped puffing on her fag for five minutes.

'Where can I get me one like that?' she growled, disgruntled, as Nathan carried Jeannie out through the greenhouse to the carpark. At the back. Out of sight.

Where no one saw him putting her into the boot of his car.

He drove to the nature reserve. She could hear bottles clinking and then he opened the boot. Stood over her with a glass of wine. She wasn't sure about this, was it going to be thrown in her face?

'Take them off.' He sipped at the wine, kissed her with it. 'Take them off.'

She took her things off. They were in the Mereside carpark, right out of the way, the furthest reach of the nature reserve. Only the Watchtower Hide to look over them. It seemed enticing, exciting, intense. She remembered their first time here. Thought there was a message in that, a reaching back. The smell of him mingling with the cool undercurrent of the water, the baked scent of the dust in the carpark. Jeannie let go with no one near, felt released, as if everything had evened up. He'd worked it out and was back with her. For now. Hold on tight. Never let go. Finish the wine.

She suggested skinny dipping. Wandered, naked with her glass, towards the skewift jetty through the reeds.

Before hearing him drive off.

He was gone for half an hour. Jeannie cowered, naked, in the water. Keeping within the reeds, uncertain whether he would ever come back.

When he did he strode along the jetty and looked down at her. 'You don't remember do you?'

'Yes. Our first time. Here. Before. I remember. I remember.'

Nathan snorted as if that wasn't important. As if that was the least of it. Jeannie panicked, if it was a test she was going to fail because she'd no idea what he meant. What was it? What else should she have remembered?

'How can you be so fucking ungrateful? You have no idea have you? How I've loved you. What I've fucking done for you.'

Jeannie couldn't answer. Could only feel tears and didn't want to cry. He could just turn round and leave her. She'd have to find her way home, stark naked up the dual carriageway. Christ, she'd be in the reading pile at the Golden Monkey Chinese Takeaway again before Friday was out.

Then he reached down into the water, grabbed her arm, lifted her, flailing like a netted fish. As he carried her back to the car she was pinpricked with cold, too shocked to ask why. Too afraid.

So when he suggested they try for a baby she thought that whatever might have been wrong, whatever she had done wrong, was over with. Forgiven. He had rounded a corner somewhere and this was their way forward.

But in the end she knew it was just an excuse. To be at her. You can't refuse me. We want a baby. Don't we? And so he broke their spell in the bedroom. They did not share each other any longer. He took. He picked her over. And he needed to do it, she told herself, over and over and over.

Chainsaw buzz. She chips and chisels and carves into the memories. It's like a jigsaw puzzle to her. There are straight edges she wants to keep so she can remember what the picture on the box was. But there are other pieces that need to be lost forever. Kicked under the rug; eaten by the dog.

Salvia officinalis purpureum

purple sage

---

aid to memory, wisdom

'What did you do to your forehead?' Geraldine asked.

Jeannie looked up, felt at her forehead as if she didn't know there was a bruise. 'Where?' she asked, and had to look away because it was clear Geraldine didn't believe her.

Or was it clear? Was it just that Jeannie didn't know whether she was standing upright these days?

Geraldine reached forward with a tender thumb. 'There, just there…'

'Must have knocked it when I was down by the summer-houses.' Jeannie brushed it aside. She couldn't say that the bruise was part of their trying for a baby.

'Turn over.' His hand in the small of her back. Her body shunting up the bed as he shunted up inside her. Until she crashed into the carved wood of their headboard but he was going to come then, no matter what, and if she really thought about it, the black stars bursting and exploding might be beautiful.

She was a black star exploding. She didn't eat well. The thought of spaghetti bolognese at her dad's house made her physically sick. She grew thin, thinner than she had ever been in her life.

She dyed her hair blonde. On a whim one afternoon after a meeting with the garden designer, Alexandra, whose hair was soft and sandy coloured. As they sat outside at the coffee shop Jeannie thought it had the tone of a Bahamian beach and the sun caught it and played with it like light on water. They were meant to be discussing the way things were going with the garden design side of Jeannie's business. Jeannie found she hadn't really been listening to a word that Alexandra had said. She'd been mesmerised by the light and shade in her hair. She stared so hard she made Alex uncomfortable.

'Are you all right Jeannie?' She had to ask three times before Jeannie heard her. Then Jeannie quickly reached for one of her smiles and mentioned just how glorious Alex's hair was, and they talked about the hairdresser and the shade she'd gone for.

Half way home from the salon she stopped off at the supermarket, saw the desert sunshine glare of the lighting bounce off her new hair, and panicked. What would he say? What if he didn't like it? What if he shaved her head? Why had she done it? She didn't even like blonde hair.

She didn't like the way her ankle and wrist bones had begun to jut out so that she was angular and birdish. She wanted to be someone else. She had no idea how it had happened, but Jeannie Gaffney had been horribly lost. There had been an accident along the way, a hit and run. She had gone wrong somewhere—not shown him how much she loved him, perhaps? Why couldn't she remember the wrong turn?

And then she was happy for a while because the blonde hair pleased him. His blonde was not going to cook, they would eat out, he would show her off. A thin figure draped in expensive clothes. She was his, and he was pleased with what he had made.

Ted Gaffney began to find that the only way to contact his daughter was to visit her at the Hanging Gardens. If he called at the house, Nathan was surly and Jeannie seemed distracted. Ted felt uncomfortable, out of place. He felt, if he was honest, as if he was creating tension, as if there was some secret challenge or test going on and his being there was counting against her. He had a terrible urge to take Jeannie's hand and lead her away.

But it wasn't up to him, not anymore, and whatever he thought he couldn't act upon it. It seemed ridiculous, paranoid. But he had telephoned on a number of occasions and Nathan answered, brusque, unwilling. The first few occasions he put it down to a hard day at work. Later he had no idea what to put it down to because the ideas that came frightened him.

And who was she anyway, this brittle blonde woman posing as his daughter? At least, as Geraldine said, there had been no more bruises.

What Jeannie thought as she organised the perennial displays, as she showed the new girl how to void a credit card transaction, as she posed for publicity pictures for the local paper with Santa and his elves, what Jeannie thought was that a policeman brings his handcuffs.

It became obvious after a year of persistent, not to say dogged, sex that she was not getting pregnant. Jeannie blamed herself, a terrible double agony of guilt and relief each month. A baby was not going to help; a baby seemed more terrifying and Jeannie knew that her terror was keeping a baby away.

And she had lied. He did not like to go near her when she was menstruating and so she added a couple of days to her cycle, to keep him at bay. She needed the rest from him, from It. But it just made him greedier. Harder. Worse.

'No.'

Jeannie had booked a stand at the regional Grow it Green Show at the Exhibition Centre a couple of hours' drive away. She had spent months preparing a stand, growing all the specialist plants that Barbara had made the Hanging Gardens famous for. Nathan was furious because it meant Jeannie would have to stay away for a few days. A 'No' moment arrived.

'No, let Debs go. You're always ranting on about giving her more responsibility. Give her this.'

Jeannie tried to argue. It was her nursery, her garden centre. This was a huge event. Networking. Business.

'Don't argue the toss with me,' he said, cold and calm. 'You arguing the toss with me? Is that it? Calm down. Will you calm down? Look at the state of you. You're not fit to be let out.' It was a free-flowing torrent towards her, speedy and quiet, flooding her words of protest.

She was calm. She was so calm. And then as he wouldn't listen she'd been so furious, wanting to beat at him, wanting to throw things and trying not to be hysterical, not to play into his hands. He laughed in her face in the end. Catching her by the wrists as she wrenched and pulled against him, not caring how much he hurt her. All he had to do was twist her around and he laughed, wrestling her, as if she was no effort at all.

'Don't try me.' Pinning her onto the table. Strapping her hands to the chair with his belt.

He thought that was settled. So he didn't notice that the Grow it Green event clashed with a stag do for one of his police buddies. He was going to be in Scotland for four days getting rat-arsed drunk and kite-surfing as criminals rampaged across the town. Jeannie knew that if she kept her mouth shut she could attend the event. She did whatever he asked. Stopped her mouth up with his cock.

Jeannie had just grabbed herself a takeaway coffee when the phone rang in the first quiet moment in two days.

The exhibition had been a huge success for the Hanging Gardens. She felt inspired and invigorated, had ideas of new things she wanted to do when they got back. Enough things to keep her so busy she might never have to go home. *This is too good to be true and you know it*. As she dug deep into her apron pockets for change, she thought it felt dangerous. Whatever happened she could never go back from this, this freedom, this feeling of lightness and sleep and daylight. And then he phoned.

She was feeling elated, reeling in the confusion of faces, plants, talk, PA announcements. Busy with change. With getting her hands dirty. Busy thinking that who knew a leather workman's apron could make you feel so indestructible, so powerful. She should always dress like this, her hair a piled-up, pinned-up mess, her face smudged with John Innes No. 3. So she didn't check the phone, was only expecting Debs or maybe Irene to be calling. A woman had bought all five of their Japanese acers and Debs had followed her home with them loaded in the back of the van, saying she'd ring to let Jeannie know where she was.

When the call came Jeannie thought she knew who it was. 'Hello? Debs?' she said. In the background the public address system announced a Pests and Prevention Q and A in Arena 2 beginning in five minutes.

'Hello?' Jeannie couldn't hear. Thought the call lost. 'Hello? Can't hear you Debs. I'll call you back.'

A hanging up. More than the call had been lost as Jeannie clicked on the screen and realised that the last caller had not been Debs. The last caller had been Nathan.

She knew now, had always known, there was no chance she could get away with it. She reasoned that the punishment would be got through, it would be worth it just for this space and time. This coffee. This would be a place she could go to in her head. A new place, safe. The smells and scents were crisp and wild in the vast exhibition hall, contained and concentrated and wonderful.

Alone in the Travelodge the last two nights, she had remembered what sleep was. Deep, refreshing sleep. She was not sticky with Nathan's spillage. The battered ache of her pelvis faded. She hadn't had to scrub her teeth five times to rid her mouth of the tang of him. She slept. He couldn't touch her.

Now it was all going to be over. On the last afternoon as she and Debs packed up the stall she found hot tears rolling down her face, couldn't keep control of herself. Hands shaking, face muscles working. Debs embarrassed to ask.

'Ignore me,' Jeannie whimpered at last, 'It's just my hormones. Ignore me.'

'Here,' Jeannie said, fumbling the keys out of her fleece jacket pocket. 'Fetch the van round, Debs. Go.' Anything to get rid of Debs. To try and stifle the thought that she did not want to go home.

Homeward, she drove slowly trying to savour the moments alone. She had only twenty-four hours before his return. She wanted to stretch them out. Maybe he wouldn't come home tomorrow, maybe he would postpone it, lulling her into thinking it was no big deal. Then he'd be back. Bang.

Then she pulled into the driveway and saw Nathan's car already parked up. Panic. Adrenaline. What lie could she try and tell? She'd been to Dad's? She could lie that the PA was at the shopping mall. The giant mall that he hated. The panic tripled when their neighbour rapped on the window as she reached for her handbag.

'He's over at your dad's.' Looking very agitated. 'Do you want me to drive you over there, Jeannie?'

Why? Why would Nathan be at Dad's? Why couldn't she just drive herself?

The phone call had pulled him home early. To catch her out. He had found the house empty and driven straight round to Ted Gaffney's house. Ted was shocked by the way his son-in-law barged in, as if he thought Jeannie was hiding out. As if his son-in-law was looking for a criminal and not his wife. There had been what Ted Gaffney politely called 'an exchange of words'. Ted Gaffney did not tell anyone how Nathan had cuffed at him, or of his white-hot rage when Geraldine put herself between them. Nathan had left then, slamming the door so hard a pane of glass shattered.

Later, Uniform was called out to a hit and run. A WPC was first on the scene, a friend of Nathan's, everyone called her simply Bailley. She thought Nathan should get out there. Because it was a woman walking, on her way home. Just parted from friends at her Wednesday night Spanish group and ploughed into, made into a rag doll at the roadside. A woman who was Geraldine.

Bailley had found the car involved. It had been driven up the dual carriageway, into the woods and set alight. Stolen. Joy riders. No hope of finding the bastards. But Bailley would be checking the town's CCTV system. She was going to go far, that girl.

Jeannie was shaking. Her fault. Why had she answered the phone? He had come home to catch her. Catch her out, and she hadn't been there. So. What had he done?

What had he done?

Nathan drove them both home. Jeannie couldn't say it out loud, couldn't ask the question. Did you? Did you do this?

She didn't have to ask. He had warned her: don't try me.

The world dimmed to black and white for the funeral.

She spent what time she could with Dad. She spent the time trying not to blurt out what she had done to him. That it was punishment for her transgression and she wanted to take it back.

She found herself in a windshear of panic that if she spent too much time with Dad maybe that would endanger him. She had to keep him safe. Nathan did not like her spending too much time 'over there'. He had taken to calling Dad and asking, 'Is she there?' as if she was an errant schoolgirl.

There was a spate of burglaries, nothing serious, just vandalism really. Enough to shake her dad up. His house broken into in the middle of the night three, five times. The alarm system faulty but the engineer couldn't seem to find the fault. 'Intermittent,' he said, the worst kind of fault. Now you see it, sort of thing.

The police couldn't get there in time. And the last time, when Dad was cornered on the stairs, he fell and dislocated his shoulder.

The phone ringing out starkly into the darkness, Nathan turning over, pretending to be asleep. Jeannie left, pulling her jacket on over her pyjamas, pulling her boots onto her bare feet. He was so white faced on the way to hospital. Jeannie knew.

Jeannie had to speak. Had to say something to Nathan.

'Stop it. Please.' Quiet. Meek.

'Stop what?' He sat on the table, one leg lifted onto the chair, casual as he reached behind him for an apple from the bowl. Bit the apple.

'Just please stop.'

He considered for a moment. Chewed at the piece of apple in his mouth, rolled the rest of the fruit around in his hand, as if it was the globe. He spat the apple onto the floor beside her, threw the rest at the sink where it cracked a new plate.

'Beg.'

'What's going on?' Dad knew exactly what he was going to say this time. Loss emboldened him. Who cared anymore? *I just care about her. She is all I have left.*

'What, the hell, is going on Jeannie?' he spoke through gritted teeth the second time. He could see her fold up before him. She dwindled visibly in the chair.

'I've been so busy. I'm sorry.'

'He won't let you come. That's it isn't it?'

She couldn't let her dad in on this. Once he knew, that would be it. The killer blow. The deadly secret.

'Why won't he? What is going on?'

'He's just careful. He cares about me. Going out on my own. That's all.' Jeannie could taste the lie as bitter as car fumes in her mouth. Dad looked edgy.

'Seems to me...' He paused as if the words were something to be coughed up. 'Seems to me, to me looking from the outside, Jeannie...that you're not allowed out.' His lips were as pinched as Jeannie's heart. All this was her fault. All this mess. She couldn't undo the past, but there had to be some way of doing the future differently.

'It's because of the...of...everything. Made him edgy. You know, Dad, you know what his work is like. The stuff he sees.'

'I don't care what he sees. I care what he does. I worry about you.'

He wanted to say that he was frightened for her but he couldn't make his mouth say it. Saying it would make it alive.

'He worries too. That's all. That's all it is.' Jeannie lied, more car fumes, making her mouth water to clean itself. Her own spit choked her. 'He wants a baby and I can't give him one and I don't know why.' She heard the words and thought that they must be true. That they had fallen from somewhere to fill the gap.

'Why is it your fault Jeannie?' Her dad spoke quietly, reasoning. 'It might be his fault.'

They were still talking about the baby weren't they? Jeannie's vision tilted, she felt sick suddenly.

'I don't know what to do,' she whispered then. And it seemed she was talking about the baby. Seemed.

Ray. Sitting puffing on a cigar at the tea shed. Jeannie could see him from the top terrace, could even smell his particularly bitter brand of cigar from inside the top greenhouse. She stood for a while looking down, watching him, hoping he'd go away. But he just kept sponging more cups of tea, insisting, 'It's free to family,' as Irene fumed. In the end she sent one of the boys up to find Jeannie with a message. 'Shift him or I'll do for him.'

It was a soggy day. The rain had been heavy all morning and everything had a scratched stainless steel sheen to it. The clouds were low over town, obscuring Cromwell Park from view and in the distance the turrets and wires of the suspension bridge had vanished. There was the background noise of water, the trickling of drains, the splash of cars on the wet roads.

'Look at the arse on that,' Ray grimaced as he watched Irene walk back into the shed with a tray of spent tea things.

Irene halted, half turned. 'Funny, I was thinking the same thing when I was looking at your face.'

Ray gave a tight whistle and a wheezy laugh. 'I like you. You've got balls,' he shouted.

'Yes. Yours if you don't piss off.'

Jeannie felt as if she was being stabbed with pins. Ray looked up at her.

'What's that face for then?' He was smirky, very pleased with himself and the undercurrent of mayhem he was causing.

'Just a social call Ray? Or did you want something?'

'Bit of cake wouldn't go amiss.' He tamped out the cigar and began to unpeel another from its cellophane wrap. 'Just thought I'd pay a visit. I had time on my hands. You know, us retired blokes. Thought I'd see what my daughter-in-law was up to.'

She took him up to the greenhouse to keep him from the public and Irene. He dawdled his way through the garden centre making idle chit-chat, cadging a birdhouse and a few trays of violas as they went. Once in the greenhouse Jeannie tried to continue with what she'd been doing, let him talk at one end of the potting bench until he got bored and then she could be rid of him. He made himself at home on an upturned crate. It seemed Linda and Shannon had abandoned him and he told Jeannie of his trawl for a new mate. Did she have any friends she could set him up with then? He'd quite like to get to know Irene's arse better.

'No kiddies then,' he said at last, getting down to the end of his smalltalk and his latest cigar. Jeannie shook her head. Did not want to think about that. Did not want him to bring those thoughts into the one place where they left her. Keep out.

'I say. Not up the duff then.'

Jeannie was not attentive enough, did not catch the tone in his voice, the preamble to something. 'You know what they say.' She tried to sound wifey.

'No. What's that they say?'

'Fun trying.'

'Is it? Is that what they say?' punctuated by the click-click of his lighter on a fresh cigar. There was an edge that wasn't quite catching her. She was too busy trying to think of pointless tasks to finish until he went away.

'No point trawling if there aren't any fish in the sea Jeannie,' he said, standing and looking at her. His voice was low and dark. Outside the cloud seemed to lower as if it could block in the windows to the greenhouse. Jeannie looked at him. Ignorant. Not getting it. He triumphed. 'Mumps. When he was in secondary school. Really bad case, he was. Looked like the Elephant Man.'

Jeannie thought time stopped and only his mouth moved in the vastness of the universe.

'He couldn't sire one on you if he fucked you till Doomsday.'

Jeannie felt the vomit rise in her throat, saw the black stars of her universe burn more intently. The familiar dull ache she felt in her pelvis seemed to increase in intensity, as if she was rotting away from the hips down.

'I've got time on my hands Jeannie. Fuck him over for once. Give me a grandchild. Only we do it my way.'

Artemisia absinthium

wormwood

_____

a useful bitter in low dosage; too much, however, is poison

They were at Bailley's housewarming party. Lots of people standing around her half-finished kitchen drinking bitter red wine that dried like ash in your mouth. Jeannie had found a quiet corner by a newly installed window. She looked out to where Bailley had lit tealights in the long thin garden. Jeannie wanted to be out there but had strict instructions not to move out of Nathan's line of sight.

Bailley had started her drinking. Jeannie didn't really want the wine, but Bailley was perched on a nearby wicker chair, intent on using Jeannie to practise her new found Victim Support skills.

'It was Geraldine who set me off on this,' she was saying. 'If it hadn't been for what happened…you know…I might not…might never have changed direction like I have…gone the victim support route…'

Jeannie couldn't believe she was hearing this. Was she supposed to be delighted that Geraldine's death had inspired such a good career move in Bailley?

Bailley topped her glass up. 'It's hard. I know.'

She knew? Had she read it on the back of a leaflet?

'You don't…I hope you don't mind me saying this but you don't…seem…well, a very happy bunny.'

Words were coming out of Bailley's mouth but Jeannie found the more wine she glugged the less she heard what they were. Instead she saw Geraldine sawing away at her cello. Dunking a biscuit in hot tea. The tealights outside beckoned like a runway. Jeannie lurched upwards and outwards through the thick polythene that was standing in for the French doors.

But bloody Bailley *followed*. The shapes her mouth made looked like a foreign language. Jeannie was embarrassed to find she had reached out, touched Bailley's lips closed.

'Sssssh.' Jeannie could hear herself now. 'Want to know a secret?' And then she couldn't decide which one to tell first. There suddenly seemed so many.

Bailley was looking at the wine in Jeannie's glass. Rather hypocritical, Jeannie thought, considering it was Bailley who'd kept it topped up. This is your fault, she thought.

'…fault.' She heard herself saying it out loud. Bailley unflinching, pitying. Nathan stooping as he pushed his way through the polythene.

'Sssssssssh.' Jeannie stumbled, Nathan caught her.

'She's just been telling me secrets.' Bailley tried to make light, tried to suck up to Nathan. Oops, the look that passed between Nathan and Bailley told Jeannie she'd said that one aloud too.

'What a Victim Support look.' Jeannie heard herself as if she was listening to her voice on the radio. She felt her mouth move, puppetish. 'Can't sire one on me then, Elephant Man.'

Bailley laughed, gave Nathan a hideous twinkling look. Did she think he was hung like a trunk? Long, like the hose on a vacuum cleaner? Reaching and sucking.

Nathan hadn't been drinking. And now she wished she hadn't. Jeannie looked up, his face blurred for a moment into two faces and she felt a strange pang, as if Nathan might be in there. A ghost in this machine.

'You're yanking my chain lately. Did you know that?' His tone was low and controlled. Very controlled. The more controlled he sounded, the angrier she knew he was. Panic.

'How?'

She hadn't done anything. Had she? Been careful not to speak to anyone without an introduction, without permission, from Nathan. Say nothing. Smile. Like the Queen.

'Have I pissed off Bailley?' she asked and heard herself answer. '*Good.*'

He was blocking her, his body filling all her sightlines. Whichever way she turned she knocked some part of herself against him. She tried to look away but he tilted her chin towards him, tender, as if she was a child. Anyone looking on would see a man being gentle with his wife, not a policeman interrogating.

'This is the least of it. What do you think you've been up to?' He was a step away and yet the words were a shove. A dig.

'Tell me then.' Leaning down to whisper in her ear. 'Confess.' Her jaw ached with what she couldn't say. If she said it, everything would crash and burn.

'How about you and Ray? Eh? Tell me about that. Start with that.'

There was a silence. The drink and the darkness blurred all the edges and Nathan loomed over her, tall as a building. The only landmark in the landscape.

'He was at the garden centre,' she said easily. 'Drinking all Irene's tea.'

'Say again?' He leaned right in close so she thought he might crack his forehead against hers.

'He was blagging freebies from Irene.'

'Forget that. I'm not on about that. I want to know what he's been saying.'

Jeannie could feel the pressure now. 'He wanted to know if I could set him up with someone new. A woman. With Irene.'

'Did you listen to him?' he spoke over her. Her head was fuzzing and she couldn't let him do that. No, it wasn't him, it was the wine. The stupid, horrible wine.

'Listen to him?'

Nathan looked relaxed, hands easy in his pockets, looking away at the party, back down at Jeannie.

'You believed what he told you didn't you?' Nathan's voice was so quiet she had to strain to hear him. She was bargaining wasn't she? He wanted to see how far he could push her. He was spoiling for a fight. 'Didn't you?'

'About Irene's arse?'

He gave her a very cold look and for the first time she returned it. If this was a game then she had, at last, some sort of trump card here. He was scornful.

'You did, didn't you.'

She smoothed at her stomach, smoothing her top down over it. Looked up at him drunkenly puzzled.

'You've been machine-gunning me for years Nathan...' She felt the spittle spattering out of her mouth as she battered lightly at him, knocking her wine glass against him, spilling wine until his hands stopped her. Couldn't stop her speaking.

'*Datdatdatdatdat*...no fucking baby. But that's not my fault...no. Not my fault...'cause you're the Elephant Man!' Her face was betraying her, she couldn't stop it stretching into a laugh. Her face seemed to think she had escaped. Was free. She felt herself tilt towards him, felt his body lean into hers, shoring her up. His eyes all over her, and she couldn't tell if he was disgusted or lusted up. And that was nothing to do with the wine. That was the…what did you call it…what was the phrase? The status quo. He lolled her head between his hands, smirked.

A couple of the other guests were wandering in their direction, glasses sloshing wine. One of the women tiptoeing barefoot through the grass saying, 'I've lost my other shoe… I've lost it…in the pond…' and laughter. Nathan leaned in towards Jeannie's face and kissed her on the mouth pushing his tongue between her lips. A hand sliding down to lift her skirt. A signal to the others who giggled and turned back towards the house. Jeannie heard *sssshhhh* and sniggers of laughter. She didn't try to stop his hands. She wanted to catch him. The wine was making her reckless.

'I know what you did,' she said at last, lifting her head to whisper into the side of his face. How she had loved the curve of his cheekbone, the wavy line his hair made across the top of his forehead. No, not him, someone else in his skin.

He traced a finger down her neck, her shoulder, down to her elbow.

'You did it, didn't you. Sssh. I know it.' She heard her voice splintering.

'Did I?' He was challenging, his eyes capturing the burning orange flickers from the tealights. 'Tell me what I did.' His voice was low, easy, calm.

'You punished me, you did.' In her mind's eye she could see Geraldine, sitting in the sun, her glasses perched on her nose. A glass of wine. White, not red.

He had caught her neck in his fist, was holding her head

as if she were a doll. 'Tell me how I punished you.'

He was leaning close and she could feel the resonance of every word on her skin. And in that moment she knew for certain what he had done. She opened her mouth.

'*Sssssssssshhhhhhhhh*.' It was a long low foolish sound. Her mouth close against his ear. She felt his hand move to the small of her back, knew he thought she was too drunk, that she could be taken home in half an hour and fucked over. No. Not tonight.

'*Sssssshhhhhh*. Hit and run.'

She did not see the punch coming and to anyone looking on it appeared, for all the world, as if Jeannie simply fainted. Her wine spilled down her front, staining her top, and Nathan, looking concerned, simply picked her up and carried her back towards the house. A vague wine-hazed sensation that she'd been here before. That this was the real Nathan come to take her back.

Jeannie remembered vomiting on the half-finished patio. It landed half on the crenellated pattern of the incomplete paving and half in the soft golden sand of the foundations. At the farthest edge there were spatters on black shoes. A woman. Tall. High heels. The woman helped her to the bathroom to clean herself up. She could hear how everyone was so kind. Especially to Nathan. With his barren wife who'd had too much to drink. Heard Bailley use the words 'sad' and 'troubled' and 'tough time'.

Jeannie knew then that he had built a story of babies. He had backup, a battalion of lies. Even if she leapt from his arms and tried to tell them all, begged for help, no one would listen. It would embarrass them all. They would have to look away.

If she had thought that the last year and a half had been a dream and there was a chance she could wake up now, the dream descended. All the lights went out.

'Please Nathan. Please.'

'Please?'

'Don't...please don't...'

'Don't? Please? Don't what? What am I doing? Spit it out Jeannie. Or swallow it.' His eyes flickered from the road to her face.

'Please don't. Please.'

He gave another snort. 'What the fuck have I done? Look at you. Off on one. You're a fucking nightmare.'

Jeannie's mind scuppered and reeled. 'I'm sorry.' She ought to laugh now, stupid, careless and mad for thinking she could win. 'I'm sorry. Sorry.'

For drinking the wine as if it was courage. For giving him what he wanted, an excuse. It was her own fault. Once more, she was to blame.

'Sorry...sorry...sorry...Take me home. Let's go home.' The shirts were clean and white weren't they? Clean and white and she'd bought the lavender water so they wouldn't smell like the iron. Only then he hadn't liked the lavender smell *like a fucking old lady* and she'd had that image in her head of the old lady astride Nathan. An old lady in thigh length boots. Knitting with his pubic hair.

'I didn't mean it...sorry. I take it back. I take it back.' Where were his socks? Weren't they paired up the way he wanted in the drawer? Socks? Were socks important? They had never seemed important. When she worked at Parks and Gardens she wore odd ones, what did it matter as long you had a sock for each foot. *What are you doing with my fucking socks? Eating them?* Jeannie thought of the garden centre. Of the thick sappy scent of the greenhouses. The wet earth after watering. Salvation. Refuge. Don't make me. Don't make me.

'It's me Nathan, don't punish anyone else. Please. Don't. Please, me. It's all my fault. Punish me.'

He gave a snorting laugh. Jeannie just wanted to turn back the gyroscope of time and feel the tender touch of his hand in the small of her back, feel the sun on her face the way it had felt that day. Up the hill to the walled garden.

'I'm sorry. Sorry...please Nathan...please...I am. I'm sorry. Look, I'm sorry. Look at me. Please Nathan.' She could hear herself bleating.

Then they sheered away from the red coals of rear lights on the dual carriageway as Nathan turned through a gate at the edge of the forest. A gate that said No ADMITTANCE. The headlights illuminated the undersides of the trees, the car bumped and clanked over the rough ground.

When they stopped in the clearing Jeannie did not move. Nathan got out of the car, slamming the door shut. He strode around the bonnet, whitened by headlights and ripped open her door. Still she didn't move. She knew better. Nathan reached across and released her seatbelt, then dragged her out onto the soft pine-needled floor. Jeannie felt she couldn't see any more. Was this real? But the dirt choked her, the rotting wood of the log stack splintered into her as she stumbled and fell against it. Nathan tugged her upwards.

'On. Your. Feet.' His hands twisting the blonde rope of her hair around his hand. Handling her upwards.

'You're a witch. You don't even know what you've done. You do this to me. You, Jeannie. Make me greedy. All those fucking Saturdays. The stuff I had to do to stay close to you.' He shook her, angry. Jeannie couldn't think, what Saturdays?

His lips brushed her neck. 'Like a chick you were that day. On the forest floor. I carried you back. Saved you. And you don't fucking remember.'

Jeannie felt a shot of adrenaline gush through her. What had he said? Remember? Carried her back?

'How can you not remember any of it, you fucking ungrateful bitch?'

Her mind sifted backwards as if her whole life was being rewound. A chick on the forest floor. They had said, it had been in the paper, a policeman had had to carry her to the ambulance. More adrenaline surged, trying to cope.

'That day Jeannie. That first day, when I felt your skin, under my hand. You were given to me.' He was looking into her eyes now. 'Took me fucking forever to find you. They said you were going to the university so I'd transferred to York. You just run me in rings. I'm just your game. Punish you? I'll fucking punish you.'

His left hand slid round her waist, skimmed across a breast and then twisted her arm into the small of her back.

'We're going to play a game,' he whispered. Jeannie wished that he would simply beat her to death or stab her, just reach for one of the logs on the stack and clonk and clonk until she was gone. It would be believable and real and manageable and, thankfully, over.

He twisted his hand tighter into her hair. It was pulling the skin. Jeannie wondered if she could just tug sharply, let her scalp rip free and keep running. Monopoly, she thought, laughter tugging at her. He plays Monopoly. I'm the dog and he's the top hat. Her breath seemed to want to stay in her lungs. Hiding. Nathan slapped her face, reviving her.

'Come back. Back to me Jeannie. Got to be awake for this one.' Slap. Slappety-slap-slap. 'This is a new game.'

As he spoke Jeannie could see the headlights making their way through the woodland towards them, the heavy vehicle bumping and lumbering. She struggled to see behind the glare and then the driver flicked on full beam. A war whoop was heard from the opened window. A thick hand banged on the car roof. Liam handbrake-turned to a stop, his face leering out at her, his eyes seeming to glint silver in the darkness. Jeannie pushed against Nathan, panicked. He held her fast.

'When I release you…Run. Understand?' His hand latched into her hair again, tugged at her head. 'Nod your head Jeannie. That's how to do it.'

Down up down up down up.

'Run. 'Cause this is a game called Hunter.'

Ambrosia artemisiifolia

ragweed

---

for courage; and put it into shoes to ease a journey

After the woods she didn't dream. She knew the darkness, and the monster that lived there. On the outside, she hid the scuffs and grazes. The bruises melted back into her.

On the inside her plan was all that held her upright, kept her focused. The focus blurred once or twice when she thought about her dad. It was like an acid inside her, the desire to run home, to bang on the door and just tell him what was happening.

But she was a grown up. She was Mrs Jeannie Flynn, successful nurserywoman with a coffee shop concession and everything, with staff who depended on her for their mortgage payments. She had students from Mr Mathieson's course at the agricultural college apprenticed to her.

She had contracts and obligations. She had made the choice. She had chosen Nathan and she had made promises, hadn't she? Promises in church and even if you didn't believe in God you could still believe in promises.

All broken. What she had done to Dad. What she had done to Geraldine. It all had to stop. That was all.

She made Debbie into Centre Manager. Debbie who had come from school with no qualifications and was the most trustworthy person Jeannie knew. Jeannie was careful how she went about it. She made certain that Debs could take on all the tasks, each week she concentrated on a different aspect of the business and how it was run. She wanted her to feel capable and confident. Jeannie did not want anyone to feel they had been left in the lurch. She planned to have a month clear when she could see Debs running the business. Then it would be time.

You could see the suspension bridge from the Hanging Gardens. It was a graceful blur of spiderweb on a hazy summer day. It was a ghostly cat's cradle in the distance on a foggy autumn day. Nathan was not going to be home till late. Jeannie walked all the way, setting off from the Hanging Gardens after work as if nothing was different. Except it was different. She was leaving her car round the back in the delivery bay. No one would notice until the morning.

She had promised herself that she would not go anywhere near Dad's house but in the end it was on her way. She made it so. She walked up the dirt lane that fed into the road. From there she could stand under the copper beech trees where Del Weston at the bungalow parked his cars. From there she could see into Dad's house without being seen. He was playing the piano. Jeannie did not have long, just long enough to take a photographic memory.

Inside the house Ted Gaffney thought he saw Jeannie out of the corner of his eye. He thought he saw her in the lane. He stopped playing. He was certain. Out there, across the road, under the copper beeches. Something was wrong. Ted Gaffney moved quickly out of the front door. But she was gone.

It took Jeannie an hour or so to get to the bridge. By that

time the rush-hour traffic had stopped and the bridge was quiet. Jeannie walked across it, aware of the emptiness beneath her. She had never liked heights. A couple of tourists had stopped to take photos, leaning, carefree, against the wire-work. Jeannie walked right across and kept going. It was going to be dark soon. If she just walked up around the houses towards Lookout Point she would have timed it just right.

By the time she had walked up through the Edwardian and Victorian mansions with their high hedges and sweeping drives towards Lookout Point, the streetlights were beginning to wink on. As she started back down towards the bridge it seemed to her that all the lampposts bowed their heads. The air chilled quickly now the sun had gone down but Jeannie didn't shiver. She walked steadily, the weight of her bag digging into her shoulder.

As a car drove over the bridge towards her, Jeannie turned to look up at the driver. In fact she realised that it would be better to be seen and so, when she heard the next car approaching she darted in front of it, across the roadway to the opposite side of the bridge. The driver pipped and braked, opened his window to shout. Jeannie ignored him. He drove on. *Pippippippiiiiip*.

She took the first shoe out of her bag and dropped it on the bridge. The second she battered against the kerb to make the heel break off. She threw the shoe over the balustrade. She watched it tumble waterwards; took out a jacket she had scrunched into her bag and threw that, the pockets weighted with a mobile phone, a set of keys. Then, she dropped the handbag where she stood. It tilted slightly and a lipstick rolled out. She watched it for a moment as it rolled across the ironwork towards the abyss below. Jeannie Gaffney did not see it fall.

She felt it.
Freefall.
And when you land, bend your knees.

Pseudotsuga menziesii

douglas fir

---

useful in matters of shapeshifting

Jeannie had some money with her. Not much, cash she'd squirrelled away from the till in the weeks before. She'd made certain of her running-away fund. But now it felt like a weight in her pockets. That first night away she stayed in a Novotel and slept so badly and dreamed so fitfully. Dreamed of Nathan in the doorway. Nathan blocking out the light. Nathan in bed beside her.

Waking with a start to headlights turning into the carpark or the rumble of an articulated lorry on the A-road close by.

Jeannie kept walking then. Walking away. Punishment. Although it didn't feel like punishment, even when she slept under newspaper or cardboard. She stayed away from doorways and shelters, aware of others there with bags and belongings, staking their pitch. Jeannie saw a man kick at the sleeping figure in a doorway, another man piss all over him. She spent a night in the wendy house in a park playground. High up it was, like a tree house. She didn't care about the smell of urine or the cigarette butts and spent chewing gum. She just felt he wouldn't look in here.

Jeannie kept walking. She washed herself in public toilets or swam in a lake in a park. Swam in her underclothes to clean them, dried herself under the driers in the park toilets.

'What you doing?' the woman clanked a galvanised bucket down. There was a powerful smell of Jeyes fluid and the water made thick steam in the cold air. Jeannie was nearly dry, scuffled herself back into her clothes.

'Got no home to go to?' The woman slopped hot water around Jeannie's feet. Jeannie felt the mop across her shoes.

There was the first time she grazed a supermarket. Waited until late in the evening when it was quieter, took a basket and put a few things into it. Filled her pockets with fruit because that wasn't tagged. Ate bread rolls. Cheese. Drank water. Plastic Barbie-pink ham. Scotch eggs. Drank more water. Left her basket at the end of the aisle. Walked easily through the doors, pockets full of bananas, as the security guard chatted up the bored looking woman with streaky blonde highlights who was manning the cigarette kiosk.

She walked, dropping down from the street to the canal path because here there were just trees and herons and moorhens. There was the reedmace and cyclists. The houseboats and narrowboats. The lock and the café in the lockkeeper's cottage where she spent more money on tea and a sandwich and washed her face and hair in their tiny cramped toilet. Used their squeegee soap.

The blonde was coming out of her hair now. She looked at it in the floral framed mirror in the tiny toilet. The mousier brown roots showed through, inching their way down her head. Once upon a time she would have been glad to see Jeannie back, but she wasn't sure anymore where Jeannie was. Someone else was inside her now. Jeannie had gone off that bridge. With that shoe.

Chainsaw buzzing again. Cut around it. Shape it out. Let it fall. Walking through the darkness and the sulphured orange or halogen blue of the night streets too tired to walk and too afraid to sleep.

Walked miles to another city. The café caught her eye because of the curled cyrillic-style writing in the window and the blood-red awning that shaded two or three round marble-topped tables even in this cold weather, the legs ending in clawed feet, clutching at the floor. Bentwood chairs. Jeannie could not sit outside, she would be too noticeable there. She moved inside. As she pushed the door she saw the sign written in an elegant hand. HELP WANTED.

The Radetzky Samovar Café made her want to cry with relief. The black wood of the chairs, the cool marble of the table tops, the scrubbed wooden floor. The high counter with a brass rail running around it. The comforting, nourishing hiss of the coffee machine, the samovar that sat on the back counter burnished with polishing. The cups. The cutlery. Everything was other and welcoming and warm. The smells of the baked goods, the savoury snacks being dished out. Jeannie thought she might just sit in the corner forever.

Help wanted, the sign had said. Frankly Jeannie thought she might never have read a truer word. She cleared her plate and cup to the counter top and asked the man behind the counter about the job. She spoke too quietly and she thought he hadn't heard her over the hysterical hissing of the coffee machine as it frothed milk. He didn't speak. Then he put two cappuccinos onto the counter top and nodded at the far table in the window.

'Number 3. In the window.'

Jeannie took the coffees and cleared away the plates and cups the two women had already finished with. She smiled, and when the older woman asked if there was any of the cinnamon cake left, Jeannie smiled again and said she'd ask.

There were two hours until closing and Jeannie cut cake, served teas and coffees and cleared tables. As he turned the sign to CLOSED the owner said simply, 'We open at eight. Can you be here for seven-thirty?'

Jeannie nodded.

'I am Boris. Owner. I will pay you five pounds an hour and you keep all tips.' He offered his hand for her to shake.

'What's your name?' he asked. She paused. Boris looked impatient, took a bill from the last customer and handed over the change as she thought.

'You have one? You going to be too quiet like this I don't want you work here.'

'Ruby,' she said. And the name must belong to her because it had popped into her head like a balloon. And she spent the next day clearing tables and washing up, and Boris watched her and knew she was indispensable. She wanted to be a workhorse.

She was. A champion workhorse. Boris began to wonder who had sent him this prize. Ruby could wipe down tables forever. It cleared her head, which she needed to be as empty as possible. The Radetzky Samovar Café was golden and warm and soothed her. At night she slept in the store room amongst the cabbages and potatoes, waiting each evening until Boris and his wife headed home. She would save up enough to rent a room, but for now she felt safe in the store. He would never look for her here.

Ruby was a force moving forward. Only there was a shard of Jeannie Gaffney left jagging out of her skin and she found herself one afternoon speaking Russian. She had heard Boris and his wife jabbering together and the memories came back of sitting in the lecture theatre on the university campus, of being in the whizzkids group for languages. Of Mrs Craven's enthusiastic need to share her passion for Russian. Jeannie would never forget the look on Boris's face when he spoke to her and she answered in Russian. His joy fed her own relief, the sloughing off, the smoothing over of herself, letting herself go into another tongue. This was something she had almost forgotten about. It was good to go back to it. She needed to be foreign, to be distanced from what had been, and in speaking Russian she had jumped off another bridge in herself.

The next month one of the customers spoke to her in Russian. Ruby didn't mind, a lot of people who came in were émigrés, like herself, people who had been forced to run away. It was only later, when he kept smiling at her that Ruby felt the hair on the back of her neck stand up. Boris came over to talk with the customer and when Ruby arrived back at the table with his borscht and some fresh-baked bread, Boris introduced Vassily, his unmarried brother.

Ruby chatted for a while with Vassily, who was perfectly nice and ordinary looking. His eyes were edgy and nervous, as if he wanted very much to make a good impression. At first Ruby thought she had panicked unnecessarily, that she simply had been introduced to Vassily as someone who could teach him English. It was as straightforward as that wasn't it? Vassily had tried a few classes at the college and found it intimidating. Maybe, a couple of afternoons a week, they could sit in the more relaxed surroundings of the café and she could teach him. Yes? Maybe so?

Yes. Maybe so. Until it became clear that Ruby's first instinct was right, the language afternoons were just a court-ship, a ritual. One afternoon, a rainy Friday. They were sitting in their usual place in the far corner of the window, the table where Jeannie/Ruby had served her first cappuccinos. Vassily had come on under her tuition and Boris and his wife were grateful. But Ruby wasn't. This afternoon they had spoken more in English and for her this seemed a backward step.

She felt edgy today and every time anyone walked past she gave a start. All the elbows and shoulders and backs of heads appeared to be just like Nathan. All the raincoats and gestures. Ruby looked at Vassily. He had a strong handsome face and kind green eyes that looked at her but didn't see her.

Ruby excused herself to go into the kitchen. She walked straight out through the back door into the rain. Later, after she had packed up her single change of clothes into a carrier bag and paid her bill at the B&B, she stopped in at a hair-dressers and had her long hair shorn. A number eight she asked for, and the stylist cried. Ruby left the salon feeling liberated. As if Nathan's fingerprints had been all over it.

Outside was a bus stop. As Ruby left the hair salon a bus hissed to a stop and Ruby knew she couldn't miss it. Or the next. Or the next. Or the next. Boarding and alighting, until the end of the line.

PART 3

IJO O DESU

That's all, the end, concluded

Zannen desu ga, shitsurei shinakereba narimasen

I'm sorry to say, I'll have to be leaving

The words came to a stop. It was dark outside now. My mouth felt very dry suddenly and Angharad reached round and fetched me a glass of water. I couldn't look at anyone by then. I could only glance at the distortions and reflections in the body of water in the glass. I kept drinking, taking water in like someone drowning. No one said a word, in fact they didn't even seem to be breathing.

'That was when you arrived here?' Mrs Atkinson spoke at last. I nodded. She nodded back, as if I had settled something for her. Silence clouded over again.

'What are we going to do about him?' Mrs Milligan said, arms folded, eyes cast, intent, to the carpeting, as if she might find the answer written there.

There were a few moments of almost total silence. Then Angharad and Ellen brewed up more coffee and tea and still there were no words, just the deep breathing of the kettle, the chank and splash and chinkcachink of stirring. Mrs Milligan opened a tin she'd brought full of caramel shortbread and everyone was very thoughtful. I fought tears, damped them down inside. I would miss this place, these people. This life.

Tea dished out, there was more pondering.

'What in hell can we do?' Angharad stirred at her tea as if all the answers would come swirling to the surface.

'Nothing,' I said very simply, very calmly. Because after all I'd been here before, at the jumping off point. 'I just have to go.' Sipping at my last chance tea.

Outrage. Angharad tutting. Mrs Atkinson shaking her head slowly. Mrs Milligan's scornful snort and vehement 'No.'

'There has to be another way. There has to be something else we can do,' Martha said, indignant. 'There has to be. For Christ's sake can't one of us come up with an alternative to running away?'

'Punish him,' said Iris, licking the chocolate off the chunk of caramel shortbread she'd just dunked.

In the lobby later, it was just me and Queen Victoria. Stony faced. Waiting. I looked up to her for some comment but she said nothing, just kept staring blankly out through the fanlight above the revolving door. Staring out at the car-roara borealis of the rush hour traffic. The headlights streetlights shoplights shimmering in the rain. And then it came. I heard the glass shattering, the wood splintering in the near distance. The clump of a chair tipping in the staff room.

The chair by the window. The one he's had to climb over as he breaks in. The bus lumbers up and I know the moment is here. The chickenwired door fobs open behind me. Fubs shut. The huge metallic rectangled bus, bejewelled with lights, hissing and spitting. Nathan's arm moves around my shoulders, his grip strong across my collarbone, shoulder, neck. His face nuzzles into my hair. 'Time to go home.'

And there is a savage tearing of duct tape.

Duct tape handsno shitwristsburn numb nocan'tno armsfuckno can't
movecan't twistcaught dark dark baggedsweat breath dark boot car
engine thrum grind stark boundbollockboundnaked sweatbreathsweat
breath breathebreathe fucking think Viiiiiiiiiibbbbbbbbbrrrrrrrrraaaa-
aattTTTTtttiiiiiiiIIIIIIiooooooooooonnnnnnnnnnnn. rrrrrrrrrrrrrrrrr-
rrrrrrrrrrrrrr rrrrrrrrrrjagjagjagjagRRRRRRRRRRRRRR elbow
snag twistachenumbnumb pins needles fuckingfingersfucking numb
AgHUgh ache breathebreathe sweat breath breathefuckingbreathe-
fuckingthinkbreathebastardbreathessspp ppppp EEEEEEEEEEEEE-
EEEEEEEEEEEEEEEEEEdSpeeeeeeeeeeeeeeeeeeeeeeeeeeeeeeeeeeeeee-
eeeeeeeeeeeeeeeeeeeeeed goingwhere fuckingthink shift kickpush graze
scuff tear numbnumbnumb moveyou bastardmoveyourself wherethe-
fuck ticketyticketyticketyticketytickety left wheelinground rolling
clonktoolsbox sharpspare ticketyticketyticketyticketytickey rightroll-
crush numbwristswrists skinburncatch shouldertwistpopthebastard-
popthebastardfuck fuckingthink agUhugUh on tickety tickety what
time clank bang crump knee sings sweat breath breathe sweat breath
can'tbreathe dark shit dark shit fuck think ache numb sweatbreath-
can'tbreathe vvvvvvIIIIIIIIIIBBBBBBBBBBBBBBBbbbbbbbbbrrrrrr
RRRRRRRRRViiiiiiiiiibbbbbbbbbbrrrrrrVVVViiiiiibbbrrrrrrrrrrrrrrrr
rrrrrrrrrrrrrrrrrrrrrrrrrrrrrraaaaaatttttttiiiiiiiiooooooooooo nnnnnnn-
nnnnn agh teeth lip blood teeth fucking chipped shit breathe sweat
sweat like a fuckingpigyou'refucked speeeeeeeeeeeeeeeeeeeeeeeeeeeeeee
eeeeeeeeeeeeeeeeeeeeeeeeeeeeeeeeeed gearsgears jab bang lurch crack
twist burn halt gears move sppeeeeeeeeeeSpeedSpeed rumbleskinrub
coldskinsweat fucking breathbreathe youfucker inoutinout hornblare
ticketyticketyticketyticketyticketytickety left pop the bastard if you
roll fuck push up up twist bump grind clank gravel long rolling
straight longlonglong POT hole bruised skin fingers numb tape
scratch bind edge tape scratch sore face burning smellsniffsmell armpit
sweat breath wet boots stop kerclick hiss torches white fuck torches
fucking hood mask gloves reach reach tugtug hands claw clonk hands
grab GRAB clutch clonk roll Out DOOOOWN aUgh.

Ellen and Mrs Atkinson tip him out of the oversized waterproofed tent bag onto the bark-strewn woodland floor. Mrs Milligan rolls him, naked, onto his back and I slash the duct-tape cuffs around his ankles with a hunting knife. He kicks out instantly, furious. As he bucks and flails at me Mrs Milligan makes a sure-handed grab for his penis. Her gloved hand grips it, uses it as if it is a handle that she tugs sharply to make him get to his feet. He stands up growling and snarling behind his duct-tape gag. Angharad reaches up and strips off the duct tape that blindfolded him and takes his eyebrows with it. His face is angry and prickled and red as his eyes water. His penis wilts and shrinks into itself. He is breathing heavily through his nose and he is watching very carefully. Now he can see that we all have guns. Big guns. Impressive guns.

Mine is the only face he can see clearly, the others are ski-masked. He sees the night vision goggles that are strapped around our heads.

It would be easy to do this differently. These clothes, the combat trousers and the fisherman vests we've all been given, smell of damp in the forest. Smell mushroomy and strange. What they bring to mind is your animal self. Right now, in the forest, that is who I need. All around the floodlights blare and scorch and the paths lead away into the edges. Beyond this sheer face of light is darkness. I step forward.

'Yulfuinpy,' he gnaws. I want to laugh. Naked, surrounded, miles from home, miles from his rugby buddies, he still thinks he can win.

'We're here to play…' I begin, my voice low and quiet.

'YullFUINGay.' He is chewing at the words, at the duct tape. In outraged fury he lunges towards me, kicks at me. Catches me. He is impressive, the sheer physical confidence of him can knock the breath out of you. He makes me flinch.

So I have to pause. I have to take a careful breath. Then,

'We're here, to play a new game...'

He catches me again in the backside with his left foot this time, a good, hard kick, despite his bare feet. And that is it. As he topples himself over, snapping and growling I am ON HIM. MY BOOT. HIS RIBS. PRESSING DOWN.

'When I say run, you run. Understand?' He kicks and wrenches at me. Once again his penis is an ergonomically designed handle and I lift him to his feet. We pull down our night vision goggles in perfect synchrony as if we have rehearsed it.

'Because this is a new game.'

He looks at me, wild, disbelieving.

'YUFUGBCH. YUFUGBCHYULPY. ILLMKUPY. FUKYOBCH.'

He tumbles against me. My hand grips and twists his penis, using all the torque available in every last centimetre of its flaccid rubberiness to twist him away from me. He hisses air in through his nose, is all snarled out, struggling to match his breath and his strangled, gagged mouth.

''Cause this is a game...' I raise my arm in the air, 'called Hunter.'

He is snorting snot, wrenching and twisting at the duct tape that binds his hands behind his back.

'Run.' I say it oh so quietly and I look right into his eyes.

As my arm falls all the lights go out and what I see in the forest is green and dense and edged bone white.

Atchen tan

English Romanichal: 'Stopping place'

She arrived so early, I had to swipe her into the museum with my new security card. It's shiny and plastic with a photograph that looks like a mug shot and it dangles on a green ribbon around my neck. As I came down the entrance steps I saw she was wearing her customary black leather coat, supple and worn, a hand-me-down from her mother. She ground out her cigarette under the polished toe of her biker boot. Silver buckles latched the boots closed, all the way up the sides like teeth.

Donya Keet's name and face have been plastered over the local paper. She's part of the Traveller group who have been battling the council to keep possession of Gabriel's Hundred, a scrabby bit of land sandwiched between the plastics factory and the dual carriageway. The council wants to redevelop the area. Already the machines are there, their steel dinosaur jaws tearing down the plastics factory. It is going to be, and I quote, *Hillside—a state of the art retail arena*. The Travellers can't stay because, as Councillor Banks puts it, no one wants to shop at a mall 'with a gang of gypsies camped out in the carpark'.

Donya has fought hard to keep their camp, fought to prove their ownership of the land but she doesn't have the documentation, the planning law is not on her side. The camp will be moved to another site and Donya knows that in a year the council will pull the plug on that site too. In the meantime, Councillor Banks' colleagues want to smooth over all the ruffled feathers and so funding has been given for a Traveller Culture Centre in the museum. Since, during my time at the library, I have already catalogued Lady Breck's journals and photographs from the turn of the century Traveller camp, putting together the Travellers' cultural and social history with Donya Keet is my first project in my new job as assistant curator at the museum.

There isn't going to be room for me at the new County Information Systems Centre that they are building on a brownfield site in the city. I am, in fact, to be replaced by a new self-service terminal *'library @ssistant'*. It is a stark black box with a glowing heart, *'Please place your book face down in the aperture...'* It is currently being tried out at Heather's branch of the County Information System Network: Eastern Outreach. Brookdale Library, as it used to be called.

Mrs Atkinson and the others have already begun parcelling up the books so that they can be moved into temporary storage before the final move next spring. They broke ground last week, Mac Tierney looming over the mayor as he wielded his silver ceremonial spade. Below the photo was an artist's impression of the new building. Wire. Glass. A fountained piazza.

'It looks like Space Station Zebra,' Mrs Milligan commented.

Mrs Atkinson always knew that the negotiations and meetings were just keeping her busy until the ink could dry on the contract with Tripp Tierney Associates. Mac Tierney has, by a roundabout route, exacted his revenge on us all. The library building is to be redeveloped into Bibliotheque, a swanky restaurant none of us will be able to afford to eat in.

Which explains why I am now employed at the museum. I know I'm here because each morning I walk up the stairs and I can see the name Ruby Robinson imprinted into a plastic name tag on my office door. I'm on the first floor, in a little corniced room with a deep half-moon window and no cupboard space.

I have sympathy for Donya, a sentiment she would scorn. I understand that you can be restless and vagabond but you need somewhere to call home. Donya's family have been returning to the Gabriel's Hundred site for over a hundred years. When the Travellers leave in a week's time for the October Horse Fair, the gates will swing shut behind them and they will be outlawed.

She has a strong accent and it took me a while to tune in. It helped that the oral history collection have some reel-to-reel tapes done in the sixties so I could listen and let the words seep inwards. She was hostile to me at first and I don't blame her. They are trying to make her into history. Then she saw what I'd done with the library exhibition. I took her through Lady Breck's journals, the photographs. How the Keets had married into the Herons, how the Kirchers feuded with the Pikes. She saw how I would go about it.

Instead of sitting in the office I thought we would go to the café. She still couldn't smoke in there, but the coffee was welcomed. As I returned from the counter she grubbed some photographs from her pockets.

'Dug 'em out. Stuff as my gran kept. Thought you could add them into the collection.'

The corners were bent a little and the prints would need conserving and probably reprinting but they were atmospheric, taken in the twenties. Kept by her gran. A social history captured in the swirling skirts of two girls posed like dancers; her grandmother Athenia and her great aunt Kezia. Another of menfolk working with a band of horses. Something about the photographs began to whisper to me.

Finally an image of an old lady, perched on the steps of her wagon, clay pipe in her mouth, clad in a greatcoat. There was a familiarity about this and instantly I realised, this is the woman from the portrait, *A Pipe of Baccy*. This was the face that greeted me each day as I turned on the stairs.

'Who's this?'

Donya squinted at the photograph. My guess is she needs glasses but she won't get them.

'That is Vancy Kircher's girl. Not much of a girl by then o' course.' She snorted. There was something about the photographs. What was it?

'Kircher's daughter?'

'Na. Ma Kircher took her in in her troubles like she was a daughter. But she wasn't blood.'

More images of the menfolk, metalworking this time, at a fire. The light. The easy, realistic poses. I recognise the style. The eye for details.

'You don't happen to know who took these photos?' I asked and already, my mind was whispering the impossible. Donya sipped at her coffee, pointed a square, stubby finger at the old lady in the photograph.

'She did. Kircher's girl.'

I looked at the image of Kircher's girl, who, in the photographs, was somewhere in her early sixties.

'What was her name?'

'Kircher. Like I said.'

'Before that. If she wasn't blood, she wasn't always a Kircher. Do you know what her name was before she took up with Vancy?'

Donya shrugged, sipped more coffee, refilled her cup from the glass cafetiere.

'Gran told me Vancy always called her Lady…but when my gran was a little 'un, after Vancy had passed, they always named the old lady Ma Breck.'

The letters were in a box sent from the library. Since I had long ago begun the task of sifting history, Mrs Atkinson had brought me the last of the boxes from the upstairs archive. Mostly it was rubbish, documents so rotted or mildewed after a radiator leak they had to be discarded. A box of school reports from 1910 proved useful and informative and then, at last, the letters.

Three thick cream envelopes tied together with parcel string. They were addressed to Lady Breck, Kite House but a strong line had been crossed through each address and the words *Not known at this address, return to St Heliers Villa, No. 5 The Heights*.

I sat for a long time with them unbundled before me.

Matilda Buller, a woman of independent means, writing home from her grand tour to her younger sister, Beatrice Buller, lately Lady Beatrice Breck.

France January 1891.
…the girl delights in every fashion my dear Beatrice. Her impeccable manner, her natural charm and diffidence and the eagerness with which she approaches each new task and situation are heartening to behold. Each day she is invigorated by

*the sights and experiences. Like an etiolated plant, too long in
a dark room, she stretches for the sun...*

Italy, March 1891.

*...the mountain and meadow charm of the Southern Tyrol.
The crossing at Lake Constance was rain lashed but the esti-
mable Miss Penny was forearmed with oilskins. Mary-Ann
anticipates my every need and is become my guardian and my
angel...*

The last. From Calais, 1893.

*...I do not anticipate that you will be able to meet our ferry at
Dover. Rather, I am concerned by your silence. Mary-Ann and
I have decided to abandon our planned stay in London and
instead will return straight to St Heliers Villa. Write to me at
home there. Beatrice, I must know of your misadventures. Tell
me every circumstance.*

> *Your loyal and true sister,*
> *Tilly*

I took the letters and sat on the turn of the stairs for a while
as, just above me on the wall, painted into the wilds of
Gabriel's Hundred in 1921, Lady Breck sat and smoked her
pipe of baccy.

TOSHOKAN SHIMARIMASU

The library is closing

There was to be a last book club in the library building. With all the books packed away and the shelving dismantled the library resembled a ballroom. As darkness fell, Martha and I put out the chairs so that we could all sit under the starlit dome. Not everyone was there; Jill, Deirdra, several others, were missing.

'No. It's the abridged book club this evening.'

Mrs Atkinson met my gaze pointedly. Then the door opened and Iris swept in.

Mrs Atkinson pulled the letter from her pocket as we poured the wine.

'This came for you yesterday.' She handed over the thin brown envelope. I looked at the nondescript printed address label, the blurred franked postmark. As Mrs Atkinson turned to give Iris and Angharad their wine I made my way to the ladies' toilets.

It was very cold. One of the cisterns was dripping water, a hollow plinking sound. The envelope tore open easily to reveal the newspaper cutting. It shivered in my hand as if it were alive.

Tickety-tickety. My heart. My breath. Angharad driving that night. *Tickety-tickety* of the rain on the windscreen. Afterwards, the *tickety-tickety* of the night creatures in the muffling quiet of the paintball forest. The mizzling rain diamonded in Iris's hair as, afterwards, she and Martha and Mrs Milligan got into her car. Angharad and Ellen, watchful as bouncers.

'How will you get back?' Angharad's keys clutched in her hand. Ellen poised at the car door.

'I should stay with you. You can't wait here alone.' Mrs Atkinson anxious. Nathan, his left eye swollen closed, turned his right eye upon her. Laughed. A low wolfish growl. But I shook my head.

'Go. It's better that you go.'

They were gone. We were alone.

Nathan lay weary, but still cursing through duct tape, on the bark-strewn floor before me.

'Finshit, Bch.'

I took his mobile from my pocket. As I scrolled through his phonebook there was a photo of a hairy arse and the sub-title *Liam*. A photo of Bailley popped onto the screen. I took a photo of Nathan, his eyes burning fury above the duct tape, his face almost obscured by the marker-pen tattoos. I clicked *send* and we waited. Nathan lolling his exhausted head backwards, wincing at the pain of his eye. Laughing. Harsh. Smothered.

As we tracked him down. As we pushed Nathan to his edges it felt as if, at the end of it all, I might be able to pounce on him. As if, with my animal self, I might be able to reach into his ribcage and find his true heart still beating there. As if, through all and everything there could be some part of him that I could recognise and salvage.

NeveragainNEVERnevERneverAGainneverRAgainNEV
erNEVERNEVErAgainNeVEREVERagainNEVERnever
everagainnevereveragainNEVERAGAINNEVER AgAiN we
had written it over and over every inch of him in permanent
marker from the library. Stained him. Blotted him out. Already
the mizzling rain had begun to sluice some of the paintball
splats and mud from him and the clear message would be
revealed. *Never again.* I wondered how long it would mark
him for. Long enough for him to understand? I wondered
how long it takes for your skin to rub and replenish and rub
and replenish until the surface is new and clean.

'Yllfuingpyfrthsbch.' The words seemed sharp enough to
cut through the tape. His look, a cold blade of fury.

'Finshit.'

A challenge. A dare.

'FINSHITBCH'

I looked at him, a wave of panic washed through me. A
knowledge.

Ijo o desu. 'It is finished.'

A moment. He rolls himself over, struggling and surging
upwards. His arms flexing furiously, unable to wrench
themselves free of the tape. His face muscles contorting as the
roar bellows out of him. The log. Clips him neatly. He falls. A
red star of blood by his eye. Fear, like a whip, smarts across
me. I reach for his belt then, spilling his belongings from the
carrier bag. My shaking hands tie his hands, secure him with
his belt.

The same belt. Supple. Buckled.

The phone rings out.

'Nat? That you? What the fuck is going on?' Bailley's
voice.

'If you want him, come for him.' I hung up, texted in the

293

map reference, neatly written out for me by Ellen on a scrap of Paintball Pandemonium headed paper. And waited.

It was almost dawn when she arrived.

He was still bound and she made no move to free him, just helped me wrap him in his mackintosh, fretting and obstructive as an oversized baby while we tied the belt around his waist. He could still be scornful even with his own blood on his face.

Still I was not prepared for the moment when, instead of opening the door, she opened the boot. I opened my mouth to speak but, as we lugged his writhing body into the hatchback, the torch beam flashed across her face. I saw at once how she was thinner. Wasted. Her gaze was unsteady as she leaned onto the boot to shut it with a muffled click.

'How did he find me?'

Bailley took a deep breath.

'Your dad. He put his house up for sale. After that...it was just a matter of digging.' She looked down, ashamed. 'Nathan wouldn't let you go, Jeannie. He was never...Nothing I did...I'm sorry for what I...' Her voice trailed off. I couldn't see the woman from the party anymore. I could see how he had dulled her; tarnished her.

'Don't be sorry,' I said.

'Too late to be sorry...' her voice thin as smoke.

Bailley's face slithered and trembled, her smile glassy.

'Too late Jeannie,' a cold dry voice, her gaze edged raw. I had a sudden vision of my wrists, Nathan's belt, the creak as he pulled it tight around the chair back.

'Can't make it right...but...' Her voice lowered, her lips pinching inwards at the sourness. 'Atonement.' The word like a stone.

'Atonement?'

Her eyes flickered away from mine, across the boot latch, '...*for Geraldine*.'

She took three steps to get into the car. Words wouldn't come to me. Only the lightning flashes of memory. The engine growling now. I took a step forward as the wheels skidded slightly on the claggy forest floor. I reached out. Afraid.

'Wait.' My hand catching for a second on the rear wing. Me, running, the mud sucking and tripping, not letting me go. Bailley pulling away. '*Wait*.'

My eyes caught by Bailley's as she gave me one last look in the rear view mirror. The headlights moving, torch-like, away through the trees.

In the cold enamel of the sink, the flames caught at the edge of the clipping.

DETECTIVE VICTIM OF PUNISHMENT KILLING
Detective Sergeant Nathan Flynn caught with a bright bronzed flare edged with black *victim of punishment killing* singed and flittered into dust *police suspect* curled and blackened *criminals he was pursuing* scorched and shrivelled *undercover operation ends in bizarre ritualistic murder*. A thin, bitter thread of smoke gasped and was gone.

'Ruby?' Martha, come to find me. Upstairs Angharad was topping up everyone's wine.

'A toast?' said Mrs Atkinson. She reached a thin, gold-papered packet from her bag. 'Ruby? Catch.'

I caught the packet. All the faces were turned to me.

'Open it, then.' Martha's eyes were sparkly with tears. I opened the paper.

'We want you to know, you're going to be missed over at Space Station Zebra,' said Mrs Milligan raising her glass.

'It's not much, just a token,' Mrs Atkinson said as I

looked up from the gold tissue paper, from the white conservator gloves within.

'To Ruby,' said Martha, and we raised our glasses.

In December 1890 Mary-Ann was taken from Kite House to Southampton by Lady Breck to become a paid companion and lady's maid to Lady Breck's sister, Tilly Buller. They never parted from that day. Of course, the same can't be said of Viscount and Lady Breck who parted quite soon afterwards.

Mary-Ann lived at St Heliers Villa, No. 5 The Heights until her death in 1958. Her name is there on the deeds from the time she was bequeathed the property by Matilda Buller in 1932. And if you'd care to look, the will is on microfiche.

In the sixties a local architect, Humphrey Burnage, bought numbers 5 and 7 The Heights and demolished them. He wanted to make way for neighbouring Scandinavian-style single-storey houses, low slung and leafy, for himself and his ex-wife Irma. Or so the estate agent told me.

Dad put his house on the market in readiness; ready for me to return, ready to leave quickly if I should need him. He will never need to know how Nathan made the dog cough up the jigsaw pieces for him. It is better that everyone believes Nathan picked up my trail from the scowling newspaper portrait that accompanied the knicker-thief story.

Dad's piano was in need of tuning after being man-handled through the doorway at No 7 The Heights. I stood in his new kitchen waiting for his new kettle to boil. As I put milk from his new fridge into two of his new mugs I saw that even in its current overgrown state, his new garden has a lovely view of the bend of the canal. Then I had to yell that I was just popping out for some sugar. The piano tuner takes five per mug, averaging three mugs an hour. Neither of them heard me, they were discussing the rights and wrongs of Shostakovich.

I walked along the curved road that is The Heights. That morning, before Dad and the removal vans arrived, I had been standing in my kitchen at No. 5 ('recently updated to an exceptional standard', the estate agent details had declared). I noticed, for the first time since I moved in, that there is a gap in the trees on the opposite bank. From there I can just make out the scaffolding where roofers are repairing the flashing on the dome of the old library.

I don't think about Nathan now. Only occasionally, if I have to take the bus. You might think it would be the memory where we are walking, that particular Wednesday, when everything seemed to be beginning, his hand so tender and gentle in the small of my back as we moved up the hill together to the walled garden.

No. I think about him on that very first day. When I said, 'My bus is here.' I can see his lips forming the words, 'Miss it.' I can feel the brown workboots I was wearing as I stepped aboard the bus. Feeling his eyes on the back of my neck. Watching as I showed my travel pass. A moment. The bus pulled away. Then I looked back, saw that he was still standing there.

Nathan, leaning against the stone pillars of Cromwell Park gates. He didn't wave. It was only a moment before he turned, walked up the hill. His back to me.

ACKNOWLEDGMENTS

A quick trawl of the internet will throw up all you need to know about the properties of herbs and plants. I browsed a few, including uponreflection.co.uk and painting.about.com on the symbolism of plants, herbs and trees. I took liberties here and there because there are contradictions from site to site, but I've used *The Encyclopedia of Medicinal Herbs* by Andrew Chevallier MNIMH as my baseline. The Patria Journal Romani resource at www.geocities.com/~patrin was a tremendous help colouring in the glimpses of Traveller life as seen by Lady Breck.

When you're writing you often cast about looking for something to help you pull it all together. Every now and again, you light on one research text that connects completely to what you had in mind and, a bit like finding that last corner piece in the jigsaw puzzle, once you've got it, you're off. So I'd like to doff my cap to Rita L. Lampkin and her *Japanese Verbs and Essentials of Grammar: A Practical Guide to the Mastery of Japanese*.

Domo arigato gozaimasu, Rita, and any mistakes are all mine.